"In this terrific series opener, Afia evokes the women's lives in all their wayward and beautiful glory, especially the abruptness with which their dreams, hopes, and fears cease to exist."

—*The New York Times*

"Tightly paced, razor-sharp, and with a wonderful no-nonsense protagonist, *Dead Dead Girls* made me fly through the pages. Ms. Afia is one to watch."

—Evie Dunmore, *USA Today* bestselling author of
*The Gentleman's Gambit*

"This book was an engaging, captivating, suspenseful, and enjoyable historical mystery and character journey."

—*Mystery & Suspense Magazine*

"Suspenseful. . . . *Harlem Sunset* excels at illustrating the culture of the late 1920s—and at capturing a woman dealing with her choices while simultaneously discovering what she wants in life."

—Shelf Awareness

"A vivid crime story and an engrossing depiction of an era."

—*Kirkus Reviews*

"Debut author Nekesa Afia brings 1920s Harlem to life in this twisty tale of murder and betrayal where nothing and no one is as it seems."

—Victoria Thompson, *USA Today* bestselling author of
*Murder in Rose Hill*

"Readers will root for intrepid, fiery Louise." —*Publishers Weekly*

"'Though she be but little, she is fierce.' Shakespeare might as well have been describing Louise Lloyd, the flawed yet fantastic protagonist in Afia's debut, set in 1920s Harlem. I loved the world that Afia created and can't wait to follow Lou and her friends on their next adventure. Come for the wonderfully diverse and twisty mystery; stay for the amazing twenties slang and fashion."

—Mia P. Manansala, Agatha Award–winning author of
*Murder and Mamon*

HARLEM RENAISSANCE MYSTERIES BY NEKESA AFIA

*Dead Dead Girls*

*Harlem Sunset*

*A Lethal Lady*

# A LETHAL LADY

~◇~

A HARLEM RENAISSANCE MYSTERY

~◇~

## NEKESA AFIA

BERKLEY PRIME CRIME
NEW YORK

BERKLEY PRIME CRIME
Published by Berkley
An imprint of Penguin Random House LLC
penguinrandomhouse.com

Library of Congress Cataloging-in-Publication Data

Names: Afia, Nekesa, author.
Title: A lethal lady / Nekesa Afia.
Description: First edition. | New York: Berkley Prime Crime, 2024. |
Series: A Harlem Renaissance mystery; 3
Identifiers: LCCN 2023057905 (print) | LCCN 2023057906 (ebook) |
ISBN 9780593548806 (trade paperback) | ISBN 9780593548813 (ebook)
Subjects: LCSH: African Americans—France—Paris—Fiction. |
Paris (France)—History—1870-1940—Fiction. |
LCGFT: Detective and mystery fiction. | Novels.
Classification: LCC PR9199.4.A3465 L48 2024 (print) |
LCC PR9199.4.A3465 (ebook) | DDC 813/.6—dc23/eng/20240104
LC record available at https://lccn.loc.gov/2023057905
LC ebook record available at https://lccn.loc.gov/2023057906

First Edition: July 2024

Printed in the United States of America
1st Printing

Book design by Alison Cnockaert

*White. A blank page or canvas. His favorite. So many possibilities.*
—STEPHEN SONDHEIM (1930-2021)

# A
# LETHAL
# LADY

# 1

IT TURNED OUT that dancing was the same everywhere. It wasn't something Louise Lloyd took for granted, but after ten months in Paris, it was something she was grateful for. Aquarius, the club closest to her apartment in the 18th arrondissement, was much like her beloved Zodiac in many ways: sweeping dance floor, big band, tables and the bar placed in as an afterthought. Every time she went, it made her homesick for something she once had.

She had spent all of the time, from club opening to club closing, on the dance floor. Her body hurt. She had been passed from blandly handsome Frenchman to blandly handsome Frenchman, not once caring that they were using her as an object, not seeing her as a person.

Louise was doing the same thing to them.

She carried her shoes, gravel and stones scratching at her stockings. It was three in the morning, and Aquarius had just closed. Rather than call a cab, it was nice enough for her to walk. She wasn't that drunk; she'd never let herself drink too much again, and the night had a hazy, dewy feeling to it. If she were back in New York, if Gilbert, then his sister, had never happened, she would have piled into a cab with Rosa Maria and Rafael, laughed at nothing, and let it whisk her back to the apartment.

Ten months on her own. She had the stack of correspondence on her desk to prove it. She was bad at letters, something she learned when her boat docked.

The past months had been quiet, in a good way. Louise had learned she liked normal hobbies, fostering a love of photography. She learned that she could survive on her own, something she thought she couldn't do. If the past two years had taught her anything, it was that she was stronger than she realized.

The room she rented was at the top of the building, maid's quarters. To access the apartment, she had to go up five flights of stairs, exit into the warm night air, and climb another set of stairs. It usually wasn't awful, but after a night of being on her feet, the last thing she wanted to do was climb them.

So, she sank down to the stairs, feeling the cool cement through the thin fabric of her dress and her stockings. She put her shoes back on, letting relief flood through her. From here, she could wait and rest, and muster the energy to take these stairs.

No one looked at her, no one cared. Paris was a lot like New York in that way. No one cared about anyone else. She was in her own little bubble, and she liked it like that.

She had work the next day; in fact, she had work in mere hours. Louise dug into her tiny purse, pulling out a cigarette and her book of matches. Compared to everything else she had done, it was a job she could do half asleep or with her head in the clouds.

And that was soothing.

Louise watched couples walk home, cars pass her on the street. She smiled and waved at her Irish neighbor. The man lived right below her and fancied himself a playwright. He was *astoundingly* annoying, but he was also the closest thing she had to a friend in her building.

She allowed him to pull her up and support her as they climbed the stairs together. He too was drunk, drunker than she was, and it turned out she was supporting him more than the other way around.

"Good night?" Ciarán asked as Louise got him to his door.

"Sure was," Louise said. "You'll be okay?"

"Always am, Tiny." He could get on her nerves, but she genuinely liked him. She liked his optimism, which only shined when he was this drunk.

He didn't return the question; he never did.

It was just as well. Louise wasn't sure how she'd answer.

# 2

ORNINGS WERE FOR stopping by Dauphine's Café. Dauphine's on Rue Bachaumont was where Louise went every
morning for coffee before work. This was partly because the lovely
café reminded her of the one she worked in back home, partly because it was the best coffee she had ever tasted, but mostly because
the Dauphine daughter, Clémence, was beautiful. Louise had had
a crush on her from the moment she moved to Paris. They had
nearly the same skin color, but Clémence wore it better. She kept
her hair long, always secured at the nape of her neck. She had a
gap between her two front teeth that she was shy about. Sometimes, she'd laugh, then clap a hand over her mouth.

Clémence was behind the counter, wearing a blue gingham
dress with her hair pulled back. She was intently reading something, her nose wrinkling, as Louise pushed the door open.

"We're closed," Clémence said.

"Would you make an exception?" Louise asked.

Clémence looked up, her face brightening as she saw Louise.
"You do this every morning."

"It's not my fault your café and my store open at the same time." Louise closed the door behind her. She was early—thirty minutes, in fact. "No one in the world makes coffee like you do."

"You Americans and your coffee. I will never understand the love affair. Come on." Clémence put her magazine away as Louise sat at the counter and began the work of preparing two cups of coffee. Clémence was a recent convert, only because of Louise.

"How was your night?" Louise asked.

Clémence rolled her warm brown eyes. She was always trying to play coy, but this is what Louise knew about her: she was an only child, and she was intent on being an actress. What she really wanted was to move to America and star in films.

Clémence began to pour the coffee, evenly splitting it between two cups. Louise was never sure if Clémence *liked* drinking coffee, or if she did it because Louise did. Adding a tiny bit of sugar, and then cream, Clémence pushed a cup toward Louise.

Even for someone who didn't like coffee, Clémence's was amazing. It was everything Louise needed in the early morning.

Clémence wiped her hands on her apron, leaning forward on the counter. They were inches away; Louise could see her perfect philtrum over her perfect lips. "You know," Louise said, "I live above Ciarán Dunne. I'm sure he knows someone looking for an actress. And he does owe me a favor. Or two." Ciarán was the most hapless person she had ever met, including herself. He managed to conjure up trouble just by existing.

"I would love that," Clémence said. "I would love anything. How did you end up living above Ciarán Dunne?"

It had been an accident; Louise had never heard of the Irish playwright before she had the misfortune of moving in above him. "I'll see what I can do." Louise winked.

⧊

BY THE TIME Louise arrived, every weekday night after work and before Aquarius, Le Chat Noir was always busy. Her group of friends was always seated on the patio, away from the smoky distractions of music; they were already locked in a myriad of discussions.

"Louise!" Doris, Black, beautiful, and talented, was the lead singer of a jazz band that hailed from Nebraska. They had gotten to Paris just before Louise had and had already taken up residence in a club nearby. Doris rose from her seat, handing Louise a glass. She was smoking, in intense discussions with Queenie and Tootsie. Toward the end of the table, which was actually several small circular tables pushed together under the awning to protect themselves from sporadic Paris rain, Ciarán and Monty were in a loud political discussion. Maude was jotting notes in a notebook.

Le Chat Noir was home, more than any home had ever been. It was the place for immigrants, most of them Black, all of them starving artists. In fact, more often than not, Ciarán was the only white face in the crowd.

It was where they met to discuss art and life. Louise was happy to sit back and watch. The best part was that she didn't have to say much. Artists, by design or necessity, only cared about themselves.

"TINY!" Ciarán got more Irish as he drank, his accent heavier. He rose, his jacket already discarded, sleeves rolled to the elbows. His face was ruddy, and he wrapped Louise up in a big bear hug, effectively lifting her off of her feet.

Seats were rearranged; Louise slipped in between Nathan and Doris. "What are you talking about?" Louise asked.

There was one thing they were talking about tonight. "Iris Wright," Doris said.

Iris Wright was an artist making her name known in all the circles in Paris. Her work was immaculate, unnerving. She painted herself and other subjects in Renoir's hazy, impressionist style. Louise had seen her work. The papers raved about her. Monty exhaled. "I don't know why we have to discuss her every night." He sipped from his glass as Ciarán patted Monty on the back.

It was true, they didn't *have* to discuss her every night, but they did. There was something about her.

It was easy to sense jealousy from Monty. "Because she's interesting," Ditsie said. "And has accomplished something you haven't been able to." One of three Moulin Rouge dancers that spend a ton of time at the cabaret before and between their shows, Ditsie was always reading something. She was with the other girls, Queenie and Tootsie. All three were varying shades of brown, impossibly long and thin. All three had glasses of water in front of them. They often seemed as if they were one person separated into three bodies. Ditsie wore a pair of cheaters, low on her nose, and she looked up at Monty over the rims. "Or do you have a showing coming up?"

She was the only person who could truly take him down a peg. Queenie giggled behind her fan. Monty sighed and turned away. "She's not even very good," Monty said with a pout. Nathan was writing, as he usually was, saying less than Louise. Louise always wondered if they would end up in a book of his, parts and pastiches of the people they actually were.

"And you think you are?" Ditsie asked, her eyes still narrow on Monty.

"Well, I think they're both good," Louise said, trying to keep the peace.

"But who is better?" Ditsie asked. In a different world, she would make quite the politician. She was unrelenting, unyielding, ready to get her way by any means possible. It was something Louise respected, admired, and feared.

"Iris." Louise lit a cigarette.

"I thought we were friends, Louise," Monty said. He stood up from the table with a huff. The women dissolved into fits of laughter. It was like being surrounded by sisters, something Louise missed. That was her fault; Minna and Josie wrote, and Louise never responded. Minna was thriving as a wife and mother, and Louise hoped she was happy with her choices.

"You know," Nathan said, leaning forward to capture everyone's attention, "they say she hasn't been seen in weeks."

"Stop it," Tootsie said.

"You're telling lies," Doris countered.

Nathan raised both hands, moving away. "I heard from a friend of a friend."

"You know how artists are," Maude spoke up. It was easy to forget that the woman was there. She was tiny, smaller than Louise, and slimmer, if that were possible. Her voice was quiet, sometimes impossible to hear. That was usually a moot point: Maude was always too busy writing to say anything. "So temperamental. She's probably spending some time in Nice or Burgundy or whatever it is rich white folks do."

Ciarán tilted his head. "Artists *are* so temperamental. So's Monserrat." Only Ciarán could invoke Monty's full name. Up until this moment, Louise had been sure it was Montague.

"Is she really rich, though?" Doris asked. Clever and introspective, Doris' main talent, aside from singing, was asking questions no one had the answer to.

"You know what I would do with all that money?" Maude asked. "Get a divorce." She raised her painted-on eyebrows and returned to the pages in front of her.

"If you could go anywhere, where would you go?" Ciarán asked.

Silly question.

For every person at those tables, they were exactly where they wanted to be.

May 18th, 1927

Lovie,

I've stopped counting the days since you've left. I've decided that in these letters, I'm only going to focus on good things. Happy things. I miss you. That's not a happy thing. Business is good. You've left us in quite capable hands. Anna has taken over running the club, and Schoonmaker's house. She seems to like it. She runs the Dove like you did. A tight ship. I know you don't want me to talk about her, I think, but my sister is also good. She's recovering well.

I thought she'd fall to pieces, but then I guess I don't know my own sister very well.

Before you ask, no, she hasn't met anyone new yet. I suppose you'll tell me when you meet someone?

I don't want to be a go-between with you two. I don't want to be caught in the middle. I'm going to give her your address, and she can write you, if she wants. And that way . . . I love both of you. You're both my sisters. And I thought maybe the two of you would be fine. Together forever. But since that didn't happen, I want to say that I'm not getting in between you two. I can't.

I guess it will be easier with an ocean in the way.

I will say this, though, I know she misses you and you must miss her, and I don't know what happened. (Do you?)

I'm not getting in the middle of it.

The summer seems to be dragging on and it's barely begun. It's not the same without you here. I keep thinking about the long nights at the Zodiac, and how I wanted the Dove to be like it. I want people to feel safe in my club. I keep turning to *the bar and thinking that's where you'll be. Eugene has taken over there, but I don't know if you've noticed, he isn't exactly very . . . bright.*

*I feel bad saying it, but it's true. Did you know? How could you not tell me?*

*I thought we would be happy together, but now I'm not so sure.*

*I am sure he'll write you, but if he doesn't, Schoonmaker sends his love. He's decided to start hosting a poker tournament, and he says that it's a shame you can't be here to help him win.*

*(Did you ever tell him I'm the one who taught you how to play?)*

*Either way, we both send our love, and we both hope that you write us soon.*

*All of my love,*
*Rafael*

# 3

L OUISE LIKED THE end of the day. It was after the afternoon rush of customers, when all she had to do was tidy the sales floor. There was something so wonderful about it. After the parfumerie closed, they would tally the sales for the day. The simplicity of Allaire's is what Louise liked best. There were glass cabinets and walls and walls of products. It was split: products for women on one side and products for men on the other.

For several months, she had been an employee at Allaire's. The parfumerie catered to rich Parisian women, and Louise found that the skills she once used as a waitress were almost the same as selling cosmetics.

She was the only clerk on the floor. Monsieur Allaire was upstairs in his office. Jessie and Clara were in the back, wrapping orders. There were twenty more minutes in the day, and Louise was straightening the glass jars of face creams. The door chime sounded behind her and, pulling the white coat she was required to wear closed, Louise turned around.

"Bonjour," Louise said. The woman in front of her wasn't

Parisian, wasn't French. Louise could tell. It was how she was dressed. A year in Paris, and Louise still stuck out like a sore thumb. This strange woman was about Louise's own height, five foot two, and had dark-brown hair, big brown eyes set in smooth white skin. Louise could have pitched her any number of face creams and rouges and lipsticks.

"Are you Louise Lloyd?" Louise was right. This woman talked with a flat, Boston accent.

"Depends on who's asking." She knew that was a dead give-away. She had had months of not being Louise Lloyd, not being a woman who solved murders or killed men who were going to kill her. She had reveled in not being someone who had to save people. It seemed as if being Louise Lloyd was something she couldn't hide from, a birthright she didn't want.

The woman was rooting through her purse. She came out with a small bundle of letters, which she held out.

Louise took them. The front of the first bore her name in writing that was familiar. Louise ripped it open and found a very short missive.

*Lovie,*

*She needs help. Help her, please.*

*—Schoonmaker*

Louise was brutally reminded, again, that she was months behind in her correspondence. She wasn't very good at writing letters and missed the times when her best friends and Schoonmaker were blocks away, instead of an ocean.

Flicking through the others, she could see Rafael's and Rosa Maria's handwriting on the envelopes.

"You need help?" Louise asked.

"He said you'd help me. My name is Lucy Wright. And I think my daughter has gone missing." Lucy Wright didn't look her in the eye.

"Mrs. Wright, I need more information," Louise said. She looked back down at Schoonmaker's letter. Maybe this was just a misunderstanding.

"My daughter is Iris Wright."

Iris Wright Montgomery, the artist her friends couldn't stop talking about, bold in the way she dared to be a woman and paint. Louise thought her work was thrilling, almost scintillating. There was something longing in Iris' touch. She painted with such affection, such love.

"Why do you think she's missing?" Louise asked.

"I haven't heard from her in months. Well, I have, but the letters don't sound like her." Lucy was pacing across the showroom floor.

"I don't . . . I can't help you," Louise said. "I work here now. I do this."

"Schoonmaker said you're the cleverest girl he knows."

"Sounds like him, but I can't help you," Louise said. She had committed to living a normal life from now on. She had the tiny apartment, the annoying neighbors, the job she loved. She was doing it. She was being a regular person.

Lucy turned to her. Louise could see the desperation, the need in her eyes.

"Please, just go check. My daughter's husband won't let me in. If Schoonmaker trusts you, I trust you." Lucy's eyes were filled with tears. Louise could never understand how Schoonmaker, a man who was lawless in everything he did, managed to make such connections. Lucy was acting on his faith.

Schoonmaker had been a great help to her. She owed him.

And this would be fast. Confirm Iris Wright was not, in fact, missing. Return to being Louise Lloyd, parfumerie employee. She'd sell a new perfume, then go dancing.

And everything would fall back into place.

"Okay." Louise exhaled. "I need to know everything about her, and I need to know what is going on. I'll meet you at Dauphine's, the café on Rue Bachaumont." Lucy nodded, and with another desperate round of thanks, she left.

Louise couldn't remember what she had been doing. She straightened her jacket again, feeling her comfortable anonymous life slip away.

⋖⋗

LUCY WRIGHT WAS waiting for her at Dauphine's when she arrived, seated at Louise's favorite table in the corner. It was right next to the window, and the sun was just past setting, making the city outside the window glow. Clémence was behind the counter; there were sheets near the till. The woman was wrapped up in words, mouthing something over and over. Clémence was always auditioning for something.

Louise placed herself in front of Lucy. The first thing she did was light a cigarette. "Now, let's get this straight. I'll help you, but you can never come to my work again. I'll give you my address." She had shed the white lab coat that was her work uniform. Now her day dress was suitably Parisian: dark red with a red rosette on her left hip.

"Thank you so much," Lucy said again and placed the stack of letters on the table. "These are her letters. They were frequent, but then they slowed. And then nothing."

Louise began to flick through them. Clémence brought two cups of coffee to the table.

"And you think she's missing because she stopped writing?" Louise asked. She wrinkled her nose, opening the last letter. It was postmarked two months ago.

"No. I don't know. I just have a feeling something is wrong," Lucy said. She lifted her cup to her lips and didn't sip from it. Around them, the café was bustling with employees after work, tourists after a day of shopping. Louise read the last letter. It was one page, handwritten. Dated in March of that year.

Louise went back to the first letter. Also handwritten, it was seven pages long.

"I agree," Louise said. "Something is wrong." She looked up at Lucy. "I think you're right to be worried."

"Like I told you, when I went to their house, her husband wouldn't let me in," Lucy said. Her eyes narrowed, a million things running through her mind. "I just need you to go to her house. And see her. And tell me. I'll pay you anything you want."

It was tempting. Louise could always use more money. But the woman was in distress, and something felt cruel about taking her money on top of that. "It's all right," Louise said. "I'll do it." She wondered what her own mother, long dead, would do if she thought any of her daughters were in danger. Louise blinked twice. "I need her address and your information. I'll follow up once I know something."

"I'll give you everything you need," Lucy said. She exhaled, a long slow breath that seemed to pull her back together. "Thank you so much."

"You may not like what I find," Louise said.

Lucy looked right into her eyes. A woman of a certain age, she was formidable. "I'm willing to take that chance. Take her letters. Read them." Louise nodded. There had to be nearly a hundred envelopes. But she couldn't say no.

Louise remained at the table after Lucy left. She slowly sipped her coffee and smoked, and the moment the coast was clear, and business had died down a little, Clémence joined her at the table. "Who was that?" Clémence asked. She was smiling. She was always smiling. She wiped her hands on her apron.

"A friend of a friend," Louise said. She lit another cigarette. Almost immediately, Clémence took it from her. Clémence had to be careful—her parents didn't approve of smoking, or her wanting to be an actress.

"Do you ever realize I know next to nothing about you?" Clémence asked. Louise was glad that the legend of Harlem's Hero wasn't interesting enough for French papers.

Louise reached over and took her cigarette back. The tables, little round things with glass tops, weren't big, and the space between them sometimes felt simultaneously like inches and a valley. "Don't you like a bit of mystery?" Louise asked.

Clémence rolled her eyes up to the ceiling. Her eyes were a warm, melted brown, the shade that made Louise catch her breath whenever she saw them. Clémence also had impressively long eyelashes, the longest Louise had ever seen. "You know I do not," Clémence said. "What did this friend of a friend want?"

On some level, Louise realized that this life was almost exactly the same as her last one. She went to a café, she went to work, she sold things for a living. She went dancing, although that wasn't illegal in Paris.

But there was no death. No murder. And she liked it like that.

She may have made a mistake by promising to look for Iris Wright. She may have ruined the perfect balance, the house of cards that was her new life. "Nothing," Louise lied. "Don't worry your pretty little head about it." She didn't like lying, but now it was a part of who she was.

Clémence took the cigarette from Louise again. The tips of their fingers brushed. Louise bit her tongue. "I have an audition," Clémence said. "I'm not confident about it. Will you help me?" She concentrated on inhaling, then exhaling.

"Whatever you want," Louise said. "I would be glad to help."

In the meantime, she would find Iris Wright.

It would be swift, and then she could return to her regular life.

*April 24th, 1928*

*Lou,*

*I will not start this letter by telling you to write me more. I will not tell you that you should at least read it. You know how much I admire you (ardently) and you know how much I hate to ask a favor (I still remember the look you gave me the last time I asked). I'm not a fool, or a man who often makes the same mistakes twice.*

*But the truth is, I need your help. You are the cleverest girl I know, and if anyone can help, I know you can.*

*I'm sending my dear friend Lucy to you. (Please, don't ask how Lucy and I are friends. The answer is, of course, something I cannot put into a letter.) Lucy's daughter, Iris, is missing. Or she suspects Iris is missing. The letters from her were a stream, then a trickle, then a drip.*

*And now, nothing.*

*Lucy fears the worst.*

*I know this must be the last thing you want to do. But you wouldn't just be doing her a favor, you'd be doing me a favor.*

*And yes, I believe you do owe me. Remember how much money you got from me before I realized you were good at cards?*

*All Lucy wants is to see her daughter. I don't know if she can trust anyone else. But you come with my stamp of approval.*

*In the event of you not reading this letter, I will send one with Lucy as well. I've given her your information, where you work and where you live. (Side note, will you please send me some of that brilliantine?)*

*I realize I'm putting you in an awkward position. I know how much you hate to say no. I'm sorry for that, I am. But I don't know anyone else who could help her like you could.*

*In the rare event you read this letter before Lucy arrives (and I realize that the chances of that are slim), I ask of you to just consider it.*

*Please.*

*Please.*

*If you ask me, I must say I think that there is something brewing. I can feel it, even though you're a world away from me. I hope Paris is everything you've dreamed of and more. I would know, already, had you sent me more than a letter to say you arrived safely.*

*Lovie, dear, I'm not angry with you. Only slightly disappointed. I didn't realize that starting a new life meant leaving your old one behind.*

*I have been watching this woman spiral to the deepest parts of her worries and anything I (or we) can do to help will be good.*

*I promise to write again, and soon. But this was urgent business that could not wait.*

*Thank you so much.*

*My love,*
*F. Schoonmaker*

# 4

◁▷

T HE ONLY WAY Louise could describe the house was foreboding. Years later, when she thought about her time in Paris, the third thing that came to her mind was that house. It looked like a small castle, with turrets and balconies, and Louise felt that she didn't fit. There was an aura around it, something that made her heart stop, her fist freeze right before knocking.

It was the type of house that was the center of gothic stories, and Louise didn't feel right standing on the porch.

But, to her surprise, when it opened, a big mutt greeted her, getting onto its hind legs, pressing its nose to Louise's chest, placing its paws on her shoulders. Louise stepped back. She never liked dogs that much. Rosa Maria had. Rosa Maria had launched a campaign to get a dog in the months that they had lived together.

There was something about the large animal that made Louise nervous.

"Maisy, down! In!" The man who appeared at the door was familiar in the way socialites are familiar. Louise had seen him—Philip Montgomery—and Iris in the papers; they had emigrated months before Louise, and were every bit the American socialites making a splash in Parisian society. It was almost impossible not to see them dining out, at parties, generally being the sun in the solar system. Everything revolved around them. They were the brightest of the Bright Young Things and Louise simply could not compare.

He was thin, wiry, dark hair slicked back from brown eyes. His face, his skin, was pale and flawless. Even though it was one in the afternoon, he was still wrapped in a dressing gown. Louise couldn't help but stare for a moment. He wasn't attractive, although Louise probably wasn't the best judge of that, but there was something about him. The dog, Maisy, obeyed his command, disappearing into the depths of the house.

"Who are you?" He leaned against the doorjamb, blocking her view of the house. He had a lazy, Southern way of speaking, an accent Louise hadn't heard many times, but it was enough to set her teeth on edge.

Louise swallowed. "Philip Montgomery? Louise Lloyd. I'm a friend of your wife's. I've recently come to Paris, and she said I should look her up."

Philip raised one dark eyebrow. "My wife never mentioned having a nigger for a friend. Wouldn't have married her if that was the case. Tell me the truth."

She swallowed hard. "Your wife's mother sent me here to talk to you. She thinks Iris is missing, and I'm inclined to agree. Now, we can discuss it out here, or you can invite me in." Louise had learned long ago that the key to dealing with entitled white men was to treat them like children.

He considered it. Louise kept eye contact, trying to stare him into submission.

Of course, he could still say no, and she'd need another plan. But appearances were more important than anything.

"What do you want?" he asked, unconvinced.

"To talk to you about your wife," Louise said.

He pulled the door open, allowing her in, and then closed it.

The dog, Maisy, sat at Philip's feet. They did not move from the foyer, a foot of space between them. "So, she what? Hired a private dick?"

Louise blinked. "I work in a parfumerie."

He laughed, and it was a real, loud laugh.

Louise felt a blush rise to her cheeks. "Mrs. Wright just wanted me to confirm that her daughter is alive and happy. Like I said, I'm a family friend."

"Well, you can tell Mrs. Wright that my wife walked out of here two months ago. And I don't know where she went." With a dramatic flourish, he opened the door. Maisy, seizing her chance, bounded out the door. Philip didn't chase her.

"You didn't report her missing?" Louise asked. There was a sinking feeling in her stomach. Something didn't seem to match up.

"I thought she'd come home." The answer was noncommittal, breezy. "She hasn't yet."

"And you haven't told anyone?" Louise dared to look around the foyer. It was clean, unforgiving. The walls were white, the floors below her feet were white too. For a moment, she wondered how easy it would be to hide a body in this place. It was too pristine, Iris' doing, or more likely, a team of maids.

"She'll come back when she feels like it. You know she's an artist; she does this a lot. I'm sure she's gone to find herself or something."

The door was closing. Louise could feel it. And she had

nothing to take back to Lucy Wright. Maybe Louise was jaded; God knew that her time as a consultant to the New York Police Department had made her so, but she didn't believe a word of this story. It was how he replied to her. How he spoke to her.

"Now, if there's nothing else, I need to go get my wife's dog."

"There is, actually. I'd like to see her studio before I leave."

"There isn't a body hidden in our attic." The way he said it sent chills down her spine. She thought it was supposed to be a joke, a callous one that wasn't funny. But he looked her right in the eye.

"I'd like to take something of hers for Mrs. Wright."

Philip exhaled. "Fine. Up the stairs."

He didn't show her the way. That was fine with her.

---

LOUISE IMAGINED WRONG when she heard the word "attic." She pictured some slightly damp place with a single flickering light-bulb.

But Iris' studio was on the third floor of the house, not exactly an attic. It had its own bathroom right next to it. The windows were large and clean, and sun shined into them. A few paces into the room, which had exquisite hardwood floors, stood an easel with a half-finished painting. There were paints and canvasses around the room, a pillow for the dog to sleep on while she worked.

Dust danced in the air, suspended in the sunlight. The room got good light. Louise wasn't an art person, not really. She liked taking photographs, and did when she found the time, but painting was a different beast. Maybe it's because her father would have deemed the pastime as frivolous. But then, anything that wasn't in service of getting a husband and being a good wife was frivolous. Maybe it was the fact that to paint, and be painted, you'd have to sit still. Louise didn't like staying still for too long—she was always trying to do something.

A framed painting on the wall showed a woman with red hair that bordered on gold, chopped to the chin, eyes bright and blue. There was an all-knowing smile on her lips. Louise stared into the ocean-blue eyes of Iris Montgomery.

Even as a painting, as a stranger, the woman was beguiling. That was the only way to describe her. Something secretive in her smile, something bold and daring in her eyes. Photographs in the paper, grainy and sucked of color, couldn't do Iris justice. The eyes of the painting seemed to follow her as Louise moved about the room, an effect that was unnerving. She tried to picture Iris in this room, painting.

There was an old piano in the corner, a record player on top of it. Most of the day and evening would be spent in this room, listening to the Victrola as she painted. Now, the house around her seemed hollow and empty. She didn't know where Philip was, and she had to act fast. She began by taking off her shoes and walking over the wood floors, trying to determine if any of the boards were loose, if there was something hidden away from view.

Then she put her shoes back on. This was Iris' domain. She doubted Philip would come up here for any reason.

And therefore, there was no reason to hide anything at all.

There was no desk. The wardrobe was filled, not with clothes, but with expensive paint supplies. She wanted something she could give back to Lucy Wright. Louise wasn't sure what she'd say to the woman. Louise could picture her desperate face, how much she wanted to see her daughter, talk to her.

And there was the story Philip had just fed her. Gone for two months.

Louise didn't see one reason to believe him.

She couldn't risk going to the bedroom. She'd get lost on her way there anyway. This was what she had, and the studio was just as secretive as its owner. Without thinking, she took the portrait off the wall. It wasn't big or awkward to carry. The house was silent. There was something both calming and off-putting about it. She had never been in a house this quiet, no one around. Not even a neighbor. Philip was still chasing the dog, the door left ajar. She had gone through the room too fast, much too unsettled to take her time. There was something eerie about the space. She didn't belong there, and she knew that. It was impossible, but she thought the room knew it too.

Should he have left her alone? Probably not.

Louise tucked the portrait under her arm and made her way back downstairs.

She thought the house, given the chance, would swallow her.

# 5

IT WAS THE way Iris painted. Louise put the painting she took from Iris' studio across the wall from her bed, where she could see it. Below her, Ciarán was typing away, humming loudly. His neighbor to the right rapped on the wall. Ciarán ignored it. It was a nightly routine, one Louise never let bother her. She turned her radio on and stared.

It was a self-portrait, and the way Iris had managed to capture her own eyes, the depths and oceans within them. Louise was drinking wine from the bottle, one leg pulled up under her. Iris painted with a softness that managed to capture something in Louise, but she could never put the feeling into words.

Was it the haziness? The feeling of impermanence? The idea that nothing could or would stay? Was it the way she painted herself, with all the care and decisiveness that men afforded themselves? Was it the mere fact that Iris was a woman making her mark in a man's world? Louise didn't know.

But it was comforting, in a strange way, to have someone else in the apartment. Louise had gone from living with her family to living in a rented room, to living with Rosa Maria. She could not stand the silence, the emptiness, even if her apartment was small.

Louise moved so she was stretched out on her stomach. She had long discarded the day's things: day dress of turquoise linen, stockings, hat, gloves, in a pile on the floor. She rolled over, windowsill within reach, and lit a cigarette.

Iris watched as she did so, judging Louise's every move. She got up, bottle and cigarette in her hands, and sat mere inches from the portrait.

Now, up close, she could see the brushstrokes, the way Iris painted. Louise had never given thought to the notion that art like this was supposed to make you *feel* something. Usually, she just felt bored. But with Iris' work, Louise could feel the artist's emotions, the patience and love poured into each portrait.

Louise was sure she would never love anyone or anything the same way Iris loved to paint.

She had never been this close to a canvas before. She reached out, brushing it with her fingertips. Iris remained unamused. The ridges seemed to come alive under the pads of Louise's fingers.

The more she looked, the more she wanted to know about the woman behind the painting.

She pulled herself back, breaking a spell that had formed around her. She took a couple of deep breaths, centering herself again. She focused on Ciarán's humming, the sun going down through her window. She stepped back, sitting at her table. The letters that Lucy Wright had passed on were all in a pile that Louise had yet to organize.

The key to understanding Iris had to be in those letters.

*July 6th, 1927*

*Lou,*

*I am finally in the pictures! I'm a background dancer on a picture called* Something Sweet. *It's almost nothing, but I love it so far. It's been months of trying and hoping and here we are.*

*Michael is thrilled for me.*

*I wish you were here to see it. I'm not even sure I'll be in it, after all of that, but it's a risk, and I took it.*

*It's a contract for three pictures, and I'll be dancing in all three of them. They also want me to start elocution classes, which I don't get, because I already know how to talk.*

*We have a little house (so you can write me at this address). There's a little porch and orange trees, and I think about how dire my life seemed even a few months ago.*

*Did I ever thank you for helping me? I know it couldn't have been easy for you.*

*Michael sends his love.*

*I'm sending a photograph, although it doesn't really do it justice. You have to see the brilliant colors: the blue of the sky, the orange of the fruit, the green of the grass. Every morning I wake up and sit on our porch, and I have to pinch myself to remember that this is my life now.*

*I didn't know that the world could be so wide or be this good. I get to have fun, dancing for money!, and I get to go home to the man I love. I feel Celia with me at every moment, and I know that she would have loved it here. I miss her every day. But she's part of me and that's the most important thing.*

*Harlem seems so bleak and empty. I think that's how you felt too. I know Minna doesn't feel that way.*

*Have you written Minna? I know she would love to hear from you. It'll be harder to keep us together now that we're spread apart, but I want us to try. And that means you and Minna have to talk; it should be easier now. Just tell her about Paris.*

*I miss you! Every moment of every day, I hope that you're finding the same happiness I am. I'll have to send you more photos, when I get the chance.*

*My love always,*
*Josie*

# 6

THE FACT REMAINED that Paris was the biggest city Louise had ever lived in, she stuck to two arrondissements, and she had no idea where to even start looking for a woman who did not want to be found.

Louise considered this as she stood behind the till, posture perfect, that morning.

Maybe Iris had left of her own volition, never to return.

Allaire's wasn't busy that morning. Mornings were slow, true, but this was slower than usual. Two customers wandered the floor. Louise knew better than to go up and *ask* if they were finding everything okay. So, she watched. Both women were white, elegant in a way Louise simply would never be. They shopped with a purpose, and Louise watched.

And pondered.

She hadn't had time to grab coffee that morning, and she had missed seeing Clémence. Louise had woken to Iris staring at her, eyes revealing nothing.

She had spent too much time reading Iris' letters. She was

funny, in a dry, sarcastic way, and she kept her mother informed about everything in her life, accompanied by newspaper clippings and diary entries.

Louise had brought some of them to work that day, just to be able to get through some of it. She tried not to think about the relationship she and her own mother would have had if she had not killed herself shortly after her twin sisters were born. Louise was the spitting image of her mother, Janie, and yet knew little about her.

Louise hoped they would have been close, like Iris seemed to be with her own mother.

"Excuse me." The woman in front of the till called Louise to attention.

"Pardon," Louise said. This woman with black hair and huge blue eyes looked Louise up and down. "My apologies."

As the woman began to lay her selections out on the counter, Louise tallied them all up, writing them in the logbook and adding up the total. This job required her to do more mathematics than she'd ever had to do in her life. "What are you reading?" The woman's voice was soft.

"Just some old letters," Louise responded. "Are you sure you want two of these?"

She nodded, a smile hooked on the left side of her mouth. "You know your face cream makes a wonderful paint remover."

"I didn't know that. You paint?" The casual conversation was the only thing Louise hated about her job. Monsieur Allaire's first rule was treating every customer as if they were family. And that included the small talk.

"A few friends and I do, yes. We swear by the stuff."

Louise had to wonder if something that was used as a paint remover was safe to use as a face cream as well. "Well, how interesting. You're at fifteen francs." The woman raised an eyebrow but handed over the money. Louise wrapped everything up in a carrier bag and gave it to her. "Have a good day."

"You too," the woman said as she departed. She left a flowery scent behind her. Louise watched her go, the chiming bells over the door announcing her departure.

An interesting meeting indeed.

⌁

CIARÁN WAS ALWAYS awake by the time she got home from work. In fact, Louise didn't know when he slept. On her way home from work, she purchased the biggest bottle of whiskey she could find and knocked on his door.

The apartment was always noisy. Ciarán had a cat, a small tabby thing that Louise had immediately adored, a record player that was thirty years old, and he was always doing something. It was distracting, and then Louise got used to it. There was little point in knocking again; Ciarán wouldn't be able to hear her. So, she pushed the door open with her fingertips, the cat immediately at her feet. She stopped to scratch him behind the ears.

His apartment was bigger than hers; he had the privilege of a bathroom. He changed his mind often. One wall was blue, another was half painted a bright, bold red. A typewriter was in the corner, under the window. The floor around the table was littered with cigarette butts and crumpled-up pieces of paper. Five years ago, Ciarán had had one hit, a farcical play about a woman locked in a love triangle. He had premiered to rave reviews, had moved to Broadway where it was turned into a musical. He seemed to be living the most charmed life. And now he spent day and night sitting at that typewriter, trying to think of another play that was innovative and amazing. To Louise, who was able to leave work at work and not be plagued by perfumes and face creams, it seemed like a very specific sort of hell.

"Ah, love!" Ciarán, in shirt and trousers, ridiculously undone for six in the evening, said. "What brings you by?"

Louise handed over the bottle, and he took it, opening it immediately. "I need your help," Louise said. Ciarán turned to her, one eyebrow raised.

"Tiny, you know exactly how to butter me up."

"Of course."

They sat at his kitchen table, virtually the only place *to* sit, excluding the bed. The apartment was barely bigger than a playing card, suitable for one person and his cat. They drank directly from the bottle, passing it back and forth. Louise wasn't sure Ciarán, as sweet and talented as he was, owned one dish.

He'd be hard-pressed to find a dish in Louise's apartment as well.

"I need everything you know about Iris Montgomery."

"Why?"

Louise wrinkled her nose. She had no normal explanation that he would accept ready. She inhaled. "Her mother asked me to check up on her."

Ciarán pursed his lips. The song changed on the radio, and he took in roughly half of it before he responded. "Why?"

"Friend of a friend asked."

"Why?" Ciarán raised an eyebrow. His eyes searched her face so intently that she knew she couldn't get out of this one.

Louise inhaled. She didn't know where to begin. "He took me and my sister in when we had nowhere to go. I owe him."

"You have a sister?"

"Three. One died a couple of years ago." Celia. Louise hadn't thought about Celia in months, doing her youngest sister a disservice. She would have to write to Minna to get her to put flowers at her grave. Minna's daughter, Louise's niece she had never met, was nearly rounding a year now and named Celia Jane, for the two women Minna had lost in her life.

That was the thing about being so far away: Louise missed all the important moments.

"And now the man who took you and your sister in needs your help?" Ciarán asked. He liked to have all the details, liked to know everything about everyone. He often said it informed his characters and the world around them. Louise loved giving him as few details about her life as possible and letting him wonder.

They sometimes spent late nights together, drinking on the little balcony that connected Louise's apartment to the rest of the building. They'd pass a bottle of wine back and forth, he would ask, and Louise would not answer.

"Can you help me or not?" Louise asked. He was her only lead. Ciarán spent enough time in both circles, the lazy bohemians and the rich ones; he could navigate both flawlessly.

And he was what she needed.

"I was planning to write tonight, you know."

"You're always planning to write, and I don't think you ever do," Louise said.

He swigged from the bottle, his free fingers tapping on the tabletop. "Well, okay. We don't know each other well, but I can introduce you to people who do." A glint in his eyes, mischievous. She knew, out of everyone, Ciarán would know how to get to Iris. "You got a nice dress?"

Louise scoffed.

"Of course you do. Get dressed, and I'll pick you up in an hour."

# 7

MADAME BLANCHET'S SALON was unlike anything Louise had ever experienced. In a dress of midnight blue, delicate beading in gold around the hem of the skirt, matching shoes, and a gold hair band, she felt incredible. Ciarán had also dressed up, as much as he was ever going to, with a dinner jacket and his hair slicked away from his eyes.

The Blanchet house wasn't the biggest house Louise had ever been in—that honor would always go to the Schoonmaker manse—but it was imposing. A housemaid with the exact same shade of skin as Louise's opened the door.

"Julie," Ciarán said, his voice almost a purr. "You, my dear, are a sight for sore eyes." He kissed the maid on both cheeks.

"Flattery will get you everywhere, Mr. Dunne." Louise could tell that Julie was trying not to appear charmed by him. "How are you?"

"I am much better now that I'm seeing you," Ciarán said with a wink. "May I introduce my colleague, Louise Lloyd?"

"Nice to meet you," Louise said.

Julie smiled at her politely. "They're expecting you and your guest, Mr. Dunne." The maid nodded her head and was out of sight before Louise could say anything else.

Ciarán jutted his chin out to the wall behind Louise. She turned and was face-to-face with Iris Wright.

The auburn hair, the dancing eyes, the blemish-free white skin, all in an eight-by-ten canvas. She was behind glass, watching every entrance and exit.

"Ms. Wright is a regular here. Just follow me," Ciarán said. He paused to light a cigarette and held his arm out to Louise.

<hr />

THE ATMOSPHERE WAS *different.* Louise was used to sitting at Le Chat Noir, getting into arguments and passing drinks around. They were late, and the rest of the group was on to the second course of a five-course dinner.

"Apologies, I'm so sorry." Ciarán turned on the charm as they entered. The host, seated at the head of the table, wearing a glittering dress of soft pink, rose to her feet.

"I'm used to it, Ciarán Dunne. You must tell me how the new play is going." She turned to Louise, expression cool.

Louise looked around the table and found that she was the only Black person, only person of color there. She swallowed hard.

"I'll tell you all about it, Coralie. May I introduce Louise Lloyd. She moved here about a year ago."

Coralie Blanchet, tall, statuesque, didn't turn her attention away from Louise. "Miss Lloyd. Are you an artist? A writer?"

Louise cleared her throat. "I'm a photographer." It wasn't really a lie. She had also finished the tube of lipstick that had come with the camera. It was a *good* gift.

"Have you shown anywhere?" a young woman at the table piped up.

"No," Louise said. "I've never thought about it."

Coralie waved toward the table. "Sit down, both of you. We have much to discuss."

Louise was placed on Ciarán's left, and to the right of the woman who had spoken up. As dinner resumed, plates being put down in front of Louise so elegantly and silently that it seemed like they appeared by magic, the woman turned to her. "I'm Margaux Blanchet." She spoke softly and wore a dress of turquoise, setting off her black hair and blue eyes. There was something about her that Louise would never be able to place, something not exactly attractive, but alluring. Her smile crooked to the left, off-center. "Welcome."

"Thank you," Louise said as she placed her napkin over her lap. She wished Ciarán had thought to warn her that she'd be the only Black person in the room. She'd have to be on her best behavior. She was practically vibrating with nerves at the table.

"All you have to do is get through dinner, and then you'll see everyone's ugly side." Margaux sipped from her wineglass. "It's tough being new."

"Well, I believe we've met," Louise said. "I sold you our face-cream-paint-remover."

Margaux's blue eyes ran over Louise's face. "Oui! Allaire's. Of course. You were very helpful."

"You're so kind," Louise said. Ciarán was already caught up in a discussion, the wine turning his cheeks a ruddy red.

Margaux nudged the woman sitting beside her, equally enthralling, with wavy black hair and a dress of seafoam green. It was sleeveless with a deep V in the back, exposing pale shoulder blades and a few moles trailing down her spine. "Estelle, she thinks I'm kind."

"And we've found the only person in Paris who thinks so." Estelle tossed her head back, her neck long and elegant. She was concentrating on lighting a cigarette, an emerald-green holder already between her lips.

Coralie tapped her butter knife against her glass, calling the table of a baker's dozen to attention. "I would like to take a moment to acknowledge Iris Wright, the beautiful soul who is not with us tonight."

Ciarán leaned back in his seat, crossing his arms over his chest, the height of bad manners. Beside her, Louise could feel Margaux shift in her seat.

"Where is she?" the man across from Louise asked.

"You know what she's like," Estelle said. "Temperamental, as all artists are."

"Not all," Margaux said. "I am a delight."

"We both know that's not true," Estelle said. A look flashed between the two women, lightning quick, with no time for Louise to discern what it meant.

Ciarán looked toward both women. "We're friends, and I wish she had told me where she was going."

"More than friends." Margaux snorted.

Coralie tapped her knife against her glass again, calling the room back to attention. "No more of that. Please, let's finish, and Adam is going to give us a reading over dessert." The man across from Louise blushed.

Louise couldn't concentrate on the dessert, a personal chocolate cake with a scoop of vanilla ice cream. She had long gotten out of the habit of eating, and getting her appetite back was harder than she imagined.

She picked up her fork, cut off a piece, and chewed the sawdust in her mouth.

All she could really focus on was the fact that Ciarán had lied to her.

THERE WERE TWENTY minutes between the last course and the readings, which, Louise was informed, would take place in the solarium upstairs.

And that gave Louise twenty minutes to look around.

Through dinner, she observed that this group of people were close. Very close. They had all these private jokes and inside stories. Louise was constantly left behind.

Aside from the beginning, Iris wasn't mentioned. Instead, Coralie, reigning supreme over the group, guided them in discussions about art and life and literature. It was exactly what Louise did at Le Chat Noir, but with better wine. Coralie grilled Ciarán on his new play, and he shrunk under the woman's imperious gaze.

The Blanchet house was full of art, paintings and sculptures and photographs. It was bursting at the seams. But there was one photograph on the wall leading to the solarium. It caught her eye, and that was because Iris was in it.

*La Mort des Artistes.* Louise stared at the photograph, taking it down. Iris was in the center of it, looking directly at the camera. The rest of the women, several of them, all young and beautiful, were dotted around. There were easels and paint. One woman's head was tipped back in full laughter.

The writing was on the back, a tiny piece of paper. It was dated, in a navy-blue ink, April of 1927. Louise flipped it over again. It stood out among the other photographs and paintings on the wall.

"Coralie has work from almost every influential artist." Ciarán, holding a flute of champagne, had come up behind her. His voice was low, his cheeks were red. She turned toward him, still holding the photograph.

Louise held it up. "Have you heard of this?" she asked. "*Death of the Artists?*"

Ciarán stared at her for a moment, then drank from his glass. His jacket had managed to disappear, his tie was undone. He took the photograph from her. "Iris, Jeanne, Estelle, Margaux, Marion, Sabine, and . . . Lili. Huh." He didn't finish whatever thought he had. He handed the photograph back. "I guess if Iris is missing, you should talk to one of them."

"What do you get out of this?" Louise asked.

Ciarán pulled out a silver cigarette case, taking out two cigarettes. He handed one to Louise and lit it for her. It was only then that he replied. "Coralie helped me stage *Darling Girl.*" Ciarán's smile was soft. "And now, I would love to have her stamp of approval on my next project."

"And what is that?" Louise asked.

Ciarán shook his head. He stepped away from her, allowing himself to fall into deep discussion with a dark-haired man in a tux.

And once more, Louise was left alone. She stared at the photograph again. She put it back where she found it, her eyes still on Iris. She was the center of the photo, and the center of the group.

Then she wandered off, trying to find another glass of wine.

# 8

THE NEXT MORNING, when Louise arrived at work, coffee in her stomach warring with the alcohol from the night before, there was an envelope waiting for her.

It was Clara who brought it to her. Louise was in the staff room, removing her jacket and hat, hanging them up.

"This came for you," Clara said. She always tried to dress right but fell a couple of steps short. Today, her shoes and hat and dress matched, all a shocking shade of pink. Her lips were painted the same shade. The color was too bright for her. She held out the envelope, where Louise could see her name, written in navy-blue ink.

"Thank you," Louise said. She took it. Clara hovered, obviously wanting to see what was inside. "I'll handle the orders today," Louise said. That was enough to get the other young woman to leave her alone. Louise dropped to the small table where they took their lunches and tore into the envelope, anxious to know its contents.

To her surprise, the first thing that tumbled out was a golden key with a small engraving of an infinity symbol.

She pulled the paper out next, unfolding it. The letter was short.

In fact, it was just an address, along with a time and instructions to dress her best.

Louise stared at it, and then shoved everything back into the envelope, and then into the pocket of her coat. She was more than intrigued.

She was also a little nervous.

⊰◈⊱

THE ADDRESS LED her to Montparnasse, a building in a section of Paris she had never been to before. How was she supposed to match the key to the apartment? There had to be at least ten thousand units.

She held the key in her gloved hand, staring up at the elevators, momentarily frozen. "Miss Lloyd." Estelle wafted in, wearing a dress of seafoam green. She hadn't cut her hair like the other Bright Young Things, and it tumbled down her shoulders. She had woven flowers into it, fresh cuts of roses and peonies.

It was stunning. Louise wished she could do the same thing. It wouldn't have the same effect.

"You're just in time," Estelle said. She leaned forward, kissing Louise's cheeks. Louise was doused with her sharp perfume. "And you look wonderful." Louise thought she sensed a bit of a pause there.

She had done her best. Her dress was royal purple, one of her best colors, long, billowy sleeves, and a skirt that just kissed her knees. She felt invincible.

"I thought I'd wait for you," Estelle said, "and you're waiting for me. How funny."

"Very funny," Louise said. "What is all this?"

Estelle winked at her and called the elevator.

It was an apartment at the top of the building. "Key," Estelle said.

Louise had forgotten she was holding it, clutched in her hand like some sort of lifeline. Louise slipped it into the lock and turned.

There was music playing, women flitting around the apartment, laughing and drinking. "Look who I found," Estelle announced as she swept into the apartment. Louise followed, unsure of what to do. Margaux, sitting at an easel, wearing an oversized men's shirt, looked up. She smiled thinly. "You should have brought your camera."

"I didn't know," Louise said.

"The instructions could have been more clear." Estelle handed Louise a glass of wine. She took it, grateful for the distraction. "Louise, this is Jeanne, Lili, Sabine, and Marion. You already know Margaux." All the other women waved. Louise looked around, getting a better sense of the place. A couple of women were sitting around, sculpting clay, sketching.

And there was a lot of drinking going on.

"Take a seat," Marion said. She was one of the women who was sculpting. Her hands were covered in clay, and she took care to wipe them on a towel.

All these women, some of whom had been at the salon the night before, were busy making their own moves, their own art.

Louise sat, feeling like a fish out of water. She thought about Rosa Maria, how she would love a place to get together with other women, other writers. "What is all this?" she asked again.

"Just women who make art." Estelle was sitting down in front of a canvas, pushing her hair out of the way.

"Why all the secrecy?" Louise asked.

"So, Louise, what do you like to photograph?" Margaux asked. She was in charge here. Margaux rose, taking off her men's shirt and revealing a spangled gold frock underneath. She moved to sit next to Louise.

"Whatever catches my eye." Louise cleared her throat. Margaux, this close, was stunning in a Pre-Raphaelite way, cold and intimidating. Her eyes locked onto Louise's. "Women, mostly." Well, one woman, but she didn't have to explain that.

Lili was one of the women who was drawing, sitting at the kitchen island, with a pencil behind her ear. She sipped from her glass of wine and exhaled. "I like you."

"She likes everyone," Estelle said.

Lili was still staring at her, her eyes, a bright green, were narrowed into slits. "You have a certain charm. Do you know that? I'd like to draw you. Hold still."

"Right now?"

Marion snorted. "She does this. If you're lucky, you'll make it into one of her larger works."

Lili got up, and then she situated herself in front of Louise, turning to a fresh page in her sketchbook.

It was quiet for a little bit, every woman working on her own projects. Margaux had returned to her canvas, Marion back to her clay. "Hold still," Lili said. Her pink lips were pursed in concentration.

Louise let a few minutes pass; she counted out the seconds as she tried her best not to move. She attempted to picture what she looked like in Lili's discerning eye. No one had ever drawn her before.

But she was here for a reason. And about an hour after arriving, three glasses of wine drank, and six cigarettes smoked, Louise broached the topic. "What do you know about Iris Wright?" The name shifted the quiet, peaceful mood of the room. She couldn't look around, but she saw Estelle pause.

"She's just traveling," Margaux said, rather quickly.

"I thought she's been gone for a couple of months," Louise said.

"Where did you hear that?" Margaux was direct. That was something Louise would appreciate if Margaux's raised eyebrow wasn't currently directed at her.

Estelle broke the silence. "Like you said, she's only been gone for a couple of months. She does this . . . all artists do. She's in Italy or Spain, soaking up inspiration. She'll be back." Those last three words were tacked on as if Estelle were trying to convince herself.

That was that.

For the next couple of hours, the apartment settled back down. No mentions of Iris, no mentions of anyone. Even Lili finished her drawing but didn't allow Louise to see it.

As they were leaving, a trail of debris in their wake, Margaux caught up to her. She was smiling softly. "Feel free to come back here whenever you want. We've made one of the bedrooms into a darkroom. But . . ." And here, she put a hand on Louise's arm. "I'd be careful about mentioning Iris. We're all close, but you can never be too careful." And with that, she swept past Louise, placing her hat back on her head.

# 9

---

AFTER WORK THE next day, Louise pulled out her camera. She was still thinking about her evening, thinking about Margaux and Estelle, and the pied-à-terre apartment. It had clouded her day at work, leading to her being distracted in the present.

She had decided to go straight home from work, something she hadn't done in months. Usually, it was first to Dauphine's, and then to Le Chat Noir, drinking the night away.

Louise kicked off her heels, pulling the box her camera was in out from under her bed. She held it in her hand, running her fingers over the abstract lightning bolts on the cover. What was she doing? Would this get her closer to Iris?

Around her, the building was quiet. Being at the top meant that she could feel every move and shift, hear everything that was going on.

She needed some film.

Louise stretched out on her bed, camera next to her, and picked up another of Iris' letters. She had started at the beginning, trying to get a better sense of who Iris was.

"Hey! Tiny!" Ciarán was at her door. He was leaning on the doorjamb, arms crossed over his chest. "What are you reading?"

"I didn't think you'd be in," Louise said.

Ciarán invited himself in, as he tended to do. He shoved his hands in his pockets. "I've been up all day." Ciarán looked around. He stopped at the portrait of Iris, kneeling down in front of it. "Beautiful."

"What do you want, Ciarán?" Louise asked. She was used to this. Every so often he would get grumpy or frustrated or bored and would seek out someone to talk to. Since they first met, Louise had become that person for him.

He strolled around the little apartment as if it were his own. "I can't believe you live like this." He picked the camera up from her bed, turning it around in his hands. "So, you really take photos? What are those?"

Louise exhaled. A lot of dealing with Ciarán was much like dealing with Rafael. Indulge, distract, and she could get back to her own work. "Letters."

Ciarán climbed into bed beside her. "That's Iris' writing."

"They're Iris' letters."

He stared at her. "Why do you have them?"

Louise didn't know how to lie to answer that, so she distracted. "How's writing going?"

Ciarán grumbled. He kept turning her camera over in his hands. "How's photography going?"

She put the papers down, trying to keep them in some sort of order. She moved so she was sitting up, her legs tucked under her. With both of them on her bed, the frame creaked with every shift. "Why don't we put everything away, and you can tell me what you know about Iris?"

Ciarán sighed. "I like Iris. She is smart and very clever. She knows how to make people look their best. She was part of the original cast of *Darling Girl*. But she didn't want to act."

Louise nodded.

"She's serious about art. She's serious about painting. When you look at her, and she's painting, sometimes she'll . . . smile, and I've never seen her look happier than when she's at an easel."

"Where do you think she is?" Louise asked.

Ciarán exhaled. Instead of answering her question, he took a moment to light a cigarette, producing his silver case from his pocket. He didn't respond until he lit a second with the butt of the first. "I don't know, Tiny. And I wish I did."

"Has she done this before?"

"Every so often, she takes these trips for inspiration. She usually tells someone when she leaves. But this time . . ." He trailed off, sorting through his thoughts. "You should talk to Estelle. I know they were close."

"What about you?" Louise asked.

Ciarán was quiet. He exhaled cigarette smoke. Louise watched as it floated up to the ceiling. "It was a bit of fun." He chose his own words carefully. "It started once after a rehearsal of *Darling Girl*. It was only a couple of times, but those girls . . . they tell each other everything. It hasn't happened for a couple of years now. They still like to tease me." He lit another cigarette, letting his words hang in the air. "I respected her. I *respect* her. She's smart. She always helped me, and I always helped her." He sat up, his eyes on hers. "How did you get caught up in this mess?"

"Favor for a friend," Louise said.

"Lot of work for a favor."

Louise didn't have a good answer for that.

⏦⏦

THE ONLY WOMAN present the second time Louise went to the apartment was Estelle. It was the middle of a Saturday, and while Louise should have been in bed, she had gotten up early, taken her camera out, and went to the apartment.

"Nice to see you," Estelle said. She was seated in front of an easel, wearing a black dress. She had taken off her shoes, and the radio was playing.

"Nice to see you too."

Estelle narrowed her eyes. "I thought you were lying about being a photographer."

"Just a hobby." Louise's cheeks burned.

"Help yourself to anything," Estelle said. "If you want to know where the darkroom is, it's down the hall and the last door on your left."

"Do you mind if I take some of you?" Louise asked. She had only taken three photographs on her morning walk, and they were all of the Moulin Rouge's red windmill.

Estelle blushed but nodded.

Louise's hands shook as she opened the cover, and she tried to steady them. She didn't think that anyone would be here this early, and she was hoping to poke around the apartment. She removed her shoes, too, finding the best place to capture Estelle's light.

She took a couple of establishing photos, and then tried to see what Estelle was working on. The canvas was blank.

"I'm having a little trouble getting started," Estelle said. "I don't even know why I came." She sighed, putting her paintbrush down. "I had a dream. It was so vivid, I thought I had to get it down immediately, and now that I'm here, I can't think of it again. Do you ever have those days?"

Louise could safely say that she had not had those days. But she didn't respond, hoping Estelle would keep talking. She picked up the paintbrush again and then threw it across the room, making Louise jump. Estelle ran her hands through her hair, letting out a groan. "Iris was supposed to help me. She would always help me."

"Maybe I can help you," Louise said.

"What do you know about painting?" Estelle asked.

"Nothing, but that doesn't mean I can't help." Louise put her camera down. Estelle exhaled.

"It's okay, but thank you for the offer." Estelle got up, opening the window. The midday sun shone in. She sat at the window bench, and Louise sat across from her.

"Do you know where she is?" Louise asked.

Estelle looked out the window. The pied-à-terre was high enough that it felt like the world was swaying below them. It made Louise dizzy. She lived at the top of her building, but this was different. Taller. She tore her gaze away from the window.

Estelle stared into the perfectly blue sky. "I don't. She'll be back though. She always comes back."

"But does she leave without telling anyone?"

Estelle laughed. "No one can ever tell Iris what to do. She does as she pleases. She'd tell me to stop whining and get back to work. She didn't get a show by sitting around."

Louise had been to that show; the gallery was still showing Iris' work. It had been the talk of her friends at Le Chat Noir for weeks. The reviews in the paper had lambasted Iris for daring to paint herself naked.

Estelle closed her eyes. "She makes it look so easy. She makes it seem like she was born with a brush in hand, and we all have to catch up. She's humble about it. She's so kind, always offering help." Estelle exhaled, tilting her head back. "I miss her."

Louise got the sense that there was something else, but she didn't want to pry. She was about to ask more when the door opened. Marion and Lili came in, breaking the spell she and Estelle were under. Estelle cleared her throat and got up from the window bench.

"I should get back to work."

And that was that. Louise didn't get another chance to ask Estelle about Iris.

# 10

〽

THE GALLERY THAT held Iris Wright's seminal art show was quiet. Louise wasn't very sure it was open, but she was coming after work, the only time she could. The doors, however, were unlocked.

Louise had seen this show. She had wandered around the different pieces, taking every bit in. She had gone with a few people from the cabaret. They had all been curious to see Iris' work.

Now, Louise began to go around again, looking for anyone she could talk to. She was the only patron that she could see. The silence hummed around her and Iris. The collection was mainly made up of self-portraits. Louise remembered the artist proclaiming that she would never do a landscape or a still life or a seascape.

There were a couple of paintings of other people, Coralie, Estelle, and Margaux. That was another thing about Iris. She only ever painted women in intimate moments. Margaux was poised in the middle of applying makeup, Estelle in a slip. These private parts of women's lives.

One painting was of a group of women, rather like the *Last*

*Supper.* With Iris in the middle, smiling softly to the viewer, with only a couple of women Louise recognized around her. It was called *La Mort des Artistes.* The same name on the photo Louise had found. The same group of women Louise had spent time with in the apartment.

This was more than a group of women who liked to make art together. That was their cover story. This felt like something else.

Just like the ones she did of herself, every painting of Iris' friends was done with the highest amount of care and love. Louise stepped up to the painting of Margaux. She had been caught mid-laugh, her face wrinkled up. If she concentrated, Louise could hear the laugh, she could feel as if she were part of the moment.

The pièce de résistance was a large self-portrait. Hung farthest from the entrance, so a viewer would have to wind their way through to it, was a full-body nude portrait of Iris leaning back on a fainting couch.

A navy-blue blanket covered her modesty. Iris had painted herself as if she were Aphrodite, a soft curve to her stomach and her breasts. She was looking directly at the viewer, daring them to say anything about her painting.

The first and only other time Louise had seen this painting, she had been shocked into silence. She had spent ten minutes staring at it, trying to capture the details hidden within. The folds of her blanket, the way her hand was posed on top. Her strong chin and defiant look. Her long legs and pointed toes coming out from under the blanket. It had made every hair on Louise's body stand at attention, set every molecule in her on fire. She hadn't been able to breathe.

And now, standing in front of it again, Louise was feeling exactly the same things.

Iris' bright eyes followed Louise around as she walked from

side to side, taking in all the details. The attention put into every painting she did was marvelous.

Indecent. Improper. Disgusting for a woman to put herself on display like that.

The more Louise learned about Iris Wright, the more Louise liked her.

"Beautiful, isn't it?"

The voice made Louise jump.

A young man in a dark suit was standing next to her, arms crossed. "The way she paints. You can tell she loves what she's doing. I'm Alphonse."

"Louise," Louise said without moving her eyes from Iris'.

"She did well for us. Made us more popular. There are a couple of pieces that have sold, but she hasn't come to collect her payment." Alphonse turned to Louise. He was cleanly dressed, handsome in the way all Frenchmen were.

"When was the last time you saw her?" Louise asked.

"A month ago, now. She promised to be back."

"Did she say where she was going?" Louise asked.

Alphonse didn't grace that with a response.

Louise knew better. To get people to open up, she had to butter them up. "How long have you worked here?" A change of tactic.

"Three years. Iris' show is my first big one. I took it over from my father when he retired." He paused to light a cigarette, offering Louise one. The thing about Louise was that she was never going to refuse a cigarette. She allowed him to light it for her, and he shook out the match.

"You didn't think she was a risk?" Louise asked.

"Of course she was a risk. My father almost lost this place, and I wanted to get it back to its former glory. Showing this work was the first step toward that."

"Did it work?" Louise asked. She had kept an eye on this show out of interest. She thought that Iris was the exact type of woman she would want to be friends with. She didn't compromise, and she knew what she wanted.

He grimaced. "One step at a time."

"And you haven't heard from her? Not at all?" Louise asked. "I can't believe she wouldn't pick up the money she's made."

"Well, she doesn't need it. She and her husband have enough money already. This is just a hobby for her."

Was it? Louise had her hobbies—well, her one hobby of dancing. She loved it, but she didn't think she spent as much time at it as Iris did with painting.

It was more than a hobby. Louise could see it was a love affair.

"If I give you my phone number, will you let me know if she comes in?" Louise asked. She had had little cards with her phone number made up, mostly for the Le Chat Noir group. She pulled a card out of her purse now, handing it over between two fingers.

"Who are you?" he asked, taking her card.

"A friend of a friend."

◁▽▷

LOUISE HAD BEEN in a couple of newsrooms in her day, and *Journal Américain* was no different. It was busy, men and women typing away. Coffee and cigarettes, it was much like the one where Rosa Maria had worked. The major difference was that this newsroom operated in both French and English.

She read this paper every morning, desperate for news about America as well as France, and she thought she knew who she was looking for.

Emme Foster.

She was the society reporter. She was the one who wrote about

Iris and Philip and their circles. Emme was the one Louise needed to talk to.

Louise stepped toward a desk with a typewriter and a phone and a little tag proclaiming the woman's name.

The reporter looked up. And her vision of who Emme Foster was didn't match the woman before her. She had brown hair of an uninspired shade and large brown eyes hidden behind a round set of glasses. When she caught Louise's eye, she raised an eyebrow but didn't stop typing.

"Emme Foster?" Louise asked. Not a *strong* start, considering her name was right there.

"At your service." American, from the Midwest. Emme's fingers didn't stop moving.

"My name is Louise Lloyd. I want to talk to you about Iris Wright."

It was then that Emme stopped typing. She stopped all motion, actually, freezing on the spot.

Louise didn't know if it was because of her name or Iris'. "I know you write about her; you're a glorified Iris stalker."

Emme snorted but nodded. "She does dominate the society pages. But she's not all I write about."

"I'm sorry," Louise said. She didn't know why she was apologizing. There was something about Emme's discerning gaze that unnerved her.

Emme wrinkled her nose to readjust her glasses, the thing Rosa Maria always did.

Louise cleared her throat, trying not to think about her ex-girlfriend. If she did that, she would be bereft for a week. "Iris' mother asked me to look into her disappearance. I thought since you write about her—"

"That I would know where she is?"

"Yes."

Emme looked around, her gaze focusing on a desk that was crowded with men. They were all laughing at this one man in the center. He was a man Louise wouldn't trust, lithe and brunette with a wide smile. But it was the way all the men flocked to him, like moths to a flame. She never trusted a man with that much power. Emme's eyes narrowed. Louise thought she felt the same. Emme picked up a package of cigarettes and a book of matches. "Not here."

Once they were situated outside in a little courtyard behind the building, with lit cigarettes, Emme turned to her. "So, Iris Wright? I can't let them overhear anything. If they think there's a good story, they'll take it for themselves. It's a fucking man's world." She exhaled, as if she were trying to calm herself down.

"Not anymore," Louise said.

Emme looked at her, a smile fighting on her lips. "Iris Wright?" she asked again.

"I'm trying to set up a timeline of when she disappeared, and I thought that you would be able to help." Louise opened her purse, pulling out a five-franc bill. It was all she had on her. "Anything you could tell me would help."

Emme removed the cigarette from her lips. Her lips were beautiful, pink and pursed. Louise watched as she thought about it. "I can tell you what I know, but it's not much."

"When was the last time you saw Iris out and about?" Louise asked.

Emme closed her eyes, taking her glasses off for a moment. "It's May, so I think the last time I saw her out was in March? There was an artist festival, and she was an artist to watch."

"When exactly was this festival?" Louise asked. "She hasn't written her mother, and she's worried."

"And her mother asked you to look into it? Are you an investigator?"

"I work at a parfumerie."

Emme's eyebrows knit together. "Right. Well. The festival was the first weekend of March."

"It's been two months without a word." Louise could feel her panic rising in her chest. That couldn't be a good sign. She didn't want to tell Lucy that her daughter was dead. But closure was better than nothing. And if this was her sister, she would want to know.

She remembered the panic she felt when Celia went missing. The crushing weight of the fear of what *might* have happened.

And her worst fear came true.

"How about this?" Emme said eventually. "I'll get you everything you need to know, and if anything comes up, I will tell you. But in my opinion? I don't think she's dead. I think she's just working on her next masterpiece."

Louise took this in. She willed this to be true. She wasn't sure she could tell another woman her daughter was dead. "One more question. Have you heard of *La Mort des Artistes*?"

Emme's smile was slight. She dropped the butt of her cigarette, crushing it under the heel of her shoe, classic, basic Mary Janes. "Barely. They're rather . . . what I have heard is that they are a group of the most intense women in art. They are an elite group. I don't know much more about them."

Louise could tell Emme who was a member and where they met. But that was all.

Emme leaned back, looking at Louise. "You know, some call them a secret society."

# 11

OUT OF ALL the women in the group, only Jeanne worked a job like Louise did. It was a clothing shop in the 2nd arrondissement, close to Allaire's.

But a clothing shop bigger than Louise had ever seen. As she entered, she was greeted by a strict French woman.

It was Jeanne's idea to have lunch together, and Louise couldn't turn the chance down to get to know the woman. The café Jeanne chose was in the middle, between their two workplaces.

Jeanne was everything Louise wished she could be. She held herself with a sort of poise that Louise could never accomplish. Her hair was long, and she wore these round glasses that made her slate-gray eyes look bright. "I'm glad you decided to join me." Jeanne lit a cigarette. Even her fingers were long, and she moved as if there was music only she could hear.

"I'm glad too." Louise usually took lunch in the break room, and being outside of it, outside of the store, made her nervous.

She looked at the menu. This was a place she couldn't afford.

Jeanne ordered a bottle of wine and then looked at Louise. "How long have you been in Paris?"

"Ten months," Louise said. "I still can't believe it. Sometimes I have to wake up and pinch myself."

Jeanne's smile was kind. "I know the feeling."

Apparently, attending that first meeting meant that, no matter what Louise wanted, she was a member.

It would be rude to decline.

Jeanne lifted her glass of wine with her left hand. Her emerald and diamond bracelet danced as she did. "I cannot wait for you to get to know all the girls. Joining the society was the best thing I've ever done." Jeanne nodded, her eyes wide behind her glasses.

"What do you think of all of them?" Louise asked.

Jeanne smiled. She seemed to be a smiley person, relentlessly cheerful. "They're all wonderful, all so talented. I'm an only child, so it feels like finally having sisters."

"I have three sisters," Louise said. "I don't know if I want any more."

"Then you have practice!" Jeanne laughed.

Louise liked her laugh. "I suppose so."

It was easy to feel at ease with the woman sitting across from her. Jeanne leveled with her. "You don't need to be embarrassed that you're a photographer. It's a new medium for us, but I'm sure you're great."

"Of course," Louise said. She was unsure how to take that, but she chose to take it as a compliment.

"Margaux and Lili will try to get you to paint. So will Iris, when she comes home."

"I can't draw," Louise said. She bit her tongue. She wanted to ask about Iris, but she couldn't jump on that. She'd look too eager.

"Well, that's a shame." Jeanne poured herself another glass of wine. She was faster than Louise, who was still nursing her first.

Even though there was a bread bowl on the table, neither of them ate. They smoked instead.

"How do you feel about Iris?" Louise finally asked. She had had to wait for the waiter to give them their bottle of wine, the second, and leave them alone.

Jeanne's smile became strained, a tiny moment that Louise noticed. "Iris is . . . nice. Good."

"Is that all?" Louise asked.

Jeanne sipped from her glass again, literally draining it before putting it down and answering. She drank more than Louise did, and that was a feat. Jeanne wiped her mouth with the back of her hand, smearing her dark-red lipstick. "Iris is nice," she said again. She was beginning to slur her words. Louise waved the waiter down, ordering some water. She pushed the bread bowl toward Jeanne, and she gratefully began eating.

Louise lit a cigarette. She had been moderating her own wine intake and had been watching Jeanne drink two glasses of wine to every one of Louise's own. Now that she was fully drunk, Jeanne's poise was gone, and Louise couldn't see what she saw in her earlier.

"She's fine," Jeanne said. "But we always had different ideas of what we wanted. And she could be controlling, and she could . . ." Jeanne trailed off, looking around. No one was looking at them. When she looked back at Louise, her demeanor had changed. "Iris and I were friends." Jeanne lit another cigarette, exhaling smoke slowly. "And I'm hoping she comes back soon."

Louise tried to keep her reaction under her skin, but she couldn't help but think this was strange. She didn't press the issue.

"Tell me about your sisters," Jeanne asked, somewhat like an excitable child.

Louise smiled. She reached over, taking the last piece of bread, soft and warm. "Well, there's Minna, and then Celia and Josie, the twins." She tried to explain her family without giving too much away. But she was running through the odd moments in her head. There were so many things Jeanne wasn't saying.

Nice and good.

One of the people closest to Iris could only summon up "nice" and "good" to describe her friend.

She knew there was something Jeanne wasn't telling her, and Louise couldn't wait to figure it out.

"I wish I had siblings," Jeanne said. It was the last few minutes of their lunch. "We should definitely do this again. We should do it every Friday." She was still tipsy but more grounded now. Louise didn't feel bad about sending her back to work.

"Maybe." Louise prevaricated. She didn't want to commit to anything. "But I'll see you at the pied-à-terre."

"Of course," Jeanne trilled. She pulled her purse up and placed a few bills on the table. Jeanne leaned forward to give her the customary double-cheek kiss. "Soon."

<hr />

LILI WAS *INTENSE*. It was the way she stared. Her green eyes managed to see everything. She and Louise were the same height, but Lili made it seem elegant. Her hair was a gorgeous chestnut brown. Her face was heart-shaped, and every thought Lili had danced across her face. When she drew, her eyes always zoned in on Louise's hair or nose or lips, individual pieces of herself that she never actually thought about. "I love your face," Lili said. She didn't like to be interrupted but would say things from time to time. "You're very beautiful."

"Thank you," Louise said.

"Don't speak."

It was her and Lili and Marion in the pied-à-terre that afternoon. Louise had come from work at Lili's insistence; she wanted to finish drawing her. Louise was in no place to disagree.

She needed to get to know these women. Something that was impossible when she couldn't speak.

At Lili's insistence, what was supposed to be a simple drawing had been changed. Louise was now sitting on a stool, topless, wearing nothing but a pair of pants, borrowed, and an ornate necklace. Her left hand was placed on her right shoulder, covering her breasts, and showcased the pendant, the necklace also borrowed. Louise hadn't wanted to do it like this, but Lili had begged, and Marion had promised nothing untoward would happen—it was just the girls—and Louise had agreed. The radio was playing, like always.

And besides, there was something freeing about it. Something incredible. Lili was left-handed, something Louise's Aunt Louise would have beaten out of her as a child, and her emerald and diamond bracelet shimmered as she moved. Louise kept still, but it was harder than it seemed. Her thoughts kept drifting, and before she knew it, she moved.

"Hand back down, please," Lili said. She always managed to know what Louise was doing, even if she was looking at the canvas, not her.

Louise lowered her arm; she scratched her nose without thinking about it.

"You're doing wonderfully," Lili said. She was dedicated and meticulous in her work; she wouldn't let Louise look at it until it was finished. They were doing a long session that seemed as though it would bleed into the night, but Louise didn't mind.

Behind her, Marion cursed. Louise heard the thud of clay hit the floor or the wall. Lili paused, looking up.

"I hate it," Marion said.

"Take a break," Lili said. She didn't stop painting.

Marion wandered over to where the easel and canvas were set up. She peered over, looking at Louise, then back at the painting. "You look good," Marion said with a nod of approval. Louise didn't react.

"She's learning," Lili said. "I know photography is so much easier, but there's something about painting. Smelling the paint, and feeling the canvas and the brush, there's nothing like it." Lili looked up. "I think we can stop there for today. Put something on."

This wasn't the only time Louise had been naked around a bunch of women, but this time it felt different. She pulled on a men's shirt and buttoned it up, instantly a little warmer.

Marion opened a bottle of wine, pouring all three generous glasses. She handed them out while Lili lit a cigarette. Marion turned up the radio, letting the music fill the room, breaking the near silence around them. She swayed for a moment, dancing along. She moved, and her special bracelet on her left wrist moved with her. "It never feels right in here without music," Marion said. "We always need to have something playing."

"Oh, I think Iris would love it." Lili's eyes were still on the easel that held her canvas. At night, when she wasn't working on it, she pushed it to the corner, pressing it against the wall. That way, no one could see it.

"What is Iris like?" Louise asked. "I wish I could have known her before she left." Marion and Lili shared a long look, one where a million things were said. Marion sat back down with her clay. She was working on something, but Louise had never seen her complete a work.

"She is—"

"Mercurial. Obsessive," Lili cut Marion off. "But she wants to be the best at everything."

"The weeks leading up to her shows are the worst." Marion put her glass of wine on the floor. "She goes through these mood swings like everything is bad, and nothing is worth showing. Or she's practically giddy, annoying all of us."

"Everyone would say she was nice, and she is, but she can also be really cruel. But if she was mean to you, it means she likes you."

"I never thought I'd like an American."

The two women held a conversation as if they shared a brain. Louise looked at Marion, who had spoken last. "Do you like me?"

"Maybe." Marion raised one fair eyebrow.

That was about as good an answer as Louise could hope for. She lit a cigarette, sitting back into the couch. "I have work tomorrow morning," Louise said to no one in particular.

"You can sleep here, if you don't want to go home," Lili said. "There are bedrooms that are actual bedrooms."

That sounded nice. And the apartment was closer to Allaire's in the 2nd arrondissement than her apartment was. But she had to go home. "One thing you have to know about me is that I can never wear the same dress twice in a row," Louise said. "But I'm grateful for the offer."

"Our house is your house," Marion said. She was wholly focused on her clay again, allowing herself to make a mess. "As long as you have the key."

"We look out for each other," Lili said. "That's the most important thing about being here." She lit a cigarette and took a long drag. "Our house is your house," Lili repeated. "And we mean that."

# 12

CIARÁN'S APARTMENT, USUALLY a hub of chaos and noise, was silent.

And that worried Louise. She thought that maybe he had passed out in a pool of his own vomit. So, as soon as she had managed to climb the stairs to her apartment, she was climbing into his.

He was alive, pacing the small room. And Estelle was watching him, perched at the kitchen table with Irving, his cat, on her lap.

"Ciarán," Louise said.

He turned toward her, his face lighting up. "Tiny, thank God. You'll know what to do."

Louise looked from Estelle to Ciarán and back. Estelle's lovely face was wet with tears.

"About what?" Louise asked.

"Show her," Ciarán directed. Estelle stood; she was wearing a solemn blue day dress. Her fashionable matching hat was sitting on the table.

"I want to talk to you about Iris," Estelle said, after a couple of minutes of shifting positions. "I'm worried too. She's sent me this." Reaching into her little beaded bag, Estelle pulled out a note. It was a light pink piece of paper, folded neatly in thirds. Louise took it, feeling their fingers brush as she did. She looked toward Ciarán, who nodded. With anticipation running through her veins, Louise flipped the paper open.

It was written in a woman's hand, the letters erratic on the page. It was clearly composed with haste. *E—I'm leaving. Find me tonight. Come with me.*

No signature.

Louise read it twice.

"It was delivered at a café." Estelle leaned against the wall, her back toward the window. She was fighting back tears, not making eye contact with Ciarán or Louise. She pulled a cigarette from her purse. Forgoing the holder, she slipped it between her lips. Ciarán was beside her, offering a match. Once Estelle had exhaled smoke through the window, she went on. "I . . . we're romantically in-volved. We have been since before her wedding. We had to hide it because her mother wouldn't approve. This is from her, I know it."

"Who delivered it?" Louise asked.

Estelle looked toward Ciarán, who nodded. "I don't know; the waiter gave it to me." She shook her head. She was blinking back tears. "We used to talk about running away and being together. I must believe this is her."

"Me too," Louise said.

"I love her. I know she's not the type. But I love her. I . . ." Estelle was saying. She trailed off, clearing her throat.

"Do you know where she would go?" Louise asked. She wanted to keep to the matter at hand.

Estelle swallowed. She took her time responding, as if there were multiple places Iris loved enough to go. She opened her mouth and then closed it, looking vaguely like a confused fish. "I can think of a couple of places. Madame Blanchet's, the gallery. The studio." She listed places with her eyes closed, using all of her energy to recall them.

"Anywhere that has personal significance?" Louise asked. There was something she didn't like about Estelle, but if she had to really face it, she would have to admit that maybe, *just maybe*, she was jealous.

Estelle opened her eyes, pursed her lips. "You know, I met her at Duke's the night she arrived. She wore this dress. Fire red, sleeveless with a plunging back." She was staring out of the window. Louise watched her every move. It was as if Estelle was on stage, giving the performance of her life. "She stood out from the crowd, and it was then I knew."

Louise understood. The breathless feeling of meeting someone who would change your life. It was how she felt, struck by an arrow, the first time she saw Rosa Maria. The idea that someone could come in, change the very course of your life, and leave was something Louise knew intimately.

"What do we do?" Estelle asked. She turned to Louise, who still had the note in her hand.

"I think there's only one thing to do," Louise said. "We go. Tonight."

◁◈▷

DUKE'S WAS A club Louise had never visited. It was much more spacious than Aquarius, but it was lacking something.

Perfectly poised couples waltzed together on the floor. The band was sensible, but not as good as Doris and her crew. A bartender, skin darker than Louise's, was behind the bar. It still shocked her, ice cold water dumped over her skin, to see Black people and white people dancing together. She had had that at the Zodiac, and at the Dove, but to see it, in the open, every place she went was . . .

Unnerving.

She wore a dramatic dress of black, a robe de style, the first dress she bought with her first paycheck from Allaire's. Black satin skirt fuller than she had ever worn, the bodice dipping down in a deep V to show her black slip underneath. Bands of beading formed delicate peacock feathers through the skirt. Louise had never felt more beautiful. She was used to sparkling, maybe not in real life, but certainly on the dance floor. She was used to being one of the brightest of the Bright Young Things. But here in Paris, she was just another woman. Well dressed, able to dance. One among many.

Estelle wore a royal-blue dress. They had come at separate times, Louise keeping an eye on the other woman as she danced and talked. She was a shadow. Quiet. Invisible.

Anywhere Estelle went, Louise did too. The bar, the tables, the bathroom. Estelle never once left her sight.

And only once was Louise tempted to dance, a quick Charleston where she had to pick her skirts up and out of the way of her feet, clad in ruby-red satin bar shoes, beaded and embroidered. They had cost a pretty penny, but they had been worth it.

It was eleven at night, and things were just beginning. This was *the* club of the night.

Iris Wright would show up.

She would have to.

Louise hadn't yet told Mrs. Wright about this development. She had to be sure this wasn't a hoax or something more sinister. It was Estelle who had the luxury of believing that Iris might show.

It was easy to really believe. Duke's, with the big band and the flowing drinks, made it so. She followed, watched, and kept to the shadows as much as she could. If Iris Wright was going to enter, she was going to see it.

It was eleven thirty when Estelle slipped up a set of stairs in the corner of the club. They were roped off, but Estelle ducked under. Louise followed, breath held, her eyes adjusting from the low lights of the dance floor to the bright houselights of the office. She knew that there were residences above this club, Paris making the most of its space much like New York City had to.

She pushed the doors open with her fingertips.

⌧

IRIS WRIGHT, AS if she had never disappeared, was sitting behind a large desk. Her hair was messy; she wore a cream day dress. She was alive. Estelle was kneeling in front of her, as close as she could get without the two merging into one being. They were whispering. Iris had a smattering of freckles on her nose, a detail always left out of her self-portraits. Her bow lips were pulled into the mysterious smile Louise had seen time and time again.

It was frightening and wonderful to see her as a real person.

"Who is this?" Direct. American. Boston. It was clear from her flat syllables. Her eyes fell on Louise, hovering near the door.

"Louise Lloyd. Your mother sent me to find you." She cleared her throat, unsure of what else to do.

"Well, shit." Iris leaned back in the chair, eyeing Louise warily. "What is she giving you?"

"Nothing. I'm doing it as a favor for a friend. She's worried about you. She came all the way from Boston . . ."

"You know she's not worried about me. She hates the fact I am who I am." Iris interrupted her, but not impolitely.

Louise wondered if this woman, bred to be a wife and a mother a world away from Louise's, could ever be impolite.

"She's here to make sure I don't do something reckless." Iris' voice was now soft, low, and melodic. She set her jaw, stubborn as anything. "I only married Philip because that's what she wanted. He didn't love me, and I don't love him. Of course I'm going to do something reckless." Iris stared at Estelle, the hardness in her eyes softening. "He only loves me because of my money. He hates everything else about me."

"Why all of this?" Louise asked. "All this fuss, taking off like this?"

Iris sighed. "I wanted to know what he'd do. Did he do anything?"

Louise shook her head.

"I once thought I could love a man like that." Iris focused on lighting a cigarette. She exhaled a long string of smoke. "He played the part well, charming my mother and father until they were throwing me into his arms. But after the wedding . . . It doesn't matter now. We are leaving." She was defiant, ready to set the world on fire.

"I just have to tell her you're okay." Louise found she couldn't speak when she looked at Iris. She seemed to be glowing from within. Forming words was the last thing on her mind. Her mouth was dry; she needed a drink.

Iris leaned forward, rooting through the desk. Louise didn't ask where she had been or where she was going. None of it seemed relevant or important enough to mention.

Iris pulled out a pen and a slip of paper. She wrote something, never pausing to think about what she wanted to say. As she wrote, her bracelet, emeralds and diamonds, hit the desk. It was missing a couple of emerald stones, a sign of wear. When she was done, she folded it into thirds, kissed the fold, and wrote her mother's name on the other side. "Give her this. With my apologies."

Louise took the paper, secreting it into her purse. "Is there anything you want me to pass on to your husband?" she asked.

Iris looked toward her left hand, even her hands were pretty, assessing her bare ring finger. "No, I think he has everything he needs." Iris looked back to Estelle, her eyes soft and warm. Iris looked back up at Louise. "Tell my mother I'm sorry, and I'll contact her when we're settled."

"Of course," Louise said. There was nothing else she could do. She had accomplished everything she had set out to do.

And Louise left Iris and Estelle wrapped in a world of their own.

# 13

◄◆►

LOUISE'S NEWSPAPERS WERE, more often than not, delivered to Ciarán below her. She had made getting her papers a routine. She would wrap herself in her dressing gown, brush her hair, and then take the staircase down to his floor. There, they would drink coffee and read the papers, Louise translating the French for Ciarán.

She always told Clémence that the cup she had at Dauphine's was her first of the day. In reality, on a good day, that was the third or fourth.

By the time Louise knocked on Ciarán's door, he was already reading her paper. He didn't subscribe to any, and that was because he had all access to hers. Irving was at her feet when Louise pushed open the door. The truth was that Louise had been feeling pretty confident that morning. All she had to do was deliver the letter from Iris to her mother, and she could wash her hands clean of this business.

But Ciarán looked pale. He was wearing trousers, no shirt,

suspenders clipped and hanging down. He was holding *Journal Américain*, and he looked sick.

"What's going on?" Louise asked. "Are you okay?"

"I . . ." He could barely muster the pronoun.

She took the paper from his hands and looked at it.

The headline, in stark, black letters. **SOCIETY MAVEN FOUND DEAD**.

Louise stared at the photo below it, feeling panic, fear, confusion grip her windpipe until she couldn't breathe.

Her eyes scanned the photograph, and then the story that followed. *Iris Montgomery, age twenty-eight, married to fellow society man Philip Montgomery, found dead over the weekend of the 20th of May. Having tumbled from the sixth story of a building, the wife, who dabbled in art, was pronounced dead at the scene. No foul play involved, according to Inspector Daniel Toussaint.*

That was it. Less than one hundred words, and barely a mention of her art career. The byline was given to a Christopher Braithwaite. Louise was infuriated on behalf of the woman who deserved better. She read the lines again and again. Then looked back to the photograph. That was how she wanted to remember Iris. With her sly smile and dancing eyes. Full of life and love.

She moved closer to Ciarán and then did the only thing she could do. She wrapped him in a hug, squeezing tightly. "I'm so sorry," Louise said.

"I didn't get to say good-bye," Ciarán's voice was soft. "I haven't even seen her since . . ." He trailed off.

Louise didn't make him finish that sentence, although she desperately wanted to know when the last time he saw Iris was.

Louise had booked the day off anyway, to talk to Lucy and deliver the letter.

And now she was dreading it.

———◁◆▷———

LUCY WRIGHT WAS staying at the César Ritz, easily the most opulent place Louise had ever stepped foot in. She was guided to the imperial suite by a polite bellhop. Louise faded among the high-class guests in her black dress, matching turban-style hat, and subdued oxblood lipstick. It was an outfit that she would have worn in her previous life as a club manager. Mature, serious.

Foreboding.

When the man knocked on the door, it was opened almost immediately. Lucy Wright, still in her dressing gown, ushered her in. The older woman was in a manic state and went directly to the bedroom.

The Suite Imperial was bigger than anywhere Louise had ever lived. She couldn't help but admire how opulent the suite was. With twenty-foot ceilings, it was large and airy. There was a full kitchen and sitting room. Louise held her breath, thinking she was too poor to breathe in this room. "Mrs. Wright," Louise said. "I am so sorry for your loss."

"What loss?" Lucy asked. She was climbing back into bed. "I assume this means you found her." Louise paused. She didn't know. Louise would have to tell her. She didn't know how to do this again. She didn't *want* to do this again.

But she had to.

Louise pulled the note out of her purse and then took a seat in the chair by the window. She cleared her throat. "I saw Iris on Saturday night," she began. "She gave this to me to give to you. But unfortunately, she . . ." The word caught in Louise's mouth, and she couldn't say it. Lucy watched her. The older woman was now under the whitest blanket Louise had ever seen. She leaned forward to take the letter from her. Louise hadn't read it. She didn't want to disrespect Iris' privacy, even though she had piles of letters from the woman.

This was different.

"Iris died over the weekend. It was in the papers this morning," Louise said. "I really am so sorry for your loss." It was quiet for a moment while Lucy read the letter. She didn't seem to hear Louise. Louise wished she had thought to bring the newspaper with her, but in a hotel as luxurious as this, they must be able to call for one.

"I'm sorry, what did you say?" Lucy asked.

Louise would never know what was in that letter. She wondered what she would write to her own mother, if she had the chance.

Louise repeated herself, and she felt the world shift from under her. Lucy stared at her, as if she couldn't quite believe what was being said. Louise saw the process of grief color the older woman's face, her entire body caving in on itself. Unsure of what to do, Louise went to the dining room and poured a glass of water, bringing it back, and setting it on the bedside table.

She sat back down in the chair she had been using, watching the older woman curl up under the piles of her blankets. She didn't know what exactly to say next, but she thought it was wrong to leave so soon.

"Louise, I need you to figure out who did this to her."

Louise could have predicted this. She knew it was coming. She heaved a sigh. "They're saying it was an accident," Louise said. The last four words of the article dedicated to her death had clearly said no foul play involved.

"Do you believe that?"

"Mrs. Wright, I think these matters are better left to the police. I can't do what you think I can . . ."

This was a woman who was used to getting what she wanted when she wanted it. As Louise saw it, she had two choices: let this rest and have Iris' legacy changed forever, or do it and be trapped in another case.

"How much did Schoonmaker tell you about me?" Louise asked. She feared the answer to this question, whatever it was.

"There were a couple of holes he left out . . . what happened to your sister exactly?"

"She died because of me," Louise said. She didn't see a way out of this. Every nerve ending in her body was telling her to leave and return to her simple Paris life.

"Would you let your sister go without justice?" Lucy asked.

And it was as if she were watching herself from above as she said, "I'll look into it."

*May 6th, 1928*

*Schoonmaker,*

*You'll have to apologize to me for getting me wrapped up in another investigation.*

 *By now, you must have heard that Iris Wright passed away. I was able to talk to her before she did. Lucy Wright wants me to investigate her death.*

 *Why did you feel the need to tell her everything about me?*

 *I'm sorry I haven't written. I've been trying to. I just can't think of anything to say that would make it easier to be away from you and Rafael and Rosa Maria and my sisters.*

 *And especially Anna's cooking.*

# 14

WHEN LOUISE GOT home, Ciarán was still sitting at his table, staring blankly at the wall. She climbed into his apartment, stopping first to feed the cat, who was yowling at his food bowl. Then Louise tapped him. "Are you okay?"

"I don't know." He didn't look at her when he responded. "I . . ." She lit a cigarette for him. He took it, still not looking at her. "My world is empty. It's turned upside down."

Louise did the only thing she could think of and pulled him close. He didn't cry, but he didn't say anything either. She had been away from the building for a couple of hours. Had he just been sitting at this table, staring into nothingness?

"I'm so sorry," Louise said. She ran a hand through his hair. He still hadn't put on a shirt. She knew what she wanted, when she felt like this. "Come on, let's get you to bed."

"No." His reply was soft and weak. Louise could guess that he was already half asleep.

"Come on." With magnificent strength, Louise pulled him up and half dragged, half led him to bed.

She sat at the foot of his bed, watching him as he settled, lying on his back, still not saying anything. Louise got up to pour him some water from the tap. Irving jumped up and joined Ciarán on the bed. They were both silent for a long time. She placed the glass of water on the bedside table. She didn't want to leave him until she knew he was okay.

"I lied to you, you know. I knew her better than I let on."

It was a surprise when he spoke. Louise was staring out of his window, trying to see the church.

"Iris and I, for a few months now . . . have been spending time together whenever we can."

Louise *knew* he had lied to her, but she wasn't expecting that. "What?"

"I know. She is married. She has Estelle. But that never seems to bother her." Ciarán let loose a heavy sigh. "She's so funny, so smart. I think I'm dreaming. Come stroke my hair again."

She stripped down to her undergarments, step-ins and brassiere, and climbed into bed with him, displacing the cat as she did. Ciarán leaned into her, and she began to run her fingers through his hair again. He closed his eyes, momentarily at peace.

Louise wished that she could turn her brain off, stop thinking. Because what was supposed to be a sweet moment turned into something darker. Louise tilted her head back. She would wait until he went to sleep to go back to her apartment.

She realized that she could be lying down with a murderer.

*August 20th, 1927*

*Lovie,*

*The Dove was raided last night! It's okay, it'll be okay. But it was really scary. I pay three hundred dollars twice a month to make sure I don't get raided.*

*We lost a lot of stock, but we'll make it out okay. No one was hurt is the biggest thing. Schoonmaker paid bail for everyone.*

*But something like that happens, and it really puts everything you have in life in perspective. I think I don't just want to be a club owner anymore.*

*I don't know.*

*I can't think about anything else. It's been hours, and my hands are still shaking. My heart is still pounding. I'm seeking refuge at Schoonmaker's house for a while. I need to get out of the city anyway.*

*Do you ever feel like sometimes you just can't breathe in the city? I guess that would be why you left.*

*Fox keeps saying that it could have been worse, and I suppose it could. He's right. We'll be closed for a couple of days, but we'll be okay.*

*I loved the package you sent me. I'm glad you sent a couple of photographs along, too. Now I can picture you in the apartment, in Paris, a world away from us.*

*I still think you should write me more! I hope you're happy. I hope you haven't replaced me and that's why you've stopped writing.*

*And you can come back whenever you want. Most people*

*have stopped talking about the Gilbert family. If that's what you're worried about, no one will remember you.*

*I keep thinking that I want everything to be exactly how it was last year. Fox keeps saying that's impossible. Things have to change. I don't know what I'm writing. I'm tired.*

*It's early. I can't remember the last time I was awake before noon. But Anna, I think you'll remember, is very particular, and that means breakfast. I'm sitting across from Fox as I write this (he's writing to you too).*

*He sends his love, as do I.*

*Write soon,*
*Rafael*

# 15

---

BECAUSE LOUISE COULDN'T meet Emme at her offices, they met at the building that housed the apartment. There was still what had to be blood on the ground from where Iris had made contact, drops of curdled brown that were now one with the pavement. Louise was early, having come right from work. She didn't have to make excuses like Emme did.

But she recognized Emme in a navy wraparound dress and matching hat, walking toward her. She was smoking and seemed to be lost in thought. There was a definite scowl on her face.

Emme greeted her with the required kiss on both cheeks. "You're early. I've never met anyone who tries to be early."

"It's a habit," Louise said. And it was, because as a child, she had to get herself ready, then Minna, then the twins. Punctuality was a virtue her father raised her with. "How was work?"

Emme rolled her eyes. "I hate those men."

Louise had wanted to ask about Christopher Braithwaite, but maybe now wasn't the best time.

Emme was still scowling. But she tipped her head back. "How far do you think she fell?"

Macabre choice for a discussion, but Louise stepped back, looking up at the rows and rows of windows. "I don't know."

"It must have hurt."

That was an understatement. Louise was barely a fan of heights at the best of times, and this had given her a new fear. The helplessness Iris must have felt as she tumbled, unable to stop. Louise turned away from the building.

"Do you really think she'd do it on purpose?" Emme talked almost exclusively in questions, wanting to get the answer to everything. Rosa Maria was like that too. The two women were more similar than Louise realized.

"I don't know, but her mother wants me to find out," Louise said.

"I researched you. I used the paper's contacts, and I looked you up," Emme said. "I'm sorry, but I had to."

Louise turned toward Emme, a little impressed. But there went her new Paris life. Whenever Emme looked at her, all the woman would see was Harlem's Hero. "I was curious. I even talked to a reporter—Rosa Maria Moreno?"

Ice shot through Louise's veins. All Louise could do was hope that Rosa Maria didn't say anything too revealing. "What did she say?"

"That everything I could read about you was true, and that you don't eat enough," Emme said.

Louise had to hold back a smile.

"You're a little incredible," Emme said.

Louise stepped closer to Emme, closing the gap. She didn't know what was going to happen.

Emme was smiling. "You're not mad?"

"You did your due diligence."

Something caught her eye, a glint in the afternoon sun. Louise pulled away from Emme, following the glint to a small garden near the building.

In the dirt was an emerald and diamond bracelet with the clasp broken. Louise kneeled down to pick it up. It was a bracelet that cost more than she earned in a year. It was delicate and beautiful, and on the back of one of the links was an engraving she couldn't quite make out. There were a couple of emerald stones missing from the setting.

"That is gorgeous." Emme was leaning over Louise's shoulder, her voice quiet.

Louise tucked the bracelet into her purse and stood, dusting dirt from her dress.

"It's Iris'," Louise said.

"How do you know?"

"I saw it on her," Louise said, recalling that night at Duke's. Emme took this in. "Who is Christopher Braithwaite?" Louise asked.

Emme sighed. "He is the man who stole my story. I was supposed to report on Iris, but when she died, it was given to *him*. He always gets what he wants, and I have to report on *parties*." She said the word with so much venom. "It's a fucking man's world," Emme said again.

Louise couldn't agree more.

⊲※⊳

THE APARTMENT WAS empty. Louise and Emme were supposed to have all the time in the world to go through the women's things.

She used her key, for the first time, letting herself and Emme in. They spread out. When it was empty, it was almost scary. The place had bad energy. Louise could feel the hair on her arms raise as she began to look. She didn't even really know what she was looking for. She could hear Emme exploring, the quiet click of doors closing behind her.

They spent an hour like this, going through rooms, all dedicated to different mediums.

Because it was quiet, she could hear when the front door opened. It seemed that the sound echoed through the place, wide in the cavernous depths of the apartment.

Without thinking, Louise grabbed Emme's hand and pulled her into the nearest room.

It was a closet, barely big enough for the two of them. They were stuck in the dark with linens that smelled as if they hadn't been washed in the past century. Louise concentrated, trying to listen, and Emme did too. It took a moment for Louise to realize that she was still clutching Emme's hand.

She could hear someone rooting around, looking for something, in another room. Which one, she couldn't begin to guess.

Louise and Emme faced each other. Lips centimeters away from each other. Louise closed her eyes, trying to think of anything other than the overwhelming desire that flooded her body. Emme removed her glasses, squeezing her eyes shut. "How long do we have to stay here?"

The husky whisper of her voice made every hair on Louise's body rise. Her heart was thudding, and she could barely hear anything else over the blood rushing through her body.

Louise took a deep breath, trying to steady herself. "I don't know." She kept her own voice just as quiet. "What if they decide to stay? What if the others come?" Her eyes were starting to adjust to the low lighting of the closet. Emme was just a little bit taller than she was, an inch if anything. Louise didn't have to tilt her head to look into Emme's eyes.

"Let's hope that doesn't happen." Emme squeezed her hand. Louise kept her eyes trained on Emme's. That, at least, was something she could do. She focused on keeping her breath steady. She was already formulating a plan. Louise could go out there, pretend she was in the darkroom, but getting Emme out would be a little more difficult.

Emme reached over, and with the softest touch Louise had ever felt, brushed her hair from her eyes. They were standing so close together that she thought she could feel Emme's heartbeat, pounding fast, just like her own. Louise breathed in through parted lips, focusing solely on trying to hear if they were still alone. She thought that if any of the society members came in, the radio would be turned on, noise pumped through the apartment like a heart pumped blood.

But nothing.

Silence.

She tried to count the minutes but got distracted.

She tried to focus on anything but the tiny closet and found that the only other thing she could think about was how close she was to Emme.

"How long has it been?" Louise asked. Emme at least wore a watch, something Louise never remembered to do. She didn't have to; Allaire's had a grand clock on the wall, and she could ask whoever else she was with to tell her what time it was.

"Five minutes," Emme said. She was breathless.

"I think we should give it another two," Louise said. "Just to be safe." She wanted two more minutes in complete silence, centimeters away from each other. Emme nodded. Her lips were parted, and her chest rose and fell with every breath. Louise could feel each movement mirrored in her own body.

And when Emme leaned in and kissed her, her heart stopped. She reacted immediately, her hands at Emme's waist. They were there, together, and suddenly, it didn't matter if they were stuck in that closet all day.

Emme ran a hand through her hair, ending at the nape of Louise's neck. She tried not to think about what this would mean.

She tasted like cigarettes and coffee, and when she pulled away, Louise nearly stumbled forward.

"I think I should leave first," Louise said. Her body was humming from Emme's touch. This was the first person she had kissed since Rosa Maria. "Just in case."

"Okay." Emme, too, was breathless.

Louise opened the closet door, hoping to find the pied-à-terre empty. She made her way down the hall to the sitting room. Whoever had been here was gone.

And a canvas that had been sitting on an easel was gone.

"Emme." Louise raised her voice. "It's clear." Nothing else, from what Louise could tell, had been taken. The front door was closed, locked.

Emme came out into the sitting room. She had put her glasses back on. "Who was it?" she asked.

"I don't know."

She was trying to calm her racing thoughts, her racing heart. "Why don't we get out of here?" Louise said. The empty pied-à-terre was unnerving now. And anyone else could come in at any time.

They didn't even find anything of use.

"Let's go get a drink," Emme said. Louise nodded her agreement. She thought about the kiss again, about Emme's lips on hers. She wouldn't mention it unless Emme did.

Maybe it was nothing.

Louise was careful to use the key she was given to lock up behind her.

Stepping back into the afternoon sun was wonderful. Emme paused to slide her sunglasses on. Louise tipped her head back, feeling the heat on her face.

She took a deep breath, trying to clear her mind. Emme was already ahead of her, always moving, doing something.

Louise had to focus on Iris.

*August 20th, 1927*

*Louise,*

*I'm sitting across from Rafael, and I'm sure he's telling you all of the big news. I'm watching him write now, and he's often stopping and starting and stopping and starting. I think it's how his brain works. I can see him going back and forth, barely finishing his sentences before starting new ones.*

*We're both a little shook up, but we'll be okay. I suggested sitting down to write to you as a distraction.*

*It's not my first raid, but it is his as an owner. I can tell he's scared now. And I don't know what to say. I suggested he stay with me for a while. He agreed. Anna is thrilled. She misses having you around, even if she won't say it. And it'll be nice to have someone else in the house again. I didn't realize how much you and Josephine changed the house. I'm glad we were all together, even if it was just for a little while.*

*Everything else is okay. We'll be able to bring the Dove back, though we may move locations. Rafael just lit a cigarette, now he's leaning back in his chair. It's early, we're having coffee. I know he got no sleep last night, but he looks so handsome.*

*You're the only one I can talk to about this; I think he and Eugene are still happy. And I don't want to ruin what we have now.*

*I'm happy for you, even though I do miss you. Rafael just said I can only write happy things in this letter.*

*It's a perfect day, and we are going to spend every minute of it in the manse.*

*All we're going to do is sleep. I think the manse needs a pool.*

*I'm keeping in touch with Josephine, and Rafael meets Minna for breakfast every Saturday. I want to look out for them, especially since you are now so far away. I want to be able to support them, because as far as I'm concerned, you are all my family now. And I want to be able to help my family. I have a lot more money than I know what to do with, and if I can help, just a little bit, then it's not a bad thing.*

*Please, send more photographs. And word that you're okay.*

*Love,*
*F. Schoonmaker*

# 16

⬦⬦⬦

THERE WAS NOTHING like the sound of a typewriter. The click-click-click of letters being put down, words being formed.

Emme pursed her lips as she typed, her eyebrows wrinkling together, and her jaw clenching as she worked. Louise was sitting across from her; they were in the newsroom.

Emme had promised her that the only people there that late would be second-stringers, and Louise hadn't seen anyone else yet. "Besides," Emme had said as she led Louise to her desk, "no one is considered part of the team until they bring a woman back and make whoopee in the empty offices." Then Emme had blushed and hadn't said much in the hour since.

Louise was poring over the letters from Iris to Lucy. It was after work, and she had a pile of them with her. She had begun chronologically and was swept up in the minor inconveniences Iris had thought important to tell her mother.

Iris rarely mentioned Philip. He got a passing mention here and there, but many of her letters were mostly focused on art.

Emme wouldn't tell her what she was working on. She had prevaricated when Louise asked. Unlike Ciarán, Emme was a decisive typer. She often stopped to write out what she wanted to say by hand before committing it to the typewriter. Ciarán could kill a tree's worth of paper writing one scene for a play. Louise glanced over. Emme's writing was tough enough to decipher right side up, let alone upside down.

Louise lit a cigarette, pushing stray hairs from her face. She was diligently taking notes every time one of the society women was mentioned in Iris' letters.

So far, the clear winner was Estelle, followed by Margaux and Jeanne.

Louise leaned back in her chair. She tilted her head back, shutting her eyes. She had a persistent headache, brought on by a long day at work and now trying to unravel Iris' life.

"You okay?" Emme asked.

Louise sighed in response. She opened one eye to find Emme staring at her. "What are you writing?"

Emme smiled mysteriously but didn't answer her question. "Do you want to talk?"

Louise leaned forward, folding like a reed in the wind. She planted her forehead on the desktop. "Yes."

Emme lit a cigarette; Louise could hear the strike of the match. Louise pulled herself up, using strength from every bit of her body. "When I had lunch with Jeanne, I thought she hated Iris. But Iris only writes nice things."

"Maybe she didn't want her mother to worry," Emme said. She exhaled smoke, her lips in a perfect circle. She looked back at the pages in front of her, as if she was going to say something. She stopped herself.

"Maybe," Louise said. She didn't know Iris that well, but she hadn't seemed like the type of person to pretend to like someone. The only thing she had was a grieving mother's insistence that this wasn't a suicide.

Maybe Lucy was wrong.

Emme leaned forward, squinting to read Iris' writing. "Maybe this is just the beginning?"

"Maybe." Louise wasn't convinced.

"How many letters are there?"

"I haven't counted, but there are a lot."

Emme frowned. "Maybe Iris and Jeanne don't hate each other yet."

She leaned back. Louise was enjoying being in the newsroom; the quiet dim room was perfect for concentration.

Emme picked up a pen, scribbling something down. Louise watched as she did it.

"Do you hate someone enough to kill them?" Louise asked.

Emme's eyes flicked up at her. "Christopher Braithwaite." Her nose wrinkled just saying the name.

Louise was sitting at his desk. It was covered in papers, writings, musings. It seemed as if Mr. Braithwaite was trying his hand at the next Great American Novel. She had scanned through pages about a girl named Marjorie.

It wasn't that interesting.

"Do you?" Emme asked.

Louise swallowed hard. Every so often, she woke in a cold sweat, thinking about that night in the deserted Zodiac. "I never want to do it again," Louise said. Her voice was low.

"Oh, I . . ."

"It was easy, just instinct," Louise continued as if Emme hadn't said anything. "It was him or me. Life or death."

"I am so sorry," Emme said. She got up and moved to wrap her arms around Louise's shoulders. "You should never have been put in that position." Her voice was soft, and she was rocking Louise back and forth.

Louise was on the verge of tears. "I'm okay now." It wasn't very convincing.

Emme pulled away, kneeling down so they were eye level. She had pushed her glasses onto the top of her head, and her eyes were wide. Louise thought about kissing her in that closet. Her heart raced. Now, Emme's pert lips were twisted into a wry smile.

"I mean it," Emme said softly. "You never should have been there."

Louise was aware it wasn't fair, but there was nothing much she could do about it now. All she could do was keep going and hope the anger and guilt would fade away.

"Louise." Emme's voice was soft. They were so close, it was so quiet, and there was no one else around them.

The things they could do. The potential and possibilities stretched out before her.

"I don't think it's a good idea." Louise's mouth was two steps ahead of her brain. "I think we should work on this and just this."

Emme's eyebrows flicked up, the corners of her mouth turning down. "You're right." She said it after two long moments, two heartbeats suspended in time. "I'm sorry. You're very right."

Emme pulled herself away, seating herself back at her desk. Louise turned back to the letters, the piles of papers that now summed up Iris' life.

Emme lit a cigarette, her pen in hand. Louise was right; it was the right call.

So then why did she feel so awful about it?

⌵⋀⌄

THE NEAREST NEIGHBOR to the apartment was directly below. Louise and Emme went down, and Louise knocked. Her heart was in her throat. Emme remained silent, writing down every detail, even though the floor was identical to the one below it.

A man opened the door. He was, Louise could tell because of his surroundings, very rich. But he didn't look very rich. His clothes were rumpled, fair hair messy. He didn't wear the uniform of service, so Louise had to assume that this man was at least one of the men of the house.

"Who're you?" Accented French, but not from France.

"Louise Lloyd. Do you speak English?" Louise said.

He looked them both up and down. "I don't want to buy anything." In English, his accent was more peculiar.

"I'm not selling anything," Louise said. She eyed him. He impatiently rubbed his eyes. It was late in the afternoon, and he was just waking up? "I have some questions about the home above you."

He closed his eyes. "Are you the police?"

"Did you talk to the police?"

Stalemate. Louise raised an eyebrow. He inhaled. "I need a drink. I guess you should come in."

Apparently, they couldn't begin to discuss murder without a glass of wine in front of them. The man introduced himself as Andy, and he smoked as he talked, carefully offering them both cigarettes every time he lit a new one.

"I live with my sister, mother, and father," Andy said. The family, he said, was from Italy, they lived in Paris over the spring and summers. That was something Louise couldn't imagine doing. Having that kind of money and freedom.

"My mother and father are in Marseille for the next couple of weeks," he explained. "My sister and I have been alone all month." He leaned back in his seat, closing his eyes for a moment. "Sorry. I'm exhausted." His eyes were red rimmed and his lips were dry: he was hungover.

"I want to know about last weekend."

"What about her?" He jerked his chin toward Emme, who hadn't said a word since they had sat down.

Emme held his gaze for a moment. "I'm just here to record the interview. I'm a journalist. I have to be impartial."

"What are you writing about?" He didn't break Emme's stare.

"Louise."

He seemed to accept this as answer. He looked back to Louise. "And you're not police?"

"I'm doing a favor for a friend," Louise said. "I'm not police."

He seemed to accept this as well. "When Iris died? I was here. I was just getting ready to leave when I heard the fall." He closed his eyes. "I thought I saw her; the windows face the same way . . . I was in the sitting room, and something caught my eye and then the sound." He fell silent.

Emme reached forward, placing her hand on his. It was a simple gesture, but so sweet and calming. "It's okay," she said softly. "I know it's scary. Just do your best to remember."

He took a deep breath, in a fashion Louise had done many times. He was centering himself, readying himself. Emme didn't move her hand.

"Did you hear anything else? Maybe someone fighting or yelling?" Louise asked.

He took another moment before responding. "They always play music up there. It bugs my parents. I never mind it, but the music blocks a lot of other noise. I don't even think I heard the window break." He took a sip from his wineglass. He had made the effort to tell them that the bottle of red in front of them was from the late eighteen hundreds and was very expensive. Louise hadn't managed to warm up to red wine, and her glass remained untouched in front of her.

"Was there anyone else with you?" Louise asked.

"My sister, Arianna, but she's not in now." Andy paused, lighting a cigarette for Louise and then himself. "She likes to stay in at night. I think she was reading."

"Where is her bedroom?" Louise asked. The apartment was similar to the one above it, but it was decorated in a way that insinuated a family actually lived in it. It felt lived in, unlike the one above, which was cold.

"Down the hall, next to mine," Andy said. If the windows faced the same way, this Arianna wouldn't have seen much.

"Can we talk to her?" Louise asked.

Andy nodded slowly. "She'll be home in a couple of hours. She works a job."

"She does?" This was Emme. Louise noticed that they were still holding hands.

"Does that surprise you?"

"A little."

Louise had to interrupt. "Did you know Iris Wright? Or any of the other women up there?"

Andy had to consider this. "I met Iris a couple times in passing, but nothing too personal. She liked Arianna. She was always kind. Polite."

"What about anyone else?" Louise asked.

"I don't know them well. They tend to stick with each other and each other only. Birds of a feather, you know." She did know. She understood that perfectly. And from what she had seen of the women, the artists that rented the pied-à-terre, that made sense. "All I can say is that Iris was always kind to me and Arianna. She's not taking the death well . . ." he trailed off. Louise thought that maybe he wasn't taking the death well either.

They had been sitting there for the better part of an hour now, and Louise felt as if she didn't know anything new. "If you think of anything else, will you call me?"

He looked at her again. For most of those minutes, he had been focused on Emme, and Emme alone.

Which Louise understood.

"Of course," Andy said. "And I'll be sure to call when Arianna is available."

Louise pulled out one of her cards, sliding it across the table. "Thank you."

It was kind of him to take the time to talk to her. Louise could only hope that Arianna was as genial.

# 17

⧓

IRIS' MEMORIAL WAS held at the gallery that had showcased her work. Her first and last show. Louise went, dressed in black, and looking for any clue as to who killed Iris.

The last time Louise had been to a funeral, she was ten years old, and she was mourning her mother. She didn't attend Celia's, not wanting to anger her father.

She regretted that now.

Ciarán was quiet next to her. She had never known him to be this quiet. Milling around were mourners, all in black. Iris' art was a little unsettling now, as if she were watching her own memorial.

"Are you all right?" Louise asked.

Ciarán was staring at a canvas. He didn't answer.

From across the aisle, she could see Emme, in black, writing something down. Emme smiled in recognition. Louise nodded back.

There were people she recognized from the Blanchet salon, but the rest of these people had to be fans. She thought she saw Monty trying to stay out of her sight.

"Ciarán! Louise!" Marion wafted over. "How are you?" She wore a men's tuxedo without the bow tie. It was chic, her dark skin glowing. Louise wished she could pull the look off.

"Marion," Ciarán said. He leaned forward to kiss her on both cheeks. "I am bereft. And you?"

"I suppose that I'm feeling the same way." Marion hugged Ciarán tightly. "I love you," she said. "I don't know if I've ever told you. But you're such a good writer, and I'm so proud of you."

Apparently, death made everyone treasure what they had. Louise could understand; a senseless death like this one made life feel finite. A woman like Iris Wright should have lived forever, and now everyone knew she was just like them: mortal.

And death could come at any time.

A hush fell over the gallery, and Louise looked up. Ciarán and Marion were still in quiet conversation as Philip Montgomery strode into the gallery. He looked perfectly put together, not the way Louise thought a husband in mourning would look. He had one hand in his pocket. Louise looked around, trying to gauge the reaction of everyone watching. Emme, by the wall and perfectly invisible, had stopped writing.

There was a collective breath being held, waiting to see what he would say. Philip looked around. When he saw Louise, he scoffed. "None of you people loved my wife. None of you *liked* her. All of you are here for appearances." Coralie Blanchet stepped forward, probably intending to stop him, but he avoided her grasp. "This is all a charade," Philip said. His voice was cold. "Stop pretending otherwise."

"Philip!" Coralie said. Her voice came out strained. "We all loved Iris. We all miss her. We're all feeling this loss."

Philip laughed, a short, harsh laugh. "You, especially. You could profit off of my wife. Make a commission with silly little things like this show. Tell her what to do and she did it. You don't miss her. You miss having someone to control." Philip's eyes narrowed. He looked around the group one more time.

"The funeral was private. Move on." With that, Philip turned on his heel and strode away, leaving the crowd in a hushed shock.

⫟

THE MOOD IN the Blanchet salon was a tense one. They had made it through dinner, Ciarán drinking copiously, and now they were in the solarium. Everyone wore black. Instead of readings and art showings, everyone talked about Iris.

Louise tried to stay invisible, never more than an arm's length away from Ciarán. And she watched.

Margaux, Estelle, Jeanne, Marion, Sabine, and Lili were sitting in a small huddle. Lili and Estelle were sobbing; Jeanne, Marion, and Sabine were talking to each other; and Margaux was staring, a blank look in her eye.

Louise sat, watching as a woman in a blue dress sobbed her way through the time Iris was nice to her, critiquing her art in a gentle way. Universally beloved, that was Iris Wright Montgomery.

"Let me go next!" Ciarán was slurring. Louise wasn't sure he had stopped drinking since he had heard the news. He got up, leaving Louise exposed. He stood in front of the fireplace, waiting for attention. "Iris was always someone who would tell you what she thought," he began. He laughed. "She told me, to my face, that my play was terrible. But then she said she could help me write a new one." A fleeting look passed over his face, one that Louise couldn't read. "She also told me I cannot dress myself and that I needed to learn to shave. But she . . . was my friend. I loved her. I feel the ache so acutely it's a wonder I can get out of bed."

From the corner, Margaux watched Ciarán, her cool expression never changing. There was a frown on her full lips. For someone usually so expressive, her face was unreadable.

Louise sat forward, trying to keep her focus on Ciarán. He had paused, unable to stop himself from crying.

"Why don't we take a break?" Coralie asked, rising to her feet, clasping her hands together as if this were any normal night.

Now Ciarán was in deep discussion with Margaux, their heads together. Margaux caught Louise from the corner of her eye and turned to her. "What are you doing here?"

It seemed that, with those five words, a hush fell over the room. Margaux's blue eyes narrowed, her lips twisting into a frown. "Louise is my guest," Ciarán said, wrapping an arm around Louise.

"I asked her." Margaux crossed her arms over her chest.

"I'm paying my respects." Louise's throat had gone dry.

"You're *spying*."

"Margaux!" Ciarán said. "She's a guest. My guest."

Margaux stared for a moment, exhaling. She looked between Louise and Ciarán. Louise stared back.

"I have to go." And with that, Margaux turned away, leaving the solarium.

# 18

THE MONTGOMERY HOUSE was alive. There was a party going on. Lights on, music spilling from open doors and windows. Zozzled flappers supporting each other over the paved driveways; men in suits, in groups, smoking and laughing, passing bottles between them. Everyone was dressed in black.

Louise was able to slip in unnoticed. She had come from the Blanchet salon, stopping only to have a drink at Le Chat Noir. That was the thing about crowded places: everyone only seemed to care about themselves. Louise hadn't seen the house on her first visit; she had gone straight up to Iris' attic studio. She followed the noise to a parlor with people streaming in and out.

She was face-to-face with a large photograph of Iris. Was this a memorial?

She took a flute of champagne, a drink she had rather gotten used to while living in Paris, off the tray of a passing waiter. She took a sip as she wandered around. There was a live band, couples danced.

If this *was* supposed to be a memorial, then it seemed very disrespectful. Louise wound her way through mourners, past the dancers and society reporters, eager beavers who were looking for a story.

She drained her champagne flute and grabbed another, feeling the alcohol buzz through her body. She was underdressed, still in the black day dress and silk cloche, and knew she stuck out.

She climbed the stairs, her breath held. This house wasn't very big, but it was the most opulent place she had been in. People were in and out of every room. It didn't seem possible that Philip and Iris knew all these people. It was claustrophobic.

The band finished their song to rabid applause. Louise remembered a time when she would be in the center of the dance floor, getting her kicks where she could get them. She climbed to the third floor of the house, where the music seemed to grow distant. This floor was dark, empty. Louise trailed a hand over the railing. The party was kept to the lower level of the house.

As long as she was there, she could try to find the master bedroom, try to uncover some of Iris' secrets.

As she wandered down the hall, there was one room that had a door ajar with a light streaming underneath. Against her better instincts, Louise pushed it open with her fingertips.

There was Philip Montgomery, leaning on a wide desk. His trousers were pulled down. A woman with dark hair was on her knees, servicing him. She and Philip made eye contact, and Louise could not pull away.

"Get up," Philip sighed. The woman rose and turned. It was Margaux Blanchet, dressed in black, dark rings around her eyes. Predictably, her lipstick was smeared, and she used the back of her index finger to wipe the sides of her mouth.

"What?" Margaux asked. Her voice was low and raspy.

Philip, now decent, stepped up beside Margaux. "You aren't welcome here."

"I wanted to talk to you about your wife," Louise said.

Philip frowned. "I want you to get out of my house. You have no right to talk to me about my wife."

"Because you loved her so much?" Louise asked.

Philip stepped toward her. He was taller than her, most people were, and he was trying to use his height to his advantage. Louise didn't back down. "I *did* love her so much," Philip said with a shake of his head. "You know nothing about my private life. And knowing you were hired by her mother to sniff around makes me like you even less." His voice was low. She looked directly into his emotionless eyes. "I am grieving, if you couldn't tell, and if you trespass here one more time, I will have you forcibly removed."

Louise exhaled. What else could she do? A younger, more reckless Louise would tell him exactly what she thought about him. And she had a lot of choice words. But she smiled. She could tell this was a man who was used to getting his way. "Of course," she said, although it pained her to say it. "You're right. I'm so sorry for your loss."

He shut the door behind her, but if he thought she was stupid enough to do what she was told, he was sorely mistaken.

⬦⚶⬦

THE DOG WAS in the bedroom. Louise could hear whining as she passed. There was scratching at the door.

And Louise opened it.

Immediately, the dog—Maisy—was on top of her, desperate for affection. Louise ran her hands through the dog's soft fur, allowing her to lick her face. "Woah," Louise said. "Sit." Eager to please, the dog did as she was told.

The bedroom was large. It was painted eclectically, one wall rose pink, another a bright green, and the final two with a light shade of purple. It was jarring to the eye, but somehow it all worked. The dog barked, calling for Louise's attention. There was a pair of bowls near the door.

Maisy raised a paw, looking at Louise with large brown eyes under comically sad eyebrows. She exhaled, kneeled, and let the dog slobber over her again.

They had two beds, and they were cleanly made. Both sides of the room were clearly denoted. Philip's side was tidy; Iris' was covered in art supplies. Philip had a stack of novels on his bedside table; Iris had nonfiction. Louise pushed the dog away, going to Iris' side of the room.

The room was cold, as if it hadn't been used in weeks. Louise got on her knees, the dog behind her, and began to rifle through the drawers. Pens, paints, art supplies. She was wading through a forest of discarded paper.

And the sketchbooks were in the second drawer. She pulled one out, flipped to the first page. It was dated 1926.

Louise pulled out another, dated 1925.

Pages showed outlines, drawings in graphite of her and Estelle and Margaux and the dog.

She pulled them all out of the drawer. It was a lot to carry, but she was going to do it.

The dog whined one more time, and Louise relented. She never thought of herself as an animal person, but the way Maisy whined at her was heartbreaking. The sounds of the "memorial" were still raging around her. Louise tapped the floor. Maisy approached, licking her hand.

"Do you miss her?" Louise asked, running her hands through

the dog's fur. Maisy climbed into her lap, and she was not a lap-sized dog. Louise wrapped her arms around the animal, and Maisy sighed, sinking into her. "I know," Louise said. "I'm sorry." Maisy sat on her lap until her legs went numb, pleased to finally have some company. Louise didn't have the heart to move her, so she picked up one of the sketchbooks.

Iris mostly thought in pictures, but her drawings and doodles were accompanied by her musings. She kept her writing straight and neat around the drawings. Some entries, all dated, were gibberish.

Maisy pulled herself from her lap, moving over to her water bowl. She drank thirstily, and Louise collected the sketchbooks. With one last kiss on the dog's head, Louise left the mansion.

October 15th, 1927

Louise,

I can't say that I don't miss you. I miss you every day. But this isn't a letter about how much I miss you.

I constantly wonder if I made the wrong choice. Life is a series of choices. I made the choice to kiss you all those years ago and look what happened to us. I think about what would have happened, if I moved with you. I thought about it. I so desperately wanted to say yes.

But we're better apart.

I know Rafael is writing you, as is Schoonmaker. And I don't think I'll write to you often. I just . . .

Do you think we only get one Great Love in our lives? Do we only have one person we fall in love with? I think I'm writing because putting pen to paper always helps me think.

If someone were to ask me, you were my great love, and no matter what I do, I can never stop thinking about you.

This is desperation in a letter.

Every day is different without you. I have a new job, and I . . . I'm not falling in love, but I want to be open to the option.

But then I think about what we could have been, and then think about what we could have done. And all the time in the world couldn't be enough.

I don't know why I'm writing. I think I just miss you. It's three in the morning, and I just came home from the Dove, and I'm a little drunk and

I don't know.

I miss you.


Rosa Maria

# 19

ARIANNA WAS MORE open to talking. Louise and Emme were back in the neighboring apartment, now seated across from Andy and his sister, the woman they hadn't met yet.

Arianna and Andy were opposites. Where he had light hair and blue eyes, Arianna was small, and her dark hair veered toward red. Her voice was light, lilting with the same accent as her brother.

Louise had so many questions for her, but she had to stick to the topic.

The wine opened this time was an airy white, paired with decadent cheese. They sat around the same table, taking up a fraction of the circle.

Arianna eyed them warily. "My brother said you wanted to talk to me?"

"About last weekend," Louise said. "You were home that night?"

"You're not police?" Arianna asked.

"Just covering every base," Emme said. Arianna's dark eyes slid to her, as if seeing Emme there for the first time.

"It's only a couple of questions," Louise added.

Arianna nodded. Louise leaned forward. Emme placed her ever-present notebook on the table.

"Did you hear anything?" Louise asked. "Yelling? Fighting?"

"I heard a scream," Arianna said. She closed her eyes for a moment. "And I heard yelling. Whatever room they were in had to be right above mine."

"Do you know who it was?" Louise asked. Next to her, Emme was writing everything down.

Arianna shook her head. "I was only really familiar with Iris."

"Do you know what time you heard the scream?" Louise asked.

Arianna opened her eyes again. "It was early—or late. I had been up reading. Maybe two or three in the morning. Then I heard footsteps leading away."

"Was there music playing?" Emme asked. She usually let Louise handle this, saying that she had to be impartial, an observer. Everyone looked toward her. She was flipping through her pages. "Andy, you said that there was music playing and that meant you couldn't hear anything."

Arianna looked at her brother. "I don't think there was music playing. Maybe they had turned it off."

Emme frowned but seemed to accept this as an answer.

Arianna continued. "I didn't know Iris well; we'd see each other in the lobby or the elevator. We'd talk. I admired her work." As did everyone Louise came across, herself included. "She was always very nice. At least, she was patient with me. She always answered the questions I had." Arianna pushed her hair from her eyes. She had a fashionable shingle bob, and the wisps that framed her face fell into her eyes. It was enviable, and made Louise want to cut her own hair that second. "It's tragic. And then the papers saying she dabbled in art?" Arianna sighed. "Disgusting."

"I agree," Emme said. Arianna looked to her with a soft smile on her lips.

Louise looked toward the siblings. Between the two of them, she had gotten information the police didn't seem to have. Or if they did, they didn't care.

And that was more valuable than anything.

⌖

THE PARIS MORGUE was cold. The idea that Louise was surrounded by dead bodies made her shiver.

She stared at the man, and the man stared back. She was smoking and waiting for Emme, feeling very self-conscious. She should have been at work, should have been doing *anything* but this. But here she was, staring at a man who looked as if he had seen better days. She could have done this alone, but there was safety in numbers.

And Louise didn't want to be around dead bodies alone.

"Sorry! So sorry! Sorry!" Emme was yelling as she ran, her heels thundering against the pavement. She was wearing her spring coat over one arm, her hand on her hat. "I couldn't get away. Christopher wanted to know where I was going, and I couldn't think of anything fast enough." She stopped running, out of breath. She slipped her coat on and turned to the man. She faced him with a smile. "My friend and I have an appointment," she said. She pulled out a card, showing it to him. "With the coroner."

Where Louise would have just tried to pay the man off, Emme used her press pass. He looked them up and down. Emme pulled Louise closer to her.

This had been Louise's idea. She hadn't exactly wanted to see Iris' body, but she had wanted to know what she had with her when she died.

He considered them through beady brown eyes. Then he cleared his throat. "Go in. He is waiting for you."

They were led to an office. Louise had been to morgues in New York, but this felt different somehow. The same shivers were running down her spine as they passed through the rows of bodies. "The morgue used to be open for public viewing," Emme was whispering as they stood in the office. "They stopped doing that about twenty years ago, but people loved seeing dead bodies."

"How do you know that?" Louise asked.

Emme's smile was sharp. "I know everything."

"Miss Foster." The coroner was a man Louise would swear she had met before. He was average height, blond hair with blue eyes. He looked like every man she had danced with at Aquarius. He went to Emme first, hugging her closely.

"Gabriel," Emme said. "May I present Louise Lloyd? She's the one I was telling you about."

Gabriel turned to her, looking her up and down. "Pleasure to meet you."

"The pleasure is mine," Louise said. She cleared her throat. "Emme's been talking about me?"

"I had to tell him. Your story is just . . . I would write about it. It's that incredible," Emme said.

Gabriel kept looking at her. "And if you're with Emme, I'm assuming you have a question or two for me."

Louise looked at Emme, who nodded. She had procured a notebook and a pen, poised to write.

"I want to ask you about Iris Wright Montgomery," Louise said. Emme was already writing, scratching notes Louise had no idea how she would decipher later. "I assume that Emme told you about my . . . work." She didn't know what to call it. It wasn't her job. It was just a favor she was doing.

"She did," Gabriel said. "Can I guess?" His French accent made every word soft. "You want to know what Iris had on her body when she died."

"Yes, I don't want to see her," Louise said. "I just want to know about her effects."

"How quickly did she die?" Emme asked, stopping her writing.

"It was fast but painful."

Louise shuddered. She couldn't think of a worse way to die. Even Emme flinched. "As for her effects, I have her shoes, her bracelet, and her purse. Her clothes and jacket were discarded."

"Bracelet?" Louise asked. "Was it a diamond one? With emeralds? A couple emeralds missing in the setting?"

The one she had found was secreted in her apartment. It was too expensive to carry around with her, and she didn't want to lose it. "It has little links? An engraving on the back?"

"Yes," Gabriel said. "How did you know?"

Louise frowned. The bracelet she had found where Iris died didn't belong to Iris.

# 20

The diamond-shaped ornament divider.

THE JEWELRY STORE was the third one that Louise visited. This one was in Montparnasse, near the place where Iris died. She had been using her lunch breaks and evenings after work to find where the bracelet came from. This place was a little more high-end than the others, the glass cases reflected diamonds and rubies and emeralds. Louise didn't like wearing a lot of jewelry, but she could be swayed for any of these pieces.

The cases were separated by type: necklaces in one, rings in the other. She looked around, finding the cases the bracelets were in.

And there it was. The diamond links accented with emeralds. Worth more than Louise currently had in her savings. She took the bracelet she found out of her purse, holding it up. It was an exact match. She would have gone to every jewelry store in Paris if she had to. She was grateful it didn't come to that.

Her day had already been long, busy with too many customers who didn't know what they wanted. So it was, in a way, a relief, to be wandering around a store she didn't work at.

"Mademoiselle," said a young woman in a white dress behind a cash register. She was a brunette with a boyish frame any New York flapper girl worth her salt would covet. "Can I help you?" Louise crossed over to her. She swallowed hard. She had a lie ready, but she wasn't good at lying. "I found this bracelet. I was wondering if you could look up who bought it."

The woman took it, holding it up. She handled the bracelet gently, as if it were an explosive or could fall apart at any moment. "The clasp is broken," Louise added unnecessarily. The woman didn't look at her, keeping her eyes trained on the bracelet.

"This is one of ours," she said. "But it's a couple years old now." She paused, pulling out a magnifying glass. "It looks like there's an engraving. Why don't I clean it off?" It was the job Louise wasn't sure she could do herself without destroying the bracelet. "Wait here, and I'll see what I can do." She turned and disappeared into a back room, leaving Louise to her own devices.

Louise wandered around the store, trying to not seem so suspicious. She knew what it would be like in New York City, people staring and whispering and shoving her out onto the street. The one place in New York she actually felt safe was Harlem.

And, of course, that was taken away from her.

She stared at the glittering baubles in the case. She would never make enough to own something like this, never have a chance to wear it. She thought about nights at her beloved Zodiac. The white women there were layered in things like this, necklaces and rings, brooches that sparkled under the light. Schoonmaker could, if he wanted, walk into a place like this and buy everything. Two of everything.

His wealth was staggering, and Louise knew very little about how he obtained it.

She stared at the gleaming rings in their case. Around her, the store was silent. She hoped that she could get what she needed. Louise passed ten minutes walking around the store when the store assistant called her back.

"Mademoiselle!"

Louise turned. She approached the clerk again. The bracelet was now gleaming like one of the showpieces.

"I got the engraving. It's simply an infinity symbol. Does that mean anything to you?"

Louise pressed her lips together. *La Mort des Artistes* used it as a calling card; it was on her key as well. But that told her nothing new. All the women wore the same bracelet. She would guess that they all had the same engraving.

The salesclerk wrinkled her nose in thought. "I can check the records for engravings, but I'm not sure you'll find the owner." She handed the bracelet back.

Louise took it, glad to be reunited with the delicate metal. She slipped it back into her purse. "Can you check the records? Please?"

"I can. It'll take some time."

"Thank you," Louise said. She dug around in her purse, looking for something she could write her information on. "I'm Louise Lloyd. I'd really appreciate it."

The clerk looked at her. "Inèz Leroux." She held a hand out.

Louise shook it, and then wrote her information on a stray business card. "One more thing. How much does this cost?"

The clerk raised an eyebrow. "Eight hundred francs."

All the air left Louise's body. A staggering amount. It would take her months to save up for that. She forced her lips into a smile despite the queasy feeling in her stomach. "Thank you for your help," Louise said, and pulled herself away.

———◁△▷———

"YOUR APARTMENT IS terrible," Emme said. She had just climbed the stairs and was at Louise's door. In her hand, she had an envelope.

"Thank you," Louise said. She had two glasses of wine poured, and Ciarán was out for the night, meaning there was pure silence below her. "Come in."

Emme did as she was told, removing her jacket to reveal an evening dress that had seen better days. She took a glass of wine and drained it. Louise did the same. "I'm going to dinner," Emme said by way of explanation.

"Do you want to borrow something?" Louise asked. "I have so many dresses."

Emme looked her up and down, her brown eyes taking in every detail of Louise's body under her wide-legged pajama pants and oversized men's shirt she slept in. "I'm not sure you own anything that will fit me," Emme said.

"Oh, come on. What's the harm in trying?" Louise asked. "Why don't I take this," she said, prying the envelope from Emme's fingers, "and you look through my clothes." She pointed to the overflowing wardrobe, organized by occasion: work, dancing, drinks. There was no way Emme could turn that down. Louise stretched out on her bed, on her stomach, watching as Emme began to go through her dresses. "How much do you spend on clothes?" Emme asked.

Louise busied herself with reading the coroner's report so she didn't have to answer.

"There's something else in there." Emme was holding a dress up to her body. It was a soft blue, and while it suited Louise, it would wash Emme out.

Louise clicked her tongue, pulling herself up from her spot. "Not that one! Try this." Louise sifted through her dresses until she found a simple gold one with fringe rounding the hem. "So alluring."

"I couldn't."

"You have to," Louise said. "I never wear it anymore anyway. It's yours."

"Where is your bathroom?"

"Just change here," Louise said. The bathroom was on the floor below, and it was a headache to go up and down all the time.

Emme did as she was told, slipping out of her dress and letting it fall to a crumpled mess on the floor. While Emme changed, Louise read the pages in front of her. It wasn't a long report and solidified what Louise already knew.

A drunk and distracted Iris had gotten too close to the window and fallen to her death. No foul play involved.

The police had investigated, and the report named Daniel Toussaint as the lead inspector on the case.

"Have you met Inspector Toussaint?" Louise asked.

She looked up to see Emme leaning into the mirror. She was wearing Louise's dress, and while it wasn't the perfect fit—Emme was right in thinking it would be too big and a little too short—the golden hue brought out her coloring, making her glow. She was running a hand through her hair. "Briefly," Emme said. She turned around to face Louise. "I should change."

"No," Louise said. "You're the bee's knees."

Emme giggled, hiding her laugh behind her hand. Emme would have to stay with the navy-blue T-bar shoes she came in. She turned back to the mirror, pressing her fingers to her face.

"Oh! Wait!" Louise said. She got up, going toward her kitchen-table-slash-vanity. The best thing about working at Allaire's was that she had an enviable range of cosmetics. She picked up a face cream, the same one Margaux had touted as the best paint remover. Louise handed the jar to Emme. "This will make your skin shine."

"You're too nice," Emme said. "I don't know what I expected with what Rosa Maria told me about you."

"I hope she said kind things."

"Only sang your praises." Their fingers brushed as Emme took the jar.

Louise tore her gaze away. "Then what were you expecting?"

Emme turned back to the mirror. Louise went back to her bed, picking up the pages that were scattered on top.

"I don't know. Not this. I don't know," Emme said. She cleared her throat, and business Emme returned. "I hope the report helps."

"It does," Louise said. "Enjoy your party."

Emme grinned. Her smile lit up her entire face. "You should come."

"I don't think so." She was itching for a night out, craving the dance floor the way people needed air. But she was going to stay in. It didn't feel right. "Don't worry about the dress; it suits you better anyway. Have fun."

Louise watched as Emme left, pulling on her coat over the gold dress. When Emme was gone, Louise picked up the discarded dress and folded it, placing it in her wardrobe for lack of a better place.

Then she poured herself another glass of wine.

She had work to do.

# 21

**I WANT TO KNOW** everything about *La Mort des Artistes*," Louise said. She was sitting across from Madame Blanchet in the solarium. The midday sun was shining in, and without everyone else, the room felt much bigger.

She knew what Emme knew. She knew what the women told her. All of it amounted to not much.

Louise wanted the whole story.

The room looked different too. The walls were painted a dark red; at night and lit by candles, they had looked black. There were Oriental rugs covering the floor, large couches and love seats to accommodate everyone. Paintings and photographs covered the wall, each in its own gilded frame.

Coralie was smoking, gracefully tapping her cigarette over an ashtray. She smiled. "Ah, yes. Why don't we start with your most pressing question?" The woman exuded power. It was palpable the minute Louise stepped into the house. Coralie was wearing a long caftan over a pair of trousers and a nicely fitted shirt. She was makeup-free and yet, seemed to glow.

Louise felt small and ungainly in comparison. "What is it?"

Coralie leaned back in her seat, a wide and elegant leather wingback chair. In certain moments, in the right light, Margaux looked exactly like her. They had the same alabaster skin, oval eyes that were bright and inquisitive. "It is a group of women who like to create art and were traditionally kept out of mainstream spaces."

"Because of men?"

Coralie nodded. "I was a member, and I mentor the current members." She stubbed out the last of her cigarette. "Come with me."

Louise did as she was told, following the older woman into the hallway. Coralie stopped at the picture Louise had looked at. "All of these women were members. Some were successful, others, less so." She pulled one photograph off the wall. "This was my first year. 1906. I was barely more than a child." She laughed. "Every year, a few talented women are invited to join the ranks."

"Why would they want to join?" Louise asked.

"Wouldn't you?" Coralie asked. "Prestige. Shows. Friendship. If you're a member then you're a member for life. Who wouldn't want that?"

Louise took it in. Of course she would want that. Even with her couple of informal meetings with the group, she could feel the love and sisterhood between them. They were all united, working toward something together. "What about Iris?"

Coralie put the photograph back. "She was a late addition. When she arrived, it was clear to everyone she was . . . a remarkable talent. And she was given entry, even though it was a little late. Not everyone was happy about that."

"Like who?" Louise asked.

Coralie didn't respond for a moment. The house was quiet, and although Louise was sure there was an army of servants infesting the house like roaches, she couldn't hear any of them. "I don't think I should say," Coralie said. She turned to head back to the solarium. Louise followed. Once Coralie was back in her chair, she looked at Louise, a frown on her lips. "There were a couple more women in contention for Iris' place in the group. But it was going to be Iris or no one."

"Who were those women?" Louise asked.

"You do have a lot of questions, don't you?" Coralie asked. Her eyes narrowed, an almost imperceptible change in her facial expression.

"All part of the job."

"You work in the cosmetics industry."

"I do," Louise said. "And I also ask a lot of questions of my subjects. The ones I photograph. And I'm curious. Who wouldn't be?"

Coralie took this in, her eyes not leaving Louise's face. "Well, I suppose you didn't hear it from me, but my own daughter wasn't thrilled at the idea of Iris joining. She wanted to invite another sculptor. But once they met, Margaux and Iris became the best of friends."

"Did they?" Louise asked.

"As close as can be," Coralie said. "Sometimes my daughter can be a little . . . selective . . . about the people around her. But once she warms up, she's a delight."

Louise didn't believe that. Margaux had always been a little cold to her. Polite, but cold. Louise shifted in her seat.

Coralie lit another cigarette. "Any other questions?"

"Can I go iron my shoelaces? Relieve myself?" Louise asked.

"Les toilettes are right down the hall." Coralie waved her hand. Louise got up to leave.

⌁

INSTEAD OF GOING to the bathroom, Louise began to look around. She was determined to find Margaux's room. Louise hoped that Margaux would be away from the house so that she could snoop around. She had waited outside of the house for Margaux to leave. Nerves skittered over skin as she pushed open doors.

She didn't find the bedroom, but she did find a cozy nook of a room that was obviously an art studio. Louise stepped inside holding her breath. Just in case, she closed the door behind her, flicking on the light. The room was so small that Louise could hold her arms out and her fingertips touched the wall. There was a small window, letting in the early afternoon sunlight. There was an easel with a canvas, a small stool, and a mess of art supplies. Louise sat down. The painting was almost finished. It was Margaux's work. Louise had seen a couple of pieces in the pied-à-terre, but this one stuck out to her.

Margaux painted her subject with tenderness, as if the subject was the only person in the world that she cared about. It was a man, lying back in bed, the sunlight spotting his skin. It was a dewy early morning, and he was smoking.

He had a chiseled chin and brown eyes, but there was something in his gaze that Louise noticed. She leaned forward, as if she could fall headfirst inside the painting.

And when her face was an inch from the canvas, she recognized him: it was Philip Montgomery. The planes of his face were familiar, and now it felt as if he were staring right at her. This was not new information, but it gave Louise a jolt all the same. She stepped back, taking in the painting, trying to see it for what it was. There was a small smile on Philip's lips, making his face seem less severe. Everywhere Louise moved in the small room, his eyes seemed to follow her. It was unnerving.

Aside from the painting of Philip, there wasn't much in the room. A men's toolbox overflowed with brushes. Louise got down on her knees and began to dig through them.

At the bottom, with dried paint and bristles that had molted like birds' feathers, was an envelope.

Louise pulled it out. It was open, torn with a letter opener. She took the letter out, and as she did, a simple silver band fell onto the floor.

The letter was typewritten, a short little missive. She scanned it. It was from Philip to Margaux. They were in *love*. She picked up the band, raising it so that she could see the inside. It wasn't engraved or anything. Just a little ring.

But that ring held all the promise between the two of them.

Louise swallowed back a sharp wave of bile. She put everything back where she found it. She wondered how long the affair had been going on.

And why didn't Iris and Philip get a divorce?

She closed the door behind her as she left. She went to the bathroom, washing her hands and then wiping them on the softest towel she had ever touched. She had to make her good-byes; she didn't want to know what Coralie was picturing since she said she was going to the bathroom.

Coralie was still in the solarium when Louise returned. She was flipping through some pages, that, from afar, looked like a novel. "Thank you so much, Madame," Louise said, clearing her throat.

Coralie didn't look up as she responded. "Of course, darling. You're welcome any time. You should bring some of your photographs sometime."

Louise blushed as she left the house. That would never happen.

# 22

FINDING INSPECTOR DANIEL Toussaint led Louise and Emme to a club in Montparnasse. It was a section of Paris that she rarely visited. She had asked Emme to come along for moral support.

And so that when Louise solved this case, Emme was first for the story.

Tit for tat.

Louise wore a red dress that she often wore to Le Chat Noir and Aquarius. It was one of her first purchases in Paris, and it made her feel invincible. Emme was in a black dress that had seen better days, trying to be invisible.

They started with drinks. The band was on the dais, not as good as Doris', but there were people dancing all the same. Louise always ordered a French 75. Now, holding her glass, she looked around the club.

Emme was at her side, her eyes narrow behind her glasses. "There." She used her glass to motion to a man surrounded by other men.

Louise drained her drink, feeling the bubbles rise to her head. She could do this. "How did you know he'd be here?" Louise asked.

Emme scoffed. "All those men are police. This is where they like to spend time. He's in the center." The man Emme was pointing to had dark hair and dancing blue eyes. He was laughing at something one of his companions had said. "Are you a good dancer?"

Louise had to fight back a laugh. "I'm the best."

She had to time her approach carefully. That meant having another drink, and then another, until she was boldly and brashly confident.

The band was starting a song Louise had heard a million times before. She loved live music, how bands and singers made the same songs sound completely different. The tempo for this one was slowed, making it perfect for a dance.

"Introduce me?" she asked.

Emme nodded. Together, they crossed the floor, and Emme tapped him on the shoulder.

Daniel Toussaint turned and raised an eyebrow. His dark eyes landed immediately on Emme. "Miss Foster," he said, just a hint of exhaustion in his voice. "How nice to see you."

"Inspector Toussaint," Emme said. "This is Louise Lloyd. She wanted to meet you."

Now his dark eyes landed on hers. Louise extended a hand. "How lovely to meet you," Louise said as politely as she could.

"Miss Lloyd." He had a trace of a French accent. His eyes narrowed as he searched her face. "You can be assured the pleasure is all mine." He took her extended hand, kissed it.

She hated when men did that. It happened more to her here in France than it did when she lived in New York. Louise drained her glass.

"Miss Lloyd has some questions," Emme said, obviously wanting to hurry this along, "about Iris Wright and her death."

"How very funny," Daniel said, "I thought that that wasn't your story." Emme's expression turned into a glower.

"It's my story . . . case," Louise said. His dark eyes found hers again. Louise decided that Rafael would be mad for this man in a second.

Detectives did seem to be his type.

Daniel laughed. "It's my case. And you are two little girls who are trying to make my life harder."

The band struck up a new song. Louise was itching to get on the dance floor. She looked the inspector in the eye. "Fancy a dance?" she asked.

He didn't answer, just led Louise onto the dance floor.

Her tango was rusty. She had only ever really done the tango with Rosa Maria, and she didn't know how to follow him. Louise didn't let go of the lead that easily. She could feel Emme watching them as he began to lead her around the dance floor.

"How long have you been in Paris, Miss Lloyd?" Toussaint asked. She could feel his hands on her body, holding her close as he led her across the floor. Following a tango wasn't as easy as Louise remembered. She had loved to tango with Rosa Maria, and that memory worsened the dull ache in her body. But he was good. It was funny to think of the New York detectives taking part in something like this instead of shutting dance halls down.

"Why don't we skip the formalities?" Louise asked. "I want to know what you know about Iris Wright Montgomery."

"Why would I help you?" Toussaint asked. His voice was soft, near her ear. Anyone watching would have thought they were in the middle of a different discussion.

"It's not about me," Louise said. "It's about getting justice."

"And what does a little girl like you know about justice?"

"Getting away with murder is wrong. I was hired to do the job you couldn't."

A soft laugh, no more than an exhale through his nose. "Who are you, really?"

"Does it matter?"

Another pause, he twirled her around. "I don't take kindly to strange women telling me I've done my job wrong."

Louise raised an eyebrow. She could feel his hand at the small of her back, guiding her into each step. "Maybe you should get used to it." It wouldn't do to make this man her enemy. She would need him, if she was going to do this.

And she had to face it: whatever *this* was, she was already knee deep. "Meet me at Dauphine's Café tomorrow. Six in the evening. I would like to talk," Louise said.

"How do you know I'll be there?" he asked.

"I hope you will be." And she realized that was all she had. All she could do was hope.

◁◈▷

THE THING ABOUT her job was that it was easy to do amidst . . . everything. That was something Louise was grateful for. Allaire's was comfortable, but it was never busy in the same way a café was. The patrons weren't as demanding, they weren't as needy. Most patrons often preferred to browse alone without being bothered. And that was something that Louise really appreciated. She didn't want to be bothered either.

With Clara behind the till and Jessie on the floor, Louise was in the back, filling orders. Her favorite place in the store was the stockroom, the stacks of boxes, the lengths of grosgrain ribbon in colors like pale pink and robin's egg blue. The seal for the wax with an ornate *A*. All of it was so luxurious. Wrapping herself up in this, expensive perfumes and face creams, things she never needed and could never normally afford, was a privilege.

Wrapping orders wasn't as easy as everyone would assume it was. The truth was that Allaire had exacting standards. She cut the wrapping paper, custom made in shades to match the ribbon, rolling it out. Everything in an order was wrapped separately, and then tied together, little boxes on top of each other, all boasting the golden *A* for a seal. She always went from smallest to largest. Face creams and atomizers went in different packages. Lipsticks and rouges were opposite shapes.

Louise was grateful to be in the stockroom. She knew Jessie hated it; they switched whenever possible. The three women who worked on the weekends, part time, were messy and left the stockroom in disarray.

But Louise liked to clean it up. And that morning, after finding out about Philip and Margaux, and meeting Toussaint, she needed to restore order to something.

So, she cleaned. And then she wrapped orders.

And she thought about what her life would be like if she had never met Iris Wright.

# 23

⏣

ALL LOUISE COULD do, as she slid into a table at Dauphine's, was hope that Toussaint showed up. It was a busy time, and she was lucky to get the table.

She found Clémence in the crowd, behind the counter, smiling as she waved in new guests. Louise didn't know if Clémence had seen her come in.

If he didn't show, Louise decided to tell Lucy Wright that she couldn't, wouldn't, do this anymore. She was in over her head. The only person she wanted to be was Louise Lloyd. She didn't want all this pressure on her to be something she wasn't.

She would be breaking her word, Schoonmaker's word, but some tasks were too monumental.

Every time the bell chimed, she looked up.

And at last, Daniel Toussaint, wearing a dark suit and a frown on his lips, entered the café.

He looked around; Louise stood to be easier to spot. She sat back down as he approached. "I shouldn't be here," he said in greeting. Very polite. Louise wondered who had raised him.

"So why are you?" Louise asked.

He sat down, folding his body into the chair. He leaned back, legs spread, the very antithesis of who Louise wanted to spend her time with. "I got the feeling you'd follow me around if I didn't. Was I right?"

"Probably," Louise said. "About Iris Wright . . ."

"Miss Lloyd, does a man not get a cup of tea before we begin?" He looked toward the counter. Clémence was standing next to her mother, watching them closely. He signaled, and Clémence crossed over.

"Good afternoon." Clémence didn't look at Louise as she spoke.

Daniel looked up at Clémence. "Can I get a green tea, please?"

"And a coffee, two sugars, no milk," Louise added.

Clémence nodded and turned away from the table. The moment she was out of earshot, Louise leaned in, keeping her voice down. "About Iris Wright," she said again.

Daniel exhaled. He narrowed his eyes. "I'd rather talk about Harlem's Hero first. Of course I looked you up. You have quite the reputation."

Louise swallowed hard. "Did you hear about my arrest?"

"Assaulting an officer."

"I will not hesitate to do it again if I feel I need to." Louise narrowed her eyes now, trying to make the threat seem real. Every so often, she relived punching then-Officer Martin right in the face. It was one of her favorite memories.

Daniel's face remained impassive, unemotional. "Then let's talk about Iris."

"Very good." Louise took a moment to light a cigarette. "Why do you think it was a suicide?"

He raised an eyebrow. "She had just been at a party with all of her friends. She had been drinking. At best, accident. At worst, suicide. Either way, there was no foul play. You can tell Mrs. Wright that with my regards."

Louise raised an eyebrow. "What if you're wrong?"

Toussaint didn't meet her eye. He was scanning the café, as if he were looking for someone more important to talk to. She didn't mention the bracelet she had found. "No one in Mrs. Montgomery's life wanted to kill her."

There was no way she was going to get through to him. Clémence brought their drinks; Louise didn't look at her as she placed cups and little bowls of sugar on the table.

Toussaint waited until Clémence left. He took a sip of his tea. Louise did the same with her coffee.

"You're just assuming," Louise said. She readjusted herself in her chair. "How do you know that for sure?"

His lips pulled into a frown. Louise got the sense he was always frowning, constantly unhappy with his surroundings. "Well, Miss Lloyd. First, I went to the scene. No one saw her fall, no one pushed her. And it's better if this case is done quietly."

Louise sat back, wrinkling her eyebrows. The woman she had met in the office at Duke's didn't seem like the woman who would throw herself out of the window. The woman she had met at Duke's was full of resolve, full of life.

And none of it made sense.

"Her mother believes this wasn't an accident."

He used his teaspoon to stir, then sipped from his cup. Each movement was deliberately done to avoid answering her. "You're believing a bereft, grieving woman?"

"I am," Louise said. She had been that bereft, grieving woman. When Celia had died. It was a feeling Louise never wanted to remember. "Did she leave a note?"

"What?"

"A note. When someone dies by their own hand, they usually say why. In a note," Louise explained.

His lips pursed. He didn't like her tone. He took another sip from his cup before he answered, pacing everything to align with what he wanted. "No. There was no note."

"I promised Mrs. Wright I would find out the truth."

Toussaint's eyes narrowed. Then his lips turned up. "Good luck with that."

CLÉMENCE WAITED UNTIL Toussaint left the table before she slid in across from Louise. Within thirty minutes, the café had settled down, only a couple of the people at tables now. "Who was that?" Clémence asked. She was always curious, always wanting to know what was going on. Her hair was coiled into a braided crown on top of her head, and Louise was immediately jealous her hair wasn't long enough to emulate the style.

"No one," Louise said.

Clémence's eyebrows wrinkled, then she smiled. "You know, I figured out what you're doing in Paris. The American president—"

"Coolidge," Louise supplied.

"Yes, him. He hired you as a spy and that man was one of your agents." Clémence raised her eyebrows, the dimples showing in her cheeks as she smiled.

"Well, I'd tell you, but then I'd have to kill you," Louise said. Clémence laughed. Louise loved hearing Clémence laugh.

"What if I tell you something?" Clémence said, now serious. She looked around, making sure she wasn't needed before continuing. "Then you can tell me something."

"Like what?" Louise's interest was piqued.

"I got married two years ago." Two years ago would have made

Clémence twenty-five. "I married him and, last year, just before you came, he left me." She didn't seem hurt or angry about this. Just sad.

Louise didn't know what to say. "Then he isn't very smart, is he?"

Clémence didn't laugh again, but she smiled. "I guess he isn't. I had to move back in with my parents and start working here again. And I don't know. I guess I just need to move on. He's not coming back." She wrinkled her nose in obvious distaste. But underneath that, Louise could see the hurt in her eyes.

"That's terrible," Louise said. It was the only thing she could think to say.

"I thought it would be different," Clémence said. "I thought he loved me." Her voice was soft, as if she were talking to herself.

Louise bit her tongue. Clémence was opening up to her. A flutter of affection skittered through her stomach. She took a sip of her now-cold coffee. She wanted to sit there and look into Clémence's eyes forever.

"Only a fool couldn't love you," Louise said. It was a bold claim, but she was rewarded with Clémence's dimples.

"Promise?" Clémence asked.

Clémence's smile always made her smile. "Promise."

⧖

DAUPHINE'S AFTER CLOSING was quiet. Louise was sitting at the counter, legs crossed, watching as Clémence placed the chairs on tables and swept the floor.

"You could help," Clémence said.

"I could." Louise leaned back so her elbows were on the counter. She was nursing a cup of coffee, one that had gone lukewarm with her watching.

Clémence stopped, leaning on the broom. She watched Louise closely. "I thought I'd do Shakespeare."

"For a comedy?" Louise knew little about acting.

Clémence sighed. "I don't know." She began to sweep again.

Officially, Louise was supposed to be helping Clémence pick her audition monologue for a new comedic play. Shakespeare felt too serious.

"I don't even know why I'm trying." Clémence stopped again, leaning the broom against the counter and sitting on the stool next to Louise's.

They were alone. It was the first thing that shattered through Louise's thoughts. Clémence's parents had left an hour ago, leaving Louise and Clémence to the clean-up and closing of the café. Clémence's parents were polite to her, but they never shared more than pleasantries. "You're auditioning for a play where a woman thinks she's a chicken. I think you're better than that."

"You've never seen me act." Despite her serious tone, Clémence was trying not to smile. It was the dimples in her cheeks that gave her away.

"Can you act like a chicken?" Louise asked. She pulled out her package of cigarettes and lit one.

Immediately, Clémence took it from her. "Do I want to act like a chicken?" Clémence exhaled. Louise shook her head, but the other woman wasn't paying attention. For a moment they were both quiet. When Clémence's parents were gone, Louise was allowed behind the counter. She stepped behind it, pouring out her coffee.

She knew where Clémence kept the alcohol.

"The way I see it," Louise said, pulling out two glasses. She collected gin, soda water, and two limes. She threw a dish towel over her shoulder. "You can either audition for what will be an awful play, or you can bide your time. Wait. Take classes." Clémence turned to watch her. "Gin rickey," Louise said, pushing a glass toward Clémence. It was the simplest cocktail Louise knew how to make. And the café didn't stock champagne.

Clémence took a sip, closing her eyes. Louise leaned on the counter. "Would you want your name attached to something terrible? It won't be good."

Clémence sighed. She was silent for a minute more. There was something she wasn't telling Louise.

But there were one hundred things Louise wasn't telling Clémence. She figured they were even. "I don't know."

Clémence leaned forward, resting her chin on her forearms. Drinking always made her a little loose-lipped, a little giggly. But tonight, she just seemed sad.

"What is it?" Louise asked.

Clémence's large brown eyes met hers. Her eyebrows creased. She avoided answering the question. "How long did you tend bar?"

"What?"

Clémence raised an eyebrow.

Louise took a sip of her own drink. "For a few months, I managed a nightclub in New York City. I was in charge of a lot of things, but I was mostly behind the bar."

"How did that happen?" Clémence asked.

"My best friend owned it, and I needed a job." Louise was about to mention Celia but bit it back. She didn't want to get into *why* exactly her sister had died. "It was fun. Possibly the best job I had." The Dove ran all night; Louise was in charge of making sure there were no surprises or hiccups. She had loved it; she had felt so powerful. And she got to work with her girlfriend and her best friend, all night, every night.

There was nothing better than that.

"Do you ever tire of being an international woman of mystery?" Clémence asked.

"Never."

She rolled her eyes, drained her cocktail glass, and then got back to the matter at hand. "I don't think I want to pretend to be a chicken." Clémence's voice was soft, preoccupied with something Louise didn't know.

"Then don't. There will be other plays," Louise said, matching Clémence's tone. "You'll be a star."

Clémence frowned. "I hope you're right."

"I am." Louise's heart skipped a beat. That was something she was sure about.

# 24

LOUISE WANTED PHILIP to be Iris' killer. He was everything she hated: a man, pompous and arrogant, who was lucky enough to be married to the most incredible woman and treated her like garbage.

She had to consider it. He could have made a copy of the pied-à-terre key, waited until all the women left, and pushed his successful wife out of the window, freeing him to marry Margaux.

The pied-à-terre was, officially, no-man's-land. Louise had asked during a meeting, all the women splayed out with different artistic mediums. They had laughed for what felt like thirty minutes.

"No man passes this threshold," Sabine had said. Margaux had nodded her agreement.

"This is a woman's place," Lili said. "No men, ever."

"You could be excommunicated," Marion had said.

But Iris was a rule breaker. It was in her genetic makeup.

Or maybe Margaux.

It took some asking around, but Louise found that while his wife was a master of art, Philip was a master of gambling.

Club Noir had one rule: no women at the tables. Louise was quite good at poker, but she wasn't there to play.

She knew how these places worked. She went right after work, still in her dark-red day dress with matching lipstick.

It was empty, except for employees. There were tables for different games: baccarat, poker, and backgammon.

She didn't know what Philip did all day. The Wright family had money, tracing back to the *Mayflower*, when Louise's family was still enslaved.

She presumed that Philip came from a rich family too, that neither of them actually had to *work* for a living.

"We're closed." The bartender didn't look up from the glass he was cleaning. He was neatly dressed, all black, with his sleeves drawn to his elbows.

"I'm not here to gamble," Louise said. He looked up at her, lips frowning in disgust. "No women."

"I just have a couple of questions," she said. She had thought about going home to get Ciarán, take him with her. But she realized that if she made the trip home, she would not want to leave. "It's about . . ." She took a deep breath. She didn't want to explain who she was or what she was doing. She looked up at him, hoping she looked just a little pitiful. "I'm trying to figure out if my man is lying to me."

He laughed. The bartender stopped cleaning glasses and leaned on the counter. He looked right into Louise's eyes. "Who's your guy?"

"Philip Montgomery."

"And you are?"

"Anna Smith," Louise said, the fake name falling out of her before she could really think about it. "I just want to know if he was here last weekend. He said he was, but I can't shake the feeling he was lying to me. I think he just wanted me to stop talking." She channeled her old housemate, Maeve Walsh. She had a way of talking, a way with men, that Louise found annoying and ridiculous.

But being able to copy her did come in handy. The bartender raised an eyebrow, an amused little smile on his face.

"I know he's married, that doesn't mean anything to me. I just want him to be honest with me."

"Okay, take a deep breath." He poured her a glass of water, pushing it toward her. What she really needed was a cigarette. She took a sip.

"Last weekend?" he asked. "He wasn't here. He's here every weekend, but that weekend he and a few other men were in London. There was a poker tournament. He lost."

"He was there the whole time?" Louise asked. "Somebody had eyes on him the whole time?"

The bartender laughed again, covering his mouth with his left hand. "Not the whole time, but he was there for two days of a tournament."

Louise felt herself crumble. If he was in London, Philip couldn't have killed Iris. They weren't even in the same country that night. She deflated. She was so sure, she wanted to go back to Lucy and tell her what happened.

And now she had no idea.

It was wrong of her to suspect Philip, based only on his sex.

She may not have liked Philip, but that didn't mean that he was a killer.

Louise took another sip from her water glass.

"Is there anything else I can do for you?" He had been helpful. Louise shook her head. "You're very kind, thank you. I just . . .

will you be discreet? The last thing I need is him knowing I was checking up on him."

He leaned on the counter, staring at her with unflinching brown eyes. "Will you make it worth my while?" he asked.

Tit for tat. Quid pro quo.

Nothing in life was free.

The only thing she had in her clutch was a five-franc bill. That was supposed to buy drinks that night, but she pulled it out.

This was more important. It wouldn't be the worst thing in the world to have a night in. He reached for it, and she moved it from his grasp. "Not a word," she said.

"I promise."

Louise handed the bill over, hoping that his word was worth it.

"ALL THE WITNESSES gave the same story." Emme was poring over the police notes, while Louise read the coroner's report again. In ten minutes, they would switch and comb over the other's pages to see if there was anything they missed.

Emme had taken the files from Braithwaite's desk. She had come to Louise's apartment grinning, nearly high from her act of espionage.

"Toussaint hates that I'm looking into this," Louise said. The discussion they had at Dauphine's still stung.

"Of course he does," Emme said. She looked up, her eyes wide behind her glasses. "You know he solved a big case a couple years ago? Then he was promoted to inspector. He hates being proven wrong, and he takes this very seriously."

In some way, Toussaint was exactly like Detective Theodore Gilbert. Long dead and buried, the man would follow her around for the rest of her life. She would think of him at the most inopportune moments, while washing her face or choosing what to wear. No matter how much she hated him, he would always be a part of her.

"Oh," Louise said. The inspector had done recon on her, and it felt like an oversight to not do the same for him. "How do you know all this?"

Emme looked back down at the papers. "I hear things. You can't work at a newspaper and not hear things." Emme closed her eyes. She tilted her head back. "Three years ago, this man is murdered. Toussaint was the one that solved it. It was almost an unsolvable case, or at least, it was in the moment. Christopher reported on it all."

Louise wondered what other things Emme heard, and what secrets she was keeping. "Why was he so insistent that Iris died by accident then? No foul play involved?" Louise lit a cigarette.

Emme didn't have an answer for that.

Louise hadn't eaten all day, but she had been drinking wine, and it was mostly the same thing. "Someone is lying." Louise exhaled through her nose, feeling a headache coming on. Sure, that could have been the bottle of wine they were splitting.

But it could also be the tangle of knots that was in front of her.

Louise didn't know what she was going to tell Lucy. The older woman's insistence that she find out what happened to Iris followed her everywhere.

The one thing she knew was this wasn't an accident.

"There were bruises on her," Louise said. "On her back. Is that anything?"

"Maybe she was pushed," Emme said.

"Maybe she was." She closed her eyes, trying to picture what Iris did in her last moments. She hoped Iris' eyes were closed.

"She landed on her back," Emme said.

It was nice to have someone to talk this over with. It reminded her of afternoons in Gilbert's office, drinking a Coke and staring at the board, trying to put a puzzle together.

How had she ended up here? How did she manage to end up in the middle of a murder *again*? This was the last thing she thought would happen.

She exhaled. "Iris, Estelle, Margaux, Jeanne, Marion, Sabine, and Lili were all at the apartment that night." She had gone over these few pages so much that she probably had them memorized, could recite it as a dramatic passage for an audition for one of Ciarán's plays. Not that she would. Maybe she could teach it to Clémence. "They met at one thirty in the morning. General consensus is that they all drank. Margaux and Sabine left first, Jeanne and Lili were next. Marion, Estelle, and Iris remained. At three in the morning, Estelle left to pack, and Marion left as well."

Seeing the facts all laid out didn't help. She would have to go through and confirm all the stories in this report. Emme was frowning, her eyes still closed. She exhaled softly through her lips, slightly parted.

It was this that Louise wanted to take a photograph of. The way the light hit her, made her glow. Louise moved slowly, moving to get her camera before Emme noticed. She took a couple of photographs, before Emme opened her eyes.

Maybe she would have something to display.

"Why did you stop?" Emme asked, opening one eye.

Louise put her camera down. "I was just thinking."

"I'm so tired," Emme sighed.

Louise sat back down on the bed. The coroner's report was full of information that, like the police report, she had memorized.

The sketches of the body would haunt her dreams for the rest of her life. The pages were crumpled and spread over her sheets.

And Louise didn't want to think about Iris for another moment. "Why don't we go see what Ciarán is drinking?" Louise asked. "He's always good for a distraction."

*November 1st, 1927*

*Louise,*

*Michael and I are going to be married!*

*Truthfully, I'm nervous. I don't know if I want to be tied down. He's a mechanic, and it's not a bad living, but I'm scared. I love him, but I'm scared. I know you probably won't understand. I think just writing to you helps, even if you've not written me back.*

*Do you read these?*

*I don't know how to picture you, or where to picture you. I just think of you floating. I know what you'd say. You'd sit me down and say, "Josie, if you're not happy, you don't have to stay with him. You don't have to do anything. I'll help you figure it all out."*

*But since you're not here, I have to figure it out for myself. I think if I marry, I'll have to stop dancing. And I don't know if I just want to be a wife yet.*

*I think about you. You would take matters into your own hands. You do it all the time. And maybe I'm scared to be as brave as you. I wake up, take a deep breath, and remember that this is good. I'm happy.*

*But just because I'm happy doesn't mean I have to be married.*

*We're finishing* Something Sweet. *Just a couple more scenes to film, and then he wants to get married fast. I don't know what his rush is.*

*To be honest, I was so taken aback that I said yes. And this ring on my finger, stable and solid. Daddy would be thrilled, I think. I haven't written him much since I've been here, and* when I have written, he hasn't replied. I know Minna checks in on him.

I know, you don't want to hear about Daddy.

The more I think about it, the more I don't think I want it to happen. Michael insisted on calling Schoonmaker the moment I said yes. I'm worried Fox wants to pay for the wedding.

I don't know what I want. And I think that's okay.

Minna says I should marry him. We get to talk on the phone sometimes, and it's nice to hear her voice. I miss her too. I know what you would say. I know what Minna says.

But it's something I have to decide for myself.

For what it's worth, I don't think being with him would be a bad life. I just don't know if it's for me. Celia was the one who wanted to get married. Celia was the one who wanted a husband and children.

And if she can't do that, do I have to?

I don't know. I miss you. I wish you were here.


Write me soon. I love you,
Josie

# 25

THE MOOD IN the store was different. It was the last fifteen minutes before they really *would* have to start closing.

Both Jessie and Clara had been in foul moods and not talking to each other. They had resorted to trading snide remarks through Louise. She was on the floor, counting the minutes until she would be able to have a drink and a cigarette.

The door chime rang, practically deafening in the silence between her and Jessie, and Louise turned around.

She and Jessie had already begun to close up for the night, dragging out the task as slowly as possible.

"Miss Lloyd?" The woman, in a chic black day dress with a scarlet cloche and matching gloves, stepped into the store. "I'm Inèz . . ."

"From the jewelry store, I know," Louise said.

Inèz looked around. She was clutching her purse to her like it contained very important documents. Jessie didn't pay them any attention.

"Over here," Louise said. She led the other woman to the till, where she could sit down. Inèz placed her purse on the counter. "I hope you didn't go through too much trouble."

Inèz shook her head. "No trouble at all." She pulled some papers out of her purse, spreading them out.

Louise looked them over. They were logs. "The engraving and the buying are two different logs. But this specific bracelet has only been engraved a few times. They've all been ordered and bought by the same woman."

"Who?" Louise asked.

Inèz looked over the pages again. "Coralie Blanchet. Do you know her?"

Of course Louise did. Everyone in high Paris society did.

And that made sense. Coralie was a member, and the mentor to the current women. And she had oodles of money, just tons of it.

"The last one was purchased by Coralie?" Louise asked.

Inèz nodded. "The seventh of May. I wasn't there, but it's in the log." That was the Monday after Iris died. Inèz pointed to the registry. The writing was thin, slanted, and in French, and Louise could barely read it.

"I really appreciate this," Louise said.

Inèz looked around the still-empty sales floor. "Would you mind if I looked around? I've never been in here."

"Be my guest," Louise said. She stayed at the till while the other woman made a dignified beeline to the women's cosmetics. She wished she could call Emme. There was a phone behind the till, but they were expressly forbidden to make personal calls.

The fact remained that she had one of those women's bracelets.

Could it be a coincidence? Could another party have pushed Iris out of the window, and the clasp on a member's bracelet broke in the same spot Iris landed?

Louise exhaled. It didn't seem likely.

One of those women was guilty.

It was hard to marry that with the group she was getting to know. They were all ambitious and clever and talented as hell. She thought that Rosa Maria would *love* a group like this, one solely dedicated to their art, their life's work.

Inèz approached the counter with her arms full of products. Louise took the order, adding on her staff discount of thirty percent as a thank-you.

Inèz grinned, making her seem girlish. "That's so kind."

"It's the least I can do; thank you so much," Louise said. "I can have those delivered, if you'd like."

"Please." Inèz took her purse back, making sure the folded pages were inside. "Good luck with what you're working on."

"Have a good night," Louise said.

That was their last customer for the day. Jessie was dusting off the shelves, and Louise began to cover the counters. Allaire had left an hour earlier, leaving them to their own devices.

Maybe he didn't want to get into the middle of Jessie and Clara fighting.

"Any plans?" Jessie asked.

"No. You?" Louise moved to the till, covering it as well. They'd sweep the floors and close the windows, calling it a night. She'd be grateful to go home and lie down. And call Emme.

Jessie shook her head. "I'm usually too tired to do anything after work. I always want to sleep." Jessie was quiet, reserved. She seemed to always be evaluating the world around her, and she never seemed to be too pleased with what was in front of her.

"Me too," Louise said. She was older than Jessie and Clara, only by a few years, and yet, it felt like a lifetime. "I'll get Clara; you can go if you want. I can finish up."

Jessie shot her a grateful smile. "Thank you." Without another word, she dashed to the employee room.

Louise waited until Jessie left to get Clara. The truth was she didn't want to hear any more sniping.

The last thing they did before leaving was turn off the lights and lock the door, officially putting an end to another day.

◁◈▷

"SO," LILI SAID. She was once again seated behind her easel. She had promised Louise that they were in the homestretch, but Louise didn't believe it. "What are your hopes? What do you really want?"

When it was just them, as it was now, Lili tended to talk a lot more. She had paint smeared on her face, the product of her rubbing the back of her hand on her cheek.

But she still didn't want Louise to respond, not to talk. So, Lili often talked, answering her own questions. "Hm. My mother was a dancer. I thought that maybe I would want to act too. Of course, she gave it all up when she met my father. She always said that being a wife and mother was what she really wanted to do."

It was hard to sit still. Louise was glad she wasn't expected to respond. Oftentimes, she would let her thoughts drift, while trying to keep that coy smile on her face.

Now that they were a few sessions into this portrait, Louise still wasn't convinced it was a great idea.

But her name would be nowhere near it. No one she knew would see it.

"My older brother is a writer; my dad was too. Family of creatives." Lili was still talking at a pace that filled the silence around them. It was soothing, and Louise knew that Lili didn't just talk to hear her own voice.

"My mother was Russian," Lili was saying. "Prima ballerina. She wanted me to dance too, but I was never good. Never had the drive." She fell silent for a moment, squeezing her eyes in a way that showed she was concentrating. If Louise could talk, she would say that this required stamina too. Maybe not as much as dancing, but Lili certainly had drive.

Louise liked watching Lili. It was an intimate sketch of who she was when no one else was looking. Louise assumed it was easy to pretend the subject wasn't there.

"You are so beautiful," Lili murmured. "This is going to be wonderful." They had spent hours sitting here, Lili talking and painting and Louise sitting.

"Have I ever told you about how I started painting?" Lili asked. She checked the time on her watch and paused. "Fifteen-minute break, and then I'll tell you."

Louise lived for those breaks. She thought Lili was calling them later and later, as a means to build up her stamina. She got up, stretching her arms over her head, even though she was bare-chested. Lili poured them glasses of water and tossed Louise a towel to wrap around herself.

"How did you join the group?" Louise asked.

Lili smiled. "Well, it was a couple of years ago, now. It was Sabine who introduced me to Margaux. We met at some gallery opening. Margaux took a liking to me, and there was a letter at my door, just like there was for you."

"What do you think about the other women?" Louise asked. She tried to make it seem like she was just curious.

Lili lit a cigarette before she answered. "Usually, it's a good group of people. Good ideas, we mix well, and it's really nice to be able to bounce ideas off of each other."

"What about the other times?" Louise asked.

Lili was the most direct in talking about the group. That was
something Louise was grateful for. She was rather straight with
her, and often talked about the petty squabbles that the women
got into while painting.

"Hm." Lili sipped from her glass. "You know what women are
like . . ." she trailed off.

"Do you fight often?" Louise asked.

"I wouldn't call it fighting. I would say there are disagreements.
Like . . . Marion and Iris. You know when you see someone and
instantly know you don't like them?"

Louise knew that well. She had despised a woman she lived
with in her boardinghouse—Maeve Walsh—for nothing in particular, but everything Maeve did got on her nerves.

"It was like that," Lili said, sipping from her glass of water
again. "Marion couldn't stand her, but Iris liked everyone. But the
harder Iris tried, the more Marion hated her."

Louise lit a cigarette of her own. They always kept a small dish
right next to the ashtrays for used matches. She appreciated the
attention to detail. Louise exhaled smoke, trying to keep Lili talking. "Iris tried, but the whole feeling of the group changed. It was
never the same. Whatever Iris wanted, Marion wanted the opposite. Neither of them would budge." Lili cleared her throat, dropping her cigarette into the ashtray. Her eyes slid over to the
window, where she stared at the new, just replaced glass. She
drained her glass of water. "Are you ready?"

"One more minute?" Louise asked.

Lili nodded. She was already moving back to her easel. "I need
to clean my brushes off anyway." She picked up the ornate vase she
used to keep her brushes and wandered over to the kitchen sink.

Preparing herself for another session, Louise sat down and finished her cigarette. She wanted to know more about Marion and Iris, but she would have to wait for another break.

Lili returned, sitting herself down in front of the canvas. She looked at Louise, who pulled the towel away, tossing it on the floor.

As Lili resumed painting, Louise was left to just think about how much Marion hated Iris.

Did Marion hate Iris so much that she killed her? Louise didn't know.

All of these women could turn violent if given a chance.

# 26

⋞⋟

IT WAS CIARÁN who eventually gave Louise Estelle's address. He had wanted to come with her, but Louise couldn't risk that. It had been a couple of weeks since the news of Iris' death had hit the media, and she already knew the story was snaking its way through polite society. And less polite society.

A mansion in the 17th arrondissement. Louise didn't realize that Estelle, like the Blanchets and the Wrights, was filthy rich. Estelle wasn't the type who seemed filthy rich; she wore it differently.

A shy little maid in a black-and-white uniform answered the door. Louise smiled as sweetly as she could. "Louise Lloyd. Here to see Estelle Callaghan. I'm a friend."

The maid opened the door, not making eye contact. "Follow me."

As they wound their way through the halls, Louise could only think that Schoonmaker could take a note or two.

They arrived at a pool room, where Estelle, wearing a rather daring swimming costume of emerald green, was lying on a chair near the edge. Her hair was stuck to her skin, every inch of her was dripping water. Without makeup, she looked much younger, almost cherubic. Her diamond and emerald bracelet was clasped around her right wrist. "Louise," Estelle said. "What a surprise. Mary, will you go make us some tea, please?"

Louise didn't intend to stay long enough to consume anything. Estelle waved an arm and moved her impossibly long legs, making room for Louise to sit. She did so, trying to keep her distance. "Lovely, isn't it?" Estelle asked. "When Father asked what I wanted in the new house, I simply had to have a pool."

Of course she did.

It was becoming clearer and clearer that Estelle and her family were new money. "It's the bee's knees," Louise said, biting her tongue. "Simply jake." She cleared her throat. "I want to talk about . . ."

"I wonder what it would be like to drown," Estelle said, without a care about what Louise wanted to talk about. "I *can* swim. I've been swimming for years. But sometimes, I paddle out and just wait." Estelle's intense eyes found Louise's. "Can you swim?"

"Not well."

A sharp exhale of air through Estelle's nose, somewhat of a laugh. "Maybe I should toss you in and see how you fare."

Louise pulled herself away from the other woman.

"Now . . . what did you want to talk about?"

"Iris."

She expected that just hearing the name would light something in Estelle, set something off in her. Maybe she would start to cry and wouldn't stop. That was how Louise would feel if Rosa Maria suddenly died. She wasn't supposed to think about Rosa Maria. Estelle did nothing. She moved her stare to the depths of the pool, then leaned over to light herself a cigarette. From somewhere far away, there was a squeal of laughter. "I have two sisters: Hazel and Hattie. They still *play*," Estelle said, as if it needed explaining. "I don't want to talk about Iris."

"I just want to know what she was like," Louise said. She hadn't gotten enough. That small taste of Iris, the way she spoke, wasn't enough. The way she held herself, seemed to glow. How bright and deep and *blue* her eyes were.

"That office was where we first kissed," Estelle said. She sighed, her whole body heaving with the effort. "That's how I knew where she'd be." She was different, and a blind person could see it. Louise watched her every move. Estelle looked everywhere but at Louise, her eyes again finding the pool. "I knew that she wanted to leave with me. She told me." She swallowed hard. Her voice was quiet. If Iris hadn't died, they would have left together. Happy ever after. "She didn't think she wanted to be an artist anymore."

"Did she ever tell you why?" Louise asked.

Estelle shook her head. "I never asked. That was just Iris. Impulsive."

"Did she have any enemies?"

"We're a sisterhood." That didn't answer her question, but Louise let it slide. She knew that meant that Iris had enemies. The pool room was cold; there were goose bumps rising on her skin. There was another squeal of laughter. Estelle rolled her eyes. "I don't know anyone who would want to kill Iris. She and Sabine had their differences, but none of us would ever do this to each other. It's us against the world. It's us before everyone."

Louise wished she had relationships like that. She used to; back in Harlem, she, Rafael, and Rosa Maria were inseparable. They were always together, so close they could read each other's mind. But here in Paris? She didn't have that bond. "The fact remains that one of you must have," Louise said.

"Iris was the type to try to take charge," Estelle said. "She was domineering, but I don't think anyone hated it. She really managed to pull us together. She made us all better." Louise had to wonder if all the women believed that, or if it was just Estelle. "She was dedicated to her work. Everyone else just wanted to sit around and drink." Estelle closed her eyes. She took three slow, deep breaths, centering herself. When Estelle opened her eyes, she focused on the still water of the pool again. "She was the love of my life. I can't believe anyone I know would ever do this. We had our disagreements, but that's just part of it, isn't it? You know artist types. So temperamental."

Maude and Ciarán had said the same thing. Louise had to wonder how true that was. It was, at least, very well known.

"Do you need anything else?" Estelle asked.

Louise hadn't exactly gotten what she had needed, but she didn't want to press Estelle.

Estelle stood. Water was dripping down from her skin. She pushed her still-damp hair from her eyes. "Then I trust you can find your way out."

Without looking at Louise, Estelle made an elegant dive into the water.

⋖⋏⋗

THE HOUSE WAS big enough to get lost in. Once Estelle resumed swimming, Louise got up, leaving the pool room. She knew she should leave, but there was the unavoidable itch to look around.

It was so quiet that Louise could hear a pin drop. She wondered how many people were on the staff. That was something she had considered, after moving to Paris. She could have worked in a house just like this.

She climbed the stairs, trying to be as quiet as possible. She already had a plan in her head: if anyone came up to her, she was going to ask where the bathroom was.

But there was no one around her. The halls were long and wide. Unlike the Blanchet house, there was no art to speak of. It made the house feel empty and lifeless. It was the opposite of the Blanchet house, where Louise could feel the creative spirit just from stepping inside. This house felt cold. From somewhere, there was the tinny sound of a radio, breaking some of the silence. The floors were soft and carpeted; Louise had removed her shoes and was holding them by the straps.

Estelle's art studio was on the second floor of the house, conveniently right next to the bathroom. Louise had been poking through every other room until she found it. She had never seen a work by Estelle. None of the paintings in the Blanchet house were signed by her.

The room was small, full to the brim with easels and canvasses. Almost every canvas was half finished. Louise looked around. Estelle painted other artists. There were portraits of Iris, sitting at her own easel. There were dancers in an embrace. There was Marion, sitting with her clay, a small smile on her face. These moments, the most human of them all, were all deftly and beautifully captured.

She had never seen art like this: it had all been serious portraits, with the sitter watching the painter. Estelle's paintings had a source of life in them that Louise had never seen before. She looked at the couple dancing. With similar hair colors and builds, the couple had to be Estelle's parents. She stepped closer, trying to see all of the individual strokes that made up the painting. That was something she had come to appreciate as well, the work and dedication that went into a piece of art.

Louise moved to look at the one of Iris. It was painted so that Iris was mostly blocked by her easel. But Estelle had managed to capture the glint in her eye, one of determination. There was a paintbrush in her right hand, poised and ready. She wondered who or what Iris was painting. She stepped closer. It was subtle, but Iris was naked behind the easel. Louise looked away. The room was small, but there was a window where the sun filtered in.

She looked around. Like Margaux, Estelle kept her things in a men's toolbox, big and red and stuffed to the brim with palette knives and brushes and pencils. Louise dug through the box, finding nothing of note.

The room was dusty, as if it hadn't been cleaned in a while. She moved the stool and a floorboard squeaked. She kneeled down and pushed it to the side. Below, the cavity was filled to the brim with papers. She pulled them out, hoping that they weren't in any significant order. Louise flicked through them, her heart in her throat. It was quiet enough that she would be able to hear anyone approach, but nerves ran through her anyway. There were letters and sketches. The letters, she knew, were from Iris. Louise was so familiar with Iris' handwriting that she now would be able to recognize it anywhere. Each letter was pages and pages long, all handwritten. She flicked through a couple of them, noting the dates. Iris had been writing to Estelle for three years. She didn't read them. The sketches were simple and small, revealing nothing. A couple of the sketches reflected paintings that were on easels, a rough draft before a more permanent version.

She looked back up at the easels. She stared up at Iris. The personal moment that Estelle had decided to commit to canvas forever, making its mark on the world.

They loved each other. Louise wondered how it happened. Iris didn't talk about the affair in letters to her mother. But it must have burned brightly, while it could. And the world was better when Iris was in it.

She put everything away, replacing the floorboard on top. She put the stool back where she had found it. Her pulse was still racing. She was thinking about Estelle and Iris. Iris and Estelle. It wasn't hard, when Iris was watching her every move, her eyes seeing all. Iris' eyes seemed to follow her as she moved around the little room. Louise stood, feeling her bones creak as she did so. She stepped out of the room, closing the door behind her. The walk to find her way out was a long one, and all she was thinking about was Estelle and Iris. They *loved* each other. Louise had to wonder if she could be that devoted to someone again. She needed a cigarette. She needed coffee.

If she had to be that devoted to anyone again, she wanted it to be Clémence.

# 27

---

I T TOOK CIARÁN too long to answer his door. Louise wasn't sure if he could hear it through all the noise. Eventually, Louise balanced her glass in her hand and pushed the door open. It was never locked.

Instantly, the cat was at her feet. She put her glass on the nearest surface and picked the cat up. "Ciarán." Louise had to raise her voice. He was intensely focused on his typewriter, smoking copiously and typing. Louise had to say his name twice to get his attention. Ciarán turned and stared at her for a moment, as if he had no idea who she was. Then he melted into a smile and got up to hug her.

She had never seen him with spirits that high. Louise buried her face into his chest, the hug made awkward because Louise was still holding the cat. He smelled like cigarettes and alcohol. "You're feeling better."

"I've got it!" Ciarán let her go, taking his cat from her arms. "My next play. And the sun was shining, and it was a beautiful day."

"What is it about?" Louise asked, picking up her glass of wine again. Ciarán leaned over, kissing her on both cheeks. He was more affectionate than usual.

"Ah, you'll have to wait until it's done." He sat back down at his typewriter. Running a hand through his hair, which hadn't seen a comb, he turned to her. "What do I owe the pleasure of your visit?"

"I want to talk about Iris."

"Of course you do. I don't think we ever talk about anyone else anymore."

"What did you like about her?" Louise asked.

Ciarán turned to her. There was a warmth in his eyes that she had never seen before. "She always told me what she thought. Exactly. It was one of the reasons I fell for her. Head over heels."

"Did you love her?"

Ciarán pursed his lips. "My question now. Why are *you* looking into her death?"

"I was asked to."

"But why?" He wouldn't let it go. He had to know the answer. He had asked a couple of times, and Louise had never given him the full story.

Louise exhaled, draining her wine. She wished she had thought to bring the bottle with her. "You first. Then I'll tell you."

Ciarán raised an eyebrow. "What do you want to know?"

"Everything."

Ciarán frowned. "She felt it all so deeply. It was all on the surface, love, hate, everything. It was what made her such a great artist. That, and she was good at interpreting what other people felt too. And she put it all on the canvas with no regrets or expectations. She was fully committed to what she chose to do. That's what she was like."

Ciarán got up, pouring himself and Louise glasses of whiskey. He handed one to her. "Your turn."

"Where should I begin?" Louise asked.

"The beginning."

Louise narrowed her eyes. She began to tell Ciarán *everything*, almost her whole story, and an hour later, peppered with his questions and comments, she was done. Telling someone about her past felt good. She was done running from who she was.

"Oh," Ciarán said when she had finished. She had never seen him speechless. He leaned back in his chair. Irving had made his way back to the table and had leaped onto it. Louise finished her whiskey. The more she drank it, the more she hated it, but she couldn't let him know that.

"That about sums it up."

Ciarán blinked. She hadn't mentioned her years-long relationship with Rosa Maria, but she kept everything else as close to the truth as possible. "Now I live here, and it was fine, until Lucy came to me." The silence was becoming a little awkward. "You don't have to say anything."

In response, Ciarán got up, poured himself another glass of whiskey, and drank it all. He muttered something, possibly a string of curse words in Irish. "My God."

"I know."

"And you're alive."

"I know."

It was the disbelief that she would never get over.

# 28

THE DAY DANIEL Toussaint first came to her job, it rained.

The Paris rain had come on fast and furious, sending people scattering from the streets. It also meant that the store was empty.

Louise was the only clerk on the floor, and she was behind the counter. They had been open for hours and had two customers. Jessie had already wrapped the outstanding orders, Clara had cleaned and organized the stockroom.

And now they were . . . waiting.

Louise had a stack of Iris' letters in front of her. She was making her way through 1926, which wasn't an easy feat. The first thing she had done was organize each letter by year and 1926 had the most by far.

She wondered what happened that year. Maybe Iris was just missing her mother more than usual.

Lucy had given her these letters to prove something was wrong. Now Louise was reading them to get a sense of who Iris was, outside of the group, outside of society. She was learning that Iris was more anxious and introspective than she let on. She wrote about every feeling she had. And the only person Iris felt she could really confide in was her mother.

The chime above the door tinkled, and Louise looked up.

Inspector Daniel Toussaint was absolutely soaked with rain. He removed his hat, looking around the store. He seemed skeptical.

"Inspector," Louise said. Allaire was in his office, above them. She had to hope her boss wouldn't come down and see her talking to him.

She wouldn't be able to explain what was going on.

Toussaint's hat dripped on the floor. She would have to mop the floor again. His trench coat was, likewise, heavy with water.

"This is where you work?" Toussaint asked. She had to bite back a sarcastic response. He began to stroll around the store, and Louise took the opportunity to hide Iris' letters under other papers.

She watched as he moved around the floor, slowly, as if he were a lion stalking his prey. He began at the women's side, looking everything over as if he didn't believe in the basics of skin and hair care.

He picked up a jar of blush, inspected it, and then put it down. He ran a finger over the soft bristles of a hairbrush. Louise waited, trying to make it look as if she wasn't watching and categorizing his every move. She wondered if he had someone, a wife or girlfriend he was shopping for. She wondered what he was doing here.

The two sides were neatly divided by some tables boasting their clients' most favored products. He stopped there, picking up the jar of face-cream-paint-remover. Then he looked up at her, still holding the jar.

"You have to stop what you're doing."

"What do you think I'm doing?" Louise asked. He had been working up to this, she could tell. "I'm at work. I'm doing my job."

He raised his eyebrows, trying to decide if she was being smart.

"You know what I mean." His response was measured. He was fighting to keep his cool.

A blush rose to her cheeks, but she held steady. When she didn't respond, he continued: "This was almost cute at first, but Miss Lloyd, you need to stop playing. This isn't a game."

He had approached the counter as he spoke, keeping his voice low and even. Now, he placed his hands on the glass, training his eyes on her. "We don't want anything happening to you."

Louise narrowed her eyes. "Are you trying to intimidate me? I already told you, I'm doing this for Mrs. Wright. She's the one who hired me. She wants the truth, and you didn't give it to her. Take it up with her."

There was something about the man that she didn't like. Louise had been content to chalk it up to her general dislike of authority figures.

But now he was *here*, in her workplace, trying to tell her what to do.

And she hated that.

"You have no idea what you're doing, do you?" he asked.

"I don't appreciate this," Louise said. "I don't come into your work and threaten you." She glared at him. "If you're not going to buy anything, I'm going to have to ask you to leave."

"Miss Lloyd!" The voice descended from on high, but it wasn't God. It was Mr. Allaire, a discerning old man who had hired her on the spot when she moved to Paris. In the ensuing months, Louise had done her best to prove to Allaire that she was a quality employee.

And this was going to ruin it.

Allaire descended the stairs, buttoning the center button on his jacket. "Who is this?" He was about her height, a man who was safely between fifty and sixty. His light hair had given way to gray, but his dark eyes were bright.

He treated every woman who worked at his store like family. More often than not that meant living up to his exacting standards, both in and out of work. Allaire had never had children of his own, he had never married, and he did have the utmost respect for the women he hired.

"No one, sir," Louise said. She stumbled over her words. Anxiety skittered over her skin. She couldn't meet Allaire's eyes.

Toussaint eased into a bright, friendly smile. "I'm sorry, sir. I was just asking Miss . . . Lloyd . . . about some products."

Louise smiled as well. "Monsieur was going to get some cologne," she supplied. "He wants to try something new. I was going to recommend your favorite."

"Of course. Allow me, Miss Lloyd." Allaire took over, sweeping Toussaint over to the men's products. She remained behind the counter. She shoved the letters on the small shelf below the register, out of sight.

When Toussaint was guided back to the till, he had four different colognes. "Miss Lloyd will help you from here. Have a nice day, Inspector."

Louise did as she was told. Toussaint watched as she added up his purchases, a frown on his lips. "Be careful, Miss Lloyd. You never know who you're up against."

◁◈▷

THE ONLY THING Louise wanted to do was go dancing. She ended up alone, at the place where she and Emme had met the inspector.

Anonymous in Montparnasse and drunk.

That was all she wanted to be.

By the time she got there, the dance floor was full. She joined right in, allowing a man to whirl her into a Texas Tommy. The handkerchief hem of her dress flared and moved as she followed the lead. With the music like a pulse, running through her like it was a part of her, she finally felt like she was at peace.

This was the only thing she was good at. Louise knew that. After everything she had been through, her talent still lay on the dance floor.

This was what she wanted.

So then, why did she feel so alone?

She spent the entire night on the dance floor. By two in the morning, the band had switched to playing slow songs; "Someone to Watch Over Me," in lilting French, flowed over the dancers. Louise leaned into a man who smelled like cigarettes and brilliantine, a usually stomach-turning combination that now felt strangely like home. They were doing an odd mix of a waltz and a foxtrot, with him effortlessly guiding her around the dance floor. The couples were beautiful, dramatic, talented. Beside them, Louise felt tiny and very American.

She had thought that dancing was the same everywhere, but it turned out it was better, like most things, in Paris.

Louise was trying not to miss things in her old life, but seeing these clubs, dancing at them, it was impossible for her not to. She missed late nights at the Dove, with Rafael and Rosa Maria, watching over the club. She missed drinking with them after the club closed, falling asleep next to Rosa Maria with everything right in the world.

The more Louise thought about it, the more she realized that she and Iris were similar: they both wanted something they couldn't have, wanted something more than they were given in life.

The fact that Iris was a rich white woman didn't mean anything. They both were women in a world where women were looked down upon.

Louise was wonderfully, happily tipsy. She'd have to call a cab back home. She had been so good about not drinking too much, but something about that night called for it. She was itchy, anxious to do something. She thought she would be content away from Harlem, away from the woman she used to be.

Now, maybe, she wanted something else?

Lost generation, indeed.

How did anyone manage to focus? How did anyone decide what they wanted to do? Louise never dared to dream when she was a child; she was busy raising other children.

But now . . .

She concentrated on her dance steps. Those had always been her anchor. When her world was in turmoil, at least she could dance.

The man she was dancing with for the last three songs was good. Better than so many men she had danced with. His lead was gentle.

But none of it was the same.

Louise blinked. Her vision was hazy, but she could see him, past her partner's shoulder.

Detective Gilbert, right as rain, in the center of the dance floor.

She remembered it like it was yesterday, her gun going off in her hands, the noise, the recoil.

So how could he be here?

She blinked twice, willing herself to look away. But he remained, staring at her.

It felt important to remind herself that she didn't believe in ghosts. And whatever this was, whatever this could be, it *wasn't* a ghost.

The music was too loud, the alcohol burning its way through her body. She was aware of every cell, every molecule vibrating, moving in a way she couldn't control. She was holding a glass, or was she? She couldn't feel or see anything but the man before her.

And she couldn't breathe.

She couldn't breathe.

He was watching her, doing and saying nothing. Louise opened her mouth, then closed it.

He always came to her when she hadn't slept, when she was piled under one hundred other things.

She thought about that day in the Zodiac. They had drunk together, as if they were friends.

She thought about the days in the office, days in the park.

After all these years, she still had things to ask. Why her? She understood, she thought she understood. But she wanted to hear him say it.

It was a type of closure she would never get.

What had he seen in her? What had pulled her to him. He was a ghost. He was dead, and she had killed him. And although she knew that, she also knew she would never be able to leave him behind.

If she were being honest, Louise would admit that this was his fault. The trajectory her life had taken, it was all his fault.

Her heart was pattering in her chest. Something, an icy grip, was locked around her, squeezing hard. She felt as if she were watching herself from above. Her soul had left her body, and she was watching, completely devoid of who she was.

She pushed her partner away, freeing herself from his grip. She pressed a hand to her mouth.

Without thinking about it, her body moving before her brain could catch up, she turned on her heel and left the club.

*January 1st, 1928*

*Dearest Lovie,*

*Happy New Year. I apologize that this letter is late, but since you never seem to read them . . .*

*I'm sorry. I miss you. We had a big New Year's bash at the club, and it was invigorating. I spent the night serving drinks, and the cops didn't close us down. We managed to dance and drink and kiss until two in the morning.*

*A wonderful way to start the new year.*

*I envy you, sometimes. You always know exactly what you want to do. And I have to assume that, since you never seem to write me or Fox, you are happy.*

*I hope you're having a fabulous life.*

*How come you can send a gift basket, but not write a letter? Lovie, which one takes* more *effort?*

*It doesn't matter. I love hearing from you any way I can.*

*I'm going to tell you something, because I need to tell someone, and I know you probably won't read this.*

*(But if you do, WRITE ME BACK!)*

*I'm in love.*

*I don't think I've ever been in* love.

*How did you know? You've been in love. (I wish you were here. We could talk about it in person. Anna isn't a very good conversationalist.)*

*Josie came to visit for the winter; she spent New Year's Eve with us. I think she's okay. She's decided to stay in California. She's strong and smart and stubborn, just like you. If anyone can make her way in the world, it's that girl. I look at her, and I wonder if I was anything like her at her age.*

*I'm doing my best to look out for her, the only way I can. If either of your sisters needs help, Fox and I will be there for them both. I know it's what you would want too.*

*I often write to you as if you've passed, and sometimes that's what it feels like. I think about you always, and I worry that if something did happen, I wouldn't know.*

*Please, send me* something.

*Yours forever,*
*Rafael Moreno*

# 29

THE OPENING OF the door pulled her out of her sleep. In fact, Louise thought she was still dreaming, the Saturday before her stretching long and languid.

"Do you think we should have called?"

"Do you think she would have answered?"

Even without opening her eyes, Louise would have recognized those voices anywhere. And when she opened her eyes, she was staring at Fox Schoonmaker and Rafael Moreno. She pinched herself, trying to make sure she wasn't actually dreaming. She had had this dream at least once a month since leaving Harlem.

But it was seven o'clock in the morning, and Rafael and Schoonmaker were really standing in front of her. Both men were still impossibly handsome, even after days of ocean travel.

"Am I dreaming?" Louise asked.

Rafael laughed—how she had missed that sound—and crawled into bed beside her, fully dressed, pressing kisses on her face. "Of course you're not dreaming."

Louise sat up. She was just a little hungover from the drinks last night, but nothing could compare to this. She waved to

Schoonmaker, still very tall, standing back with his hands in his pockets, and leaned over to give him a kiss as well. "What are you doing here?" Louise asked.

"Well, you never write back," Rafael said.

"We worried you had died or something," Schoonmaker added.

"So, we took a ship, and five days later, here we are standing in front of you," Rafael finished. It was nice to just be close to him again. His hair had gotten a little longer, he was sporting a little bit of stubble. Now he awkwardly wrapped his arms around Louise, pulling her close. He even smelled the same.

"You didn't have to come all this way," Louise said against Rafael's chest.

"We did. You wouldn't write us back."

She had only been good about her correspondence for the first month or two. She didn't blame them for coming to Paris to find her. If she were in their position, she would do the same thing.

"And," Schoonmaker added, pulling out his gold cigarette case, making every move look sophisticated, "I'm out of pomade."

"Come see me at work," Louise said. "I will make sure you never run out of pomade again." Schoonmaker smiled, and looked around, easily distracted. "I have to say, Lovie, this is not where I thought you'd be living."

"It's all I can afford," Louise said.

"Do you even have a bathroom?" Rafael asked.

"It's communal, downstairs." Louise knit her eyebrows together.

Schoonmaker crossed to her little desk, one she hadn't sat at for a very long time. "That's where all of our letters are, huh?" Schoonmaker asked. "Are any of those open?"

"Yes," Louise said. "I think?"

Rafael pulled himself up from her bed, crossing over to the desk. He flicked through the envelopes. "Two of these are open."

"I really am sorry," Louise said.

Rafael turned back to her, a smile widening over his face. "I'm just glad we're here." He reached into the inner breast pocket of his suit. "Letters from Josie and Minna."

"How is Josie? How is Michael?" Louise asked. The last time Louise had seen her youngest sister, she had been putting her on a train to California. She had read the letter to say that Josie had arrived, with their new address, but hadn't read anything else.

"You're behind. You need to catch up," Rafael said. Louise frowned.

"Michael proposed, Josie decided she didn't want to be married," Schoonmaker said. It hit her like a train. "But she's good. They're both good. Read your letters."

"And Minna is well too," Rafael said pointedly. "They both miss you." He trailed off, as if he was going to say something else. She was only partially sure she wasn't dreaming.

She nodded, reaching for a package of cigarettes. "How long are you staying?"

"As long as you need us," Rafael said.

"And if that means moving you to an apartment where you have your own bathroom, so be it." Schoonmaker was sitting at her little desk, totally dwarfing it with his size.

She looked at both of them, her best friends. She had been wishing for this moment, and now that they were here, she had no idea what to say. "I don't want you to leave at all."

"Then we'll stay," Rafael said. He reached for her, pulling her close. Just the feel of him so close to her was enough to nearly set her to tears. Below them, Ciarán began typing. That was earlier than normal, but Louise could tell that he was on a roll, discovering something in his writing.

"What is that?" Schoonmaker asked.

"My neighbor. He's a playwright, and he's working on something new." Every new detail was turning them off to her apartment. "Ciarán Dunne."

"Him?" Rafael asked. Schoonmaker groaned. "His first play wasn't even good," Rafael continued. He reached over and picked up her package of cigarettes. "The musicale was good, but that's because of the music. He didn't do any of it. And, after reading the pages, I thought that the story was weak." Rafael frowned.

"Will you be nice to him?" Louise asked.

"No promises."

Louise laughed. She would have to keep them apart. "I have to go to work." In fact, she was going to be late; she would have to skip going to Dauphine's if she was going to be on time. "I'll leave you my key. If anything, Ciarán can let me in. I should be home around five."

"We're at the Ritz," Schoonmaker said. "Why don't you come for dinner after work, and we can talk more later?"

"Perfect," Louise said.

Rafael chose her outfit, a summery blue number she had never worn. After she had dressed, Rafael put both his hands on her shoulders, surveying her. "You have to let me cut your hair." It was just touching her shoulders now, but she liked the length. She pinned it from her face for work. He kissed her on both cheeks. "I am so happy to see you."

<hr/>

SHE HAD FORGOTTEN the effect her friends had on other people. After nearly being late to work, Louise's day crawled until the last hour before closing, when Schoonmaker strolled in.

With a hand in his pocket, he looked perfectly Parisian, effort-less. And it was seconds before Clara, who was on the floor with Louise, swooned over him.

Louise was behind the till, her second favorite role in the store. It had been quiet all day, an uncharacteristically slow day. In a way, she was grateful for it. The arrival of her friends meant that she was giddy, and it was hard to concentrate.

"Lovie," Schoonmaker said the moment he stepped through the door. It was only him and Rafael who insisted on calling her by her middle name. It had been nice, being only known as Lou-ise, but she knew that she could kiss that good-bye.

The moment Schoonmaker crossed to the till, Clara deflated. He had barely even *looked* in her direction.

"What can I help you with?" Louise asked, keeping a smile on her face.

Schoonmaker leaned on the counter in front of her. "You look like a real grown-up. With a job!" he said.

"I am a real grown-up with a job." Louise allowed him to kiss her on the cheek. When she saw him, she felt her heart glow with happiness. "And I have a question for you."

"Show me around and I'll answer every question you have."

Louise stepped out from behind the counter. She could feel Clara's eyes on her, seething with jealousy. Schoonmaker offered his arm, allowing Louise to escort him. "I can't believe how much you've grown," Schoonmaker said. He kept his voice low, his head bent toward Louise.

"I haven't grown, but I don't think you'd be able to tell."

Schoonmaker laughed, a rumble in his stomach. "I mean in maturity, Lovie. You've grown in maturity."

They looked at the men's selection. Admittedly, the men had a smaller range of products to choose from than the women did. Louise stepped up to the wall. "This, you'll want. And maybe a new shaving kit?"

"Do you work on commission?" Schoonmaker asked, his red eyebrows rising.

"I do not," Louise said. "Is he okay? Rafael, I mean. Is he okay?"

Schoonmaker laughed softly. His smile was quick and sweet. "He's thriving. He's been worried about you, but we all are. The raid really threw him."

"The what?"

"The Dove was raided, but we're fine. We moved locations. He wants to write a musical or something. He's just searching for something. We all are."

"When was the Dove raided?" Louise asked. She was so caught up in herself that she forgot that the people in her life were probably feeling the same way she was.

"Last year. It's okay, we're fine. We're stronger than ever."

"How could he not tell me?" Louise asked. Schoonmaker was silent for a moment. He was avoiding her eye contact, and she knew what he was about to say. "You did tell me, didn't you?" she asked.

"If you had read the letters . . . But he is going to get on you about that. I don't want to add to it," Schoonmaker said. He looked around the store. In the last dregs of business hours, the store was nice and quiet. Almost empty. "I wanted to talk to you alone," Schoonmaker said, breaking the silence around them. They were both facing the wall of men's products, Louise already weighed down with items. "I wanted to apologize . . . I know that—"

"You don't have to apologize for anything," Louise said.

Schoonmaker turned to her, his arms crossed over his chest. "Please, let me finish. I've had five days to think about this." Louise waved him over to the counter, setting everything down. "When Lucy came to me, she was desperate, and you were the only person I knew I could trust. But I'm sorry for putting you into that position. I shouldn't have, but I did and for that, I am so sorry."

"You had no choice. I understand," Louise said. She was making the tally of products, writing everything out line by line so she didn't have to look up at him. If she did, she was scared she would burst into tears. She felt the incoming wave, and she was doing all she could to hold it back. It had been a highly emotional day, and she was still slightly hungover. "I'm not mad!"

"Good," Schoonmaker exhaled. He leaned on the counter in front of him, looking right into her eyes. "I wouldn't be able to take it if you were furious with me."

"I'm not. But you could buy a couple more things." Louise eased into her sweetest smile.

"You are a shrewd negotiator, Miss Lloyd. What else?"

She guided him around the store, Clara still forlornly watching them. She was pretending to dust the shelves, but Louise could tell that Clara's eyes never left Schoonmaker as they gathered more pomade and shaving kits and perfumes and lotions for Josie and Minna. "Is that all?" Schoonmaker asked.

"That's all," Louise said. "I can wrap all of this, but I won't be able to until tomorrow."

"Just have it delivered to the hotel," Schoonmaker said. "I'll deal with it all there."

She added everything together, and it was the most she had ever managed to sell in her year of working at Allaire's. Schoonmaker didn't even react when she said, "Three hundred francs." He just laughed and pulled out the bills he needed. "You do look amazing. More mature."

"You said that."

"I can't believe it," Schoonmaker said.

"If you want to wait, I can go back to the hotel with you," Louise said. "We just have to close up. Wait outside?"

"Looking forward to it," Schoonmaker said. He turned, finally acknowledging Clara. He winked at her, and she blushed, immediately turning away and hiding her face. "Have a lovely rest of your day, both of you."

# 30

---◆---

I N 1926, WHILE Louise was being blackmailed into solving the Girl Killer murders, a world away, Daniel Toussaint was solving a case of his own.

It was the case that propelled him to where he was presently.

In June of that year, a man had been murdered in cold blood.

And what seemed like an open-and-shut case started off slowly and then froze.

As Toussaint investigated, he found two things. The first was that the wife had been at work all night, and her employer had corroborated her alibi. The second was that the husband had seemed to make a game out of hitting his wife.

Louise read all of this, what Emme could get for her out of the office. This was the first thing she should have done; looked into the background of the inspector. After all, that was what he had done to her.

She knew what she was hiding. She wanted to know what he was.

"Everyone I know says he's the greatest man in the world."

Emme said this without even the slightest hint of hyperbole. "Kind, caring, and intelligent. Not to mention . . ."

"He's a total sheik?" Louise asked. It was nice enough for them to be outside, the sun shining down on them as if they owed it money. They were seated outside of Le Chat Noir, with glasses of wine and plates that hadn't been touched.

"That," Emme said. She tipped her face back. Her eyes were obscured by dark, round sunglasses.

"What do you think about him?" Louise asked. Emme didn't respond for a moment. Louise had a stack of papers, articles and notes about the inspector.

It was reading on top of reading, but it would be worth it if she could figure this all out.

"I think he's self-serving. He always has an ulterior motive. But . . ." Emme said. She trailed off, lighting another cigarette. Emme was the only person she knew that smoked as much as she did.

Louise felt her stomach curdle. She took a sip from her glass, letting the wine slither down her throat.

"You've met him. What do you think?" Emme asked.

"I think he's . . . fine." Louise put her glass back down. She picked it back up again, unsure of what to do with herself. "He seems to care very much about his job."

Emme nodded, a slight frown on her lips. She had removed her sunglasses and was looking Louise directly in the eye. "Isn't that how they all seem?"

She couldn't disagree.

Emme turned back to her own notebook. She was writing an article on the investigation, and, by extension, Louise.

The idea of it made her skin crawl.

Emme was diligent in all of her note-taking. And now, pen to paper, Louise knew Emme was jotting details down about her.

Emme seemed skeptical of most things. She was always asking things, always trying to make sense of what was going on around her. It was that drive that would make her a brilliant reporter, if only the men in charge would be able to see it.

"One more thing," Emme said. "That woman, the wife of the man who was murdered, works in Coralie Blanchet's house now."

"How do you know that?"

"Her name is Julie Cooper."

Louise had met her, the first night at the salon. Ciarán had seemed overly friendly with her. Julie had barely looked at Louise. She hadn't seen Julie in her following visits to the Blanchet house.

"Really?" Louise said.

Emme shrugged. She was taking her own notes, in a strange shorthand language Louise would never be able to decode. She was writing Iris' death and the investigation as a series of articles. Louise had had to make her promise not to spend too much time on her.

She turned back to the pages in front of her. "I don't think I like him," Louise said.

"Toussaint? I suppose he's something of an acquired taste. I think he does really have his heart in the right place."

Louise doubted that.

⋖⋈⋗

THE LAST THING Julie Cooper wanted to do was talk to Louise.

They had been sitting at the kitchen table for a solid ten minutes now, Louise chain-smoking and Julie watching the stove with an intensity Louise had only seen on the dance floor.

She didn't have to lie, exactly. It was Julie who had answered the Blanchet door. Without Ciarán to charm her, Louise had had to tell mostly the truth.

Julie had escorted her to the servants' quarters, which included the kitchen, and there they sat.

"I don't know anything about Ms. Iris' death," Julie had said.

Louise mustered a small smile. She wanted to make sure the other woman knew they were on the same side.

But she had to rationalize. Would she want to tell a perfect stranger her secrets? Her past?

Louise lit an eleventh cigarette. "I don't want to know about Iris' death." She tried to keep her voice soft. Gentle. Kind. "I want to know about Inspector Toussaint."

"He's been very kind to me."

"Tell me about him," Louise said.

"When my husband died . . . he helped me a lot." Her answers were never more than ten words long. Louise inhaled.

"Can you tell me about the case?"

Julie looked down at the table. No matter what she did, she was careful not to meet Louise's eyes. The woman was nervous. "I'm not a reporter. I just . . ." Louise trailed off. What did she want from this woman? "I want to know what his character is like."

At that, Julie smiled. A small one, but a smile all the same. "He was very thorough. He was very committed to solving the case."

"What happened?"

"My husband died. I was about to go down for his murder, but his business partner was guilty. We were all at home that night, he had come over to talk or something. They arrested me because he had fled." She took a moment. It had been two years, but the pain of the whole ordeal hadn't gone away. It was something Louise could empathize with. She wondered what her life would be like had Detective Gilbert been more like Inspector Toussaint.

Well, she'd still be a waitress in a Harlem café. Celia would be married. She and Rosa Maria never would have parted ways.

Her life would be different in so many ways.

"He was dedicated, and really cared about me." Julie looked up at her now, and there was something breathtaking about her eyes, her face. Her hair wasn't pulled back so severely today, and it made her look younger.

"So, you would say he's a good guy?" Louise asked. Julie had offered Louise tea, coffee, a glass of wine. Louise had declined all of it. Now she wished she had some wine.

Julie looked back toward the stove. Sauces were simmering, and it was making Louise hungry. "One second." Julie got up, beginning to stir the pots. She still wore her wedding ring, a small silver band. "It was Toussaint that helped me get my job in this house too. I was fired after the death. There was a small trust, but I still need to support myself."

"I understand." Louise had been supporting herself for as long as she could remember.

"So, I'm grateful," Julie said. She sat back down, wiping her hands on a soft tea towel.

"Can I trust him?" Louise asked.

Julie didn't respond for a moment. She seemed to be considering this answer more carefully than any of the others.

Eventually, after Louise had moved to her thirteenth cigarette, Julie answered. "I trust him with my life."

That had to be good enough for Louise.

# 31

THE TABLES AT Le Chat Noir were full when they arrived. Already, she could see Ciarán, Nathan, and Monty in deep discussion; Ditsie, Queenie, and Tootsie laughing as Doris danced and the band sang a cappella. Even Maude had put her pencil down, laughing at the girls.

It was home. It was everything.

They stopped as Louise arrived, as she made the introductions. Ditsie, always watching, always making notes, narrowed her eyes at Louise. "You never talk about your past."

"She never writes to us about her present," Rafael said with a scoff. Tootsie eased into a smile, a sign she liked him.

Louise sat down, taking a sip of wine from Monty's glass. "Well, I'm about to."

"Get ready," Schoonmaker said.

Thirty minutes later, with only a couple of inserts from her friends, Louise had managed to tell her whole story. Ciarán, having already heard the story, managed to come up with follow-up questions he didn't have before. But the majority of the group was silent.

"Has anyone ever written a book about you?" Maude asked.

Louise scoffed. "No one wants to read about a girl who can barely feed herself."

"Have you eaten today?" Doris asked.

"Sure." She took another sip of Monty's wine.

"That's our Lovie," Rafael said fondly. "Always drinking, never eating."

Louise exhaled. As glad as she was to have her friends around, she was worried that everyone would stop calling her Louise. Schoonmaker had ended up in a discussion with Maude and Nathan, who were probably pitching him something. Rafael was talking to Doris, finding out about their band. And it felt right. It felt like how it was supposed to feel. She didn't realize just how much she missed her friends until right now. "You have nice friends," Tootsie said. She was leaning back in her chair, her head tipped back. She was always relaxed. Louise had only ever seen her put any effort into anything when she was on stage.

"It was a nice surprise," Louise said. Doris laughed at something Rafael said. He looked rather pleased with himself.

⊲╫⊳

AND, AFTER DRINKS, she and Rafael spent time alone. Louise couldn't remember the last time it was just the two of them.

He looked the same. He had brought champagne and pastries, and they were sitting on her bed, facing each other.

Rafael could *talk*. He had talked nonstop for the past forty-five minutes, and every minute that passed was one that brought him close to asking her about her life.

". . . And so, that means I owed a lot of money to some very powerful people." He gesticulated as he talked, nearly spilling his wine on her sheets.

All Louise had to do was smile and nod, and for a while, at least, he was sated. They had eaten through the croissants and most of the beignets. She was concentrating on licking chocolate off of her fingers. It had been a long day at work, and she hadn't had the will to think about Iris afterward.

This is what she needed.

"How did you pay them back?" Louise asked.

Rafael lit a cigarette. They had, between them, already finished a package and a half of cigarettes.

"I went to Paris." Rafael raised an eyebrow. Louise had to stifle a laugh. Below them, Ciarán was clicking away. "I hate your apartment."

"It's grown on me."

"And Ciarán below you! Are you kidding?" Rafael frowned. They hadn't gotten along as well as she hoped. Well, Ciarán had no idea, but Rafael hated him. Louise had run a lot of interference.

"That's the best part." Louise settled back into her pillows, rolling her neck around as she did so. "He's grown on me too."

Rafael looked around. His dark eyes landed on her, boring into her. Louise could never lie to him, no matter how hard she tried. "What is going on? It's just you and me, Lovie. You can tell me anything."

She held her breath, unsure of what to say. "I am so tired. I thought moving would be what I needed, but I still feel lost."

Rafael stood, stretching, and moved around the small apartment.

"I feel like I'm doing the same things I've always done."

Rafael sat down next to her. He wrapped an arm around her. "What do you want to change?"

She didn't know. She had thought she had longed for anonymity and a new life.

But now that she had it, she was in exactly the same place.

Louise leaned into him, smelling his distinct scent, one she knew came from Allaire's now.

"I was reading a letter Josie wrote me."

"Finally, huh?"

"Hush. She talked about wanting a big, whole life." Louise lit a cigarette. She was in the middle of composing a letter back to her youngest sister, an epic that was already several pages long. She realized her reluctance to read and write letters back was a result of fear.

Reading those words over again struck something in her.

*I have a big and exciting life. Now that I think about it, and I do a lot, it's all I've ever wanted. I want to climb mountains and jump and fly. I want to make mistakes and fight and win.*

She wanted that. She didn't know how else to describe it.

"I want everything," Louise said. There was something in her that was ready to go, ready to do . . . something.

She didn't know what.

She leaned back, her head against the wall. Rafael was looking around, taking in every detail of her apartment. "I think you'll find it." He took her cigarette from her fingers, and she remembered all the times at the Zodiac, at the Dove, at Maggie's, that they had done this, passing cigarettes and bottles of alcohol between them like it was nothing. He held it to his lips, silent for a moment. He did look the same, but in some moments, he seemed eons older than he really was.

Wizened.

"Fox and I just want to make sure you're okay."

"I can't believe you call him *Fox*."

"His name?"

Louise rolled her eyes.

"It's true," Rafael continued. "We didn't know what else we were supposed to do. Josie wanted to come, too, but with her schedule . . ."

"My little film-star sister," Louise said.

Rafael nodded, with a smile. "We all love you, and you know it's fine if you don't have everything figured out. We're the lost generation for a reason."

"I didn't finish that one."

"I don't think I've ever seen you finish a book."

That was fair. Rafael got up. He crossed over to her tiny kitchen. Below them, Ciarán was quiet. He turned around. "You do have such a view, though."

That was the best part. She couldn't see the Eiffel Tower, but she could see the Moulin Rouge, and Le Chat Noir, and the buildings around it. This was home, for now, for better and for worse.

"What does it say about me that my little sister is more fearless than I am?"

Rafael barked a laugh. "If there's anything the Lloyd sisters are, it's fearless."

She lit another cigarette. Rafael made drinks. "For what it's worth, I tried to tell him not to ask you. But Lucy was desperate, and you know how he gets."

Louise did know. Schoonmaker's heart was the biggest thing about him. He was so careful to help anyone who needed it.

And if he asked, she couldn't say no.

"It's not that," Louise said. "I'm glad he asked. The inspector on the case is . . ."

"Better or worse than Gilbert?" Rafael asked. He climbed back onto her bed, handing her a glass. She took a sip: gin fizz.

"Better or worse than the man who killed six girls, including my sister, and tried to kill me?" Louise asked. "Better."

Rafael nodded solemnly. "I had to ask."

She laughed. He did too. "He's . . . odd. I don't know if you'll meet him, but he's very determined to keep me away from Iris' case."

"Huh." He took a sip from his glass. Louise wanted to tell him everything, but it would have to wait.

# 32

⟁

WHEN LOUISE STUMBLED on the truth, it was an accident. It was the early morning. She was sitting on top of her bed, smoking a cigarette. She craved coffee but hadn't yet had any. She was nursing a hangover, thanks to a late night at Le Chat Noir, but there was something that was bugging her.

It was early enough that Ciarán below her was quiet. She knew that he, too, had had a long night, playing cards or something with his theater friends. He had come home at two in the morning, giddy and whistling, which Louise had taken to mean he had had a very good night.

Louise was, once again, reading about the Cooper case. She was trying to not let it distract from Iris' case.

But Toussaint had been so annoying; it would feel so good to have something on him.

Louise flicked past pages. It was all research Emme got for her. Everything outlining the Cooper case. Statements, autopsy, reports.

Everything Toussaint had collected for the case.

He hadn't been the inspector on the case; that was a man named Marcus. Toussaint was one rank below, doing all the hard work. Emme had said that there was one case he had brought to a close, and then was promoted.

As Louise read, she relived the night of May 6th, 1926.

The call for police came at two thirty in the morning. A neighbor had made the call. Julie Cooper was found, shocked, at her husband's side.

The interview with Julie had been recorded at three in the morning. It was typewritten, and seven pages long.

But the pages numbered three, four, five, and six were missing.

The first time Louise had gone over it, she thought it was an oversight.

But now, she thought it could be something more.

She leaned against her window. The sun was already bright, and she was grateful that she didn't have to go into work.

"Tiny!" It was Ciarán, on the landing of the stairs.

"You came in late last night," Louise said.

"I came in rich last night. Can I get one?" He motioned to her silver cigarette case.

"Come in," Louise said.

Ciarán let himself in, closing her door behind him. He helped himself to her cigarettes.

Indulge, distract.

"When are you taking me to dinner with your winnings?" Louise asked.

Ciarán laughed, loud and boyish. She loved his laugh. He sat down. "Whenever you want, Tiny. What are you doing?"

"I'm trying to make sense of something." It was rare they spent any time in her apartment. They could never quite comfortably fit in it. Ciarán helped himself to two of her cigarettes and sat down at the table; the surface was filled with yet more information on Toussaint. He picked up a page, scanning it. Emme's notes were always neatly typed, no need for corrections anywhere.

"Is this about Iris?" Ciarán asked.

"A little."

"Are you going to make me guess?"

While she was tempted to play a guessing game, it wouldn't be worth it.

Louise looked up. She had papers all over her lap. "It's strange that a couple of pages are missing, right? This is a police report, but most of the information is missing."

"Who is it with?"

"A woman whose husband was murdered. Her interview says that she was at home at the time of the murder, but I can't get anything else."

Ciarán pursed his lips. "Is this what it was like?"

"What?"

He knit his eyebrows together. "Solving a case with the police."

"A little. It's less glamorous than people think it is."

He considered this, cigarette between his lips. "So, what is all of this?"

Louise exhaled. "I don't know if it's relevant." She was exhausted now and wanted nothing more than to go back to sleep. "This woman swears that someone else killed her husband. The accused swore he was away from the house when the killing occurred."

"Someone is lying," Ciarán said with a sage nod, as if he had discovered the meaning of life.

The interview with the accused murderer was not missing pages, but it did seem weirdly stilted. Louise had read the pages several times; it was a longer interview, filled with this man swearing over and over he was innocent. She could practically feel the desperation through the pages, and then on the last, a quick and stilted confession.

Along with a photograph of the murder weapon, described as an eight-inch knife from the house where the victim was killed.

"Something isn't matching up," Louise said. Ciarán, too, was reading. She could tell that he was on the autopsy.

"He was stabbed seven times." He looked up with wide eyes. "Hell of a way to go. A couple wounds on his arms and hands. He was trying not to die."

She pushed her hair from her face. "Wouldn't you?" Louise asked. She exhaled, tilting her head back. "There's not even a very good motive." If there was, she couldn't find it in the pages she had. It just seemed as if everyone had decided that this one man was guilty and didn't take another look.

"I should write a murder mystery play." Ciarán was smoking and musing, moving on from being helpful to her work. "I could keep you on as consultant."

"No, thank you," Louise said. That was the last thing she wanted to do.

Ciarán frowned. "You're lucky I'm rather happy with what I'm writing now."

"What *are* you writing now?"

He winked. "A play."

Louise exhaled. She needed coffee. She turned back to her pages. Her vision was starting to double. But she had gotten somewhere.

At the very least, she had a suspicion she had to confirm.

And that meant going back to the Blanchet house.

# 33

◁▽▷

THE FIRST THING Schoonmaker did when he and Rafael were settled in Paris was hold a party. Schoonmaker invited everyone he knew, which was Louise.

Louise, in turn, invited everyone she knew.

Nights like this made her miss the manse, the parties Schoonmaker would have there. But this was a close second.

There were drinks, food, and of course, dancing. Almost immediately, Louise found herself in the center of the makeshift dance floor, in a frenzied Charleston. Across from Rafael, it was easy to pretend they were back at the Zodiac, making everyone stare. She was wearing a velvet cocktail dress, bands of stones in her hair. In lieu of a band, they were playing records, yelling along to the lyrics.

Just like home.

Schoonmaker was behind the bar. He didn't dance, much to Louise's insistence he join them.

Ditsie, Tootsie, and Queenie were wearing matching dresses and hairbands, smoking in the corner. Ciarán and Monty were talking, Doris and her band were crowing around the piano. Clémence was with Schoonmaker; they seemed to adore each other. And Emme was alone, on the sidelines, watching everything. Her notebook was always present, and she had been writing everything down.

Louise had brought her camera, but it had been abandoned for the dance floor. She would have to pick it up.

For the first time in what felt like ages, certainly before the whole Iris saga began, she let herself go.

She always felt at home on the dance floor, the music running through her; she couldn't stop smiling. She and Rafael matched their steps, moving in perfect unison. It took a moment, but Louise could always read his mind, know what he was going to do next. Sweat dotted her forehead, her hair was stuck on her lipstick, and she didn't care. She didn't care at all.

After five songs, kicking her shoes off and tossing them somewhere, Louise had to take a break. She needed another drink. Ditsie was there to take her place. Rafael could dance for hours, and Louise had to regain that stamina. She wandered over to the bar, where Clémence and Schoonmaker were in an intense discussion.

"You serve drinks all day. Go dance," Louise said.

Clémence blushed. "Fox and I were just talking about you."

"I'm trying to make sure you're being taken care of over here," Schoonmaker said. He reached over, ruffling Louise's hair. Louise stuck her tongue out. With that, Schoonmaker went to pause the music.

He was tall enough—so, *so* tall that everyone could see him. He cleared his throat. "If you ask anyone, they'll tell you I don't love making speeches. I prefer being behind the scenes. But I just wanted to thank you all for joining me and my friends. We're new in town, and it's nice to have such a warm welcome." Everyone cheered.

Louise took the chance to climb onto the coffee table. She clapped twice to get their attention. "I would just like to say I love you all. I'm not the easiest woman to get to know . . ."

"An understatement," Ciarán called, his hands cupped around his mouth. Everyone laughed. Louise felt a blush rise to her cheeks.

"Even so, these two men are my best friends and I am so glad you're giving them a proper welcome." She looked at Schoonmaker and Rafael, now standing next to each other. Rafael had an arm wrapped around Schoonmaker's waist. She cleared her throat, pulling herself back together. "Let's dance!"

A cheer as the music started back up. Everyone threw themselves into the next dance, and she was reminded of what she loved most.

Rafael and Queenie, Ditsie and Schoonmaker, even Emme and Ciarán.

Louise returned to the makeshift bar, next to Clémence. Clémence was watching Schoonmaker, her eyebrows raised. "He . . ."

"Is terrible, yeah," Louise said. Schoonmaker didn't have the innate sense of movement her friends seemed to have. His limbs jerked wildly, as if he had no control over them. It made Ditsie dissolve into laughter.

"They're great," Clémence said.

Louise poured herself a drink. "I didn't know how much I missed them until they were here. Last year, I lived with Schoonmaker, for a little bit, and he . . ." Louise stopped talking. She didn't like getting emotional, and she didn't know how to put into words how much those two men meant to her.

She watched Queenie and Rafael, him leading her in an intricate pattern.

"They wanted to spend time with my new friends," Louise said instead. "I think parties are the only way they know how to do that."

Even though Schoonmaker loved to help people, as much as he could with his immense wealth, it also made him nervous. Like he never knew if people liked him or his money.

He compensated with parties, with people around him. And Louise was grateful that she was one of those people.

"Was it like this where you're from?" Clémence asked.

Louise smiled softly. "Yes. We could go dancing every night, if we wanted. Rafael has a club, and I used to manage it."

"Lovie!" That was Rafael, calling to her from the center of the dance floor. She had no choice but to allow herself to be pulled back into the fray, back where she needed to be.

The party continued into the early hours of the morning. Anyone who tried to shut it down, instead got swept right in with them. And for a moment, Louise knew that she was right where she needed and wanted to be.

Nothing could be better.

⧌

RAFAEL TOOK HER home. By the time they got to her tiny, sad apartment, neither of them wanted to do anything but sleep.

So, they climbed into Louise's bed together.

Half dressed, and very drunk, Louise and Rafael faced each other, the bed tilting them together. He reached over, pushing stray hair from her eyes. "I'm exhausted."

"I know," Rafael said. He kept his voice soft, but it seemed to spread around the empty space as if he had shouted it.

Louise rolled over so she was lying on her back and opened her eyes to stare at the ceiling.

"I can't believe you use the camera," Rafael said. It had been a birthday gift, from him and his last boyfriend.

"I love it," Louise said. "I love everything you've done for me."

"I know." He laughed, and she could feel it deep in her stomach. He fell silent for a moment. She breathed in his soft, so familiar scent, something she had got him from her work. The closeness they had on the dance floor didn't often translate anywhere else—his thinking was too chaotic for that—but now she thought she felt it.

"You don't have to do this," Rafael said. "You can always come home. You can live with Fox . . ."

"I don't want to do that." Louise sat up, pulling her knees to her chest. "I don't want to go back." She didn't know she was thinking it as she said it, but it made sense. "I can't."

There were so many things she wanted to say, but she bit her tongue. She reached over him to the windowsill, picking up the package of cigarettes she kept there. She lit one, exhaling smoke. Rafael watched as she did so, a frown on his usually unserious face. "You're telling me you're happy?"

"Yes."

His frown deepened. "Once more, with feeling, please."

She rolled her eyes. "I just wanted to do something different."

And here she was, solving another murder.

He didn't say it, although she knew he was thinking it. She exhaled smoke and continued. "Think about it like this. You have everything I want. Schoonmaker, the Dove, Rosa Maria. I just wasn't happy there."

"And you're happy here?" Rafael asked again. He was sitting up now, too, his hair messy and eyes wide. He was backlit by the lights of Paris, sitting with his back against the window. Louise bit her tongue. "I don't think I understand." He sounded sad. Louise forced herself to look at him, right in the eye. For the longest time, a decade of her life, it was he and Rosa Maria who knew her the best. He had changed, and she had too.

Rafael picked up a cigarette for himself, and for a couple of minutes, in silence, they smoked. When he was done, he pulled her close, and Louise felt herself relax. "You are my closest friend," he said. "I just want to know you're safe and happy. That means you need to write more and tell me the truth. I may not understand, but I will listen." She always had to be aware, aware of her surroundings, aware of who was around her. She hadn't let herself put her guard down in a long time.

She exhaled, trying to see it from his point of view. He was worried about her, and she didn't help that at all.

"I am glad you're here."

"I think we'll be here for a while. For as long as you need us," Rafael said.

She wanted to ask about Rosa Maria, but that would send her into a spiral, and she couldn't deal with that. Rafael ran a hand over her hair, much like she had done for Ciarán the day they found out Iris had died. She exhaled, trying to focus on everything good.

"You've had too much to drink tonight," Rafael said. His voice was a whisper near her ear. She nodded but didn't say anything. She could feel her heart racing, under the pressure of everything she had to do.

But she had Rafael. And that was enough. That was important. She moved so they were facing each other again.

"How did you and Schoonmaker . . ."

Rafael sat up again, and she did too. They were close enough to whisper, and it brought back nights in the Harlem apartments,

drinking and curled up in bed, talking about nothing and everything.

"That is a long story," Rafael said. He lit another cigarette, for
her and then for him.

"We have nothing but time," Louise said. "I've known he liked
you. He told me last year."

"And you didn't tell me?" Rafael asked.

"It wasn't my secret."

Rafael rolled his eyes. "I had just ended things with Eugene,
and I was sort of lonely. We were at the Dove, in the office, we
were fighting about something and then he just kissed me. I didn't
even realize, but we've been together ever since." Not that long of
a story. She was happy for them. She reached up, kissing his
temple.

It was hard to feel like she hadn't missed everything significant
in her friends' lives.

# 34

THE SECOND TIME Louise sat in front of Julie, in the same kitchen, at the same time of day, the same pots and pans on the stove, the same silence between them, Julie told the truth.

Louise sat, watching the other woman closely. All she needed was for this skittish woman to confirm her suspicions, and she would have something on Toussaint.

The only thing that was different this time was that Ciarán was by her side. He had *begged* to come with her. Louise had almost declined, but she remembered how Julie had lit up in his presence and thought that he would be an asset.

Julie had a glass of water in front of her. She stared at it as if it contained the answers to the universe. Louise was jumpy, anxious, the result of too much coffee. She hadn't slept in two days, and she was feeling the exhaustion, the creakiness, right down to her bones.

"Julie, all we want to know is the truth," Ciarán said gently. He was leaning forward, all of his attention on her. He spoke so softly, reaching across the small table to take her hand.

Julie had been, initially, excited to see Ciarán. But as he raised the reason why they were there, she had begun to shut down.

"What happened?" Louise asked. It was her third time asking this. She had explained everything she thought she already knew—the strange interviews, the evidence, the weapon from the house. All she needed was to put it all together in some way that made sense.

Julie looked up, briefly meeting her eyes. She was playing with her wedding ring, the solemn band she still wore, still chained her to a man who was dead. "I was married in 1920. By 1921, my husband was hitting me." Her voice was so low, Louise could barely hear her. She talked fast, too, trying to get the whole story out at once. "He hated me. He thought I was just some dumb girl, and one day, I couldn't take it anymore."

Julie stared at the ring on her finger. "It's true. I stabbed him seven times while he begged for his life." She looked up, hard brown eyes meeting Louise's. She exhaled, looking back down at the table. "Toussaint did his best to help me. He looked me in the eye and said that he would find a way out of this for me. He was the first man who believed me. Anyone else I tried to tell didn't care, or they said that he was such a kind man, a *caring* man, that he would never raise a hand to the woman he married. It didn't matter that I was sitting there, telling them the opposite. Do you know how many times I heard that? How many people blamed me? 'What did you do wrong?' they asked. As if accidentally burning dinner warranted a broken arm.

"Toussaint was the only man who listened to me. Who understood. And he saved my life. Can I have a cigarette?"

Immediately, always a gentleman, Ciarán lit one for her.

Julie exhaled, closing her eyes. "I am grateful for that. He set Peter up to take the fall for me. He swore no one would find out."

Louise nodded. "Why Peter?"

Julie took a deep breath. "Peter was already a violent man. Years before my husband, he had killed his own wife. He and my husband had been working together forever. Things weren't always above the law with them. I wish I knew that before I had married him." Julie sighed. Her eyes were closed. "Two dangerous men. It was me. Peter just took the fall. Daniel did that for me. I owe him everything."

"Why here? Why this house?" Ciarán asked. Louise was grateful he had come with her. He felt important, a crucial part of the case. She hadn't had the heart to tell him otherwise.

"Why this house?" Julie repeated. She shrugged. "I don't know. I'm grateful to be here."

"Who else knows?" Louise asked. She was breathless. Everything she thought about Toussaint, everything she had assumed about the man was wrong.

He had put himself on the line to save someone he didn't know. And that, to Louise, was admirable.

"Coralie does. Margaux does. No one else. We've been careful."

"We won't tell anyone," Ciarán said. He said it so seriously. Louise knew he was a man of his word. He looked at Louise, who nodded her agreement. She was lost for words, and that didn't happen often.

"I'm happy here. I have a new life. Peter is in prison; my husband is dead. I don't want anything to change that," Julie said. Her voice was soft but firm. Louise understood that. How many times had her life been changed in irreparable ways? How long had she wanted stability?

"I won't do anything to disturb that," Louise said. She wondered what would happen to Toussaint if this got out. She knew Emme would be dying to know.

But she was now sworn to secrecy.

And her word meant more to her than anything else.

"Thank you so much for your time," Louise said. She rose to go, her mind racing. She had gotten what she wanted. And it hadn't changed anything.

# 35

WHEN LOUISE VISITED the gallery again, wanting to get lost among the art, she found the walls bare and empty.

All of Iris' art was gone, and Alphonse was presiding over a flock of men and women, all quietly discussing something. She hung back, knowing she should turn and go. He was busy. There was no art to get lost in. But her sudden turn caught his eye. "Miss Lloyd."

She stopped. "I was just leaving. I didn't realize you were . . ."

"It's not a problem," Alphonse said. "We're getting ready for our next show. Margaux Blanchet will be debuting her work."

"Margaux? Really?"

"We're going to announce it soon."

Louise smiled. "So, it's privileged information?" She liked talking to him. She liked the airy space of the gallery, the sun shining down on them. She had been thinking of it all day during her workday. "What happened to Iris' work?" she asked.

He watched her for a moment, a slight frown on his face. "You are very curious about things, aren't you?"

"I suppose I can't help it."

His eyes were still on her, his face unreadable. "Then come with me."

He led her through a side door, which led to a hallway. Alphonse pulled a key from the key ring in his pocket. He opened the door and allowed her to step in.

It was cool and dark. All the pieces from Iris' show were piled on top of each other, free from their frames and glass.

Louise stared at them all. She didn't know where to start. Alphonse closed the door behind them. Smart of him. She would probably try to abscond with a painting if he hadn't.

He turned on the lights and the room flickered to life. It was more claustrophobic with the lights on. Every painted set of eyes was watching her.

She kneeled down next to the nude portrait. Now that she was close to it, Louise could see that the canvas wasn't nearly as big as she thought it was. Up close, she looked at the texture of the paint strokes, trying to find the layers within it.

Alphonse kneeled down next to her. "Her best work," he said. "She was unafraid. Look at how she paints the light hitting her skin. Look at how boldly she paints herself."

It all looked the same to Louise. She crept a little closer, trying to isolate the sunbeams.

And he was right. Instead of straight streaks, the sunlight was painted in little swirls. It was a breathtaking little touch Louise would never have noticed had it not been pointed out. "Beautiful."

"She was a talent," Alphonse said. He was silent for a moment. "She was once in a generation."

"And now you're hosting Margaux Blanchet?" Louise asked.

"Oui."

Louise leaned back on her heels, her eyes still locked on the painting.

Estelle. Margaux. Iris.

The three of them, thick as thieves.

"Can I see the ones of Estelle Callaghan and Margaux Blanchet?" Louise asked.

Alphonse rose. "It may take a moment."

"I have all day."

He went through the canvasses, handling them as gently as a newborn baby. He pulled them out, put them against the wall with the door, the only one with nothing on it. He stood next to her, crossed his arms over his chest. "What are you looking for?"

Louise bit the inside of her cheek. Estelle's portrait was bigger and showed the woman sitting in a bed. The sunlight streamed in, making her hair glint. Louise looked closer, finding the little swirls in the sunlight. Once she recognized it, she couldn't not see it.

Margaux's portrait was painted with Margaux at a desk. She wore a sailor blouse, square collar and ties around her neck. She was painted inside, with a book in her lap.

There was less care placed into the portrait, like Iris couldn't wait to finish it.

"I don't know," Louise responded slowly. Alphonse stepped back. She copied him.

"Look at the painting now," he said. His voice was low. She had thought about these paintings a lot, allowed them to take up real estate in her head. "Look closely at the strokes," Alphonse said. "See?" Louise didn't know anything about fine art, something that was becoming more and more apparent every day. With distance, the strokes blended together with ease and harmony. She couldn't see the swirls in the sunlight.

There was one thing Louise could see clearly. Iris Wright loved Estelle Callaghan just as much as Iris loved herself.

---

LOUISE GAVE EMME a key to her apartment. It was a logical step, and Emme would come over after the workday to talk about the case.

Louise typically made it home after Emme arrived; the nature of their jobs meant that Emme could leave earlier whereas Louise had old man Allaire's exacting standards to measure up to. And that evening, she didn't count on Rafael and Schoonmaker being at her apartment too.

The setting she found was intimate. Emme had kicked her shoes and cardigan off, Rafael was pouring wine. Schoonmaker was telling a story in his captivating way. Louise almost didn't want to interrupt, but it had been a long day. Allaire was in a mood, a blustering one that affected her and her coworkers. When he got like that, there was no talking to him, no reasoning with him. So, Louise was later than she wanted to be. Then, of course, she had visited the gallery. She was looking forward to having a quiet evening. But this was better. It was worlds better.

It was nice, coming home to see her friends. Her friends! The presence in her life she had been missing over the past months, this hole she had been living with.

"The lady of the hour," Rafael said, looking up and into her eyes. He was grinning, and Louise stepped into the apartment, closing the door behind her. She leaned against the door.

"Fox was just telling me about how you helped him win a poker game." Emme's cheeks were flushed; she was nearly drunk. The apartment was warm, not used to having four people in it. The radio was playing, and if Ciarán below her was making any noise, she couldn't hear it.

"When you were living at my place, remember?" Schoonmaker asked. He was as giddy as a schoolboy, and his mood was infectious.

Louise nodded. "It's not as dramatic as he says. There were just a couple of nights where he had this big party, and none of the men thought a little girl like me could beat them at poker . . ."

"So, what does Lovie do," Schoonmaker continued, picking up her story flawlessly, "but makes all those men wish they'd never been born." He laughed, the sound filling the room.

"Impressive," Emme said. Her face was impossible to read. Louise watched her carefully as Rafael handed her another round of drinks. Louise always noted how people reacted to her friends, the rich and tall and brilliant Schoonmaker only matched by the quick and clever and funny Rafael.

Her friends, sitting in her apartment.

"How was work?" Emme asked. She always asked questions. She was always trying to find something out, even if there was nothing to discover.

"Long." Louise sighed. She sat down on her bed. This many bodies in her apartment left very little room for her. "And, hey, Margaux Blanchet is having a show."

"Really?" That got Emme's attention. She leaned forward, taking a sip from her glass of wine.

Louise lit a cigarette, exhaling smoke toward the ceiling. "She's debuting at the same gallery Iris did."

"Oh," Schoonmaker said. "I thought I would have time to see Iris' work."

"How did you know Iris?" Another question from Emme.

"I didn't know her well. I'm more a friend of her mother, Lucy.

She's a friend of my family." Schoonmaker never talked about his past. Louise had the privilege of knowing that, before Prohibition, before being the Club King of Manhattan, Fox Schoonmaker had been Franklin Smith, a whole different man. He had five siblings, and Louise didn't know if any of them were alive.

For all intents and purposes, Louise and her sisters were his family. Rafael and Rosa Maria were his family.

They were all family. And that was the way Schoonmaker wanted it.

The past was a hindrance to who they wanted to be. Thinking about it too much, longing for it, only held them back. To be their best possible selves, they had to forget everything and move on.

Schoonmaker took a sip from his glass of wine. "When Lucy wrote to me asking for help about Iris, I knew I had to ask Lou. She's the only person I would trust for this."

"And then Lovie never answered, so Lucy came to Paris," Rafael added. They were so in sync; it was hard to feel as if Louise hadn't missed out.

"Lovie?" Emme asked. Another question.

"My middle name."

"Louise *Lovie* Lloyd?"

Louise nodded. "And then, these two came to Paris for a . . . vacation?"

"And to see our Lovie!" Rafael said. He was sitting next to her on the bed. He leaned over and kissed her forehead. He still wore the same cologne. "Our good old Lovie."

Emme was smiling, but her eyes were narrowed, as if she were trying to figure something out. But she didn't ask another question.

"Have you talked to Lucy?" Louise asked.

"It was the first thing I did," Schoonmaker said. "She's wrecked with grief. I'm not sure she even knew I was there."

"I have to go see her again." Louise hated the fact that she had been the one to tell Lucy her daughter was dead. It seemed as if Iris was the only thing tethering Lucy to this earth. And she felt guilty, like she could have done more to help.

She had been able to give Lucy the letter Iris wrote. And that had to count for something.

Schoonmaker nodded gravely. "I think she would like that." And Louise had to believe that Lucy would, and that she would know Louise was there.

And Louise would have to tell her something.

# 36

⟨⟁⟩

THE SECOND TIME Inspector Toussaint visited her work, the sun was shining. It was busy; Louise had been on the floor all morning, working through lunch, attending to the needs of the ladies of Paris.

It was so busy that even old man Allaire had come down from his office to help out. His version of helping included charming every woman who crossed his path, laying compliments on relentlessly until they were ready to buy whatever he suggested.

With Clara behind the till and Jessie with her on the floor, the store was busy at opening and remained that way until the late afternoon.

Allaire permitted them to take shorter lunch breaks, fifteen minutes each, and by the time Clara took hers, last, the store had settled down.

And then Toussaint walked in. He wore no overcoat, allowing Louise to judge the quality of his navy-blue suit, the same color as ocean depths. His clothes were always sensational, beautifully tailored, and the best fabrics. His shirt underneath was a stark, bright white, a color Louise would spill on if she wore it. His hat sat low on his brow. By now, Allaire had disappeared back into his office. Jessie was still behind the till. She looked up as he entered, raising an eyebrow. Jessie had long confirmed that she was working here until she got married. But, with no prospects on the horizon, that seemed to be further and further away.

"Jessie, can you take over the orders?" Louise asked politely.

Jessie looked her over, disappointment coloring her face. There were only three women on the floor now, talking in rapid French, taking their time selecting their products. Toussaint was taking his time also, obviously waiting for Louise to be alone. "Fine, but you owe me," Jessie sighed.

Louise stepped behind the till. She knew that with the rush of customers that morning, there would be many orders to pack up, and she would be grateful to take Jessie's place.

Just as soon as she talked to Toussaint.

"You really have to stop doing this," Louise said. She pressed her hands flat on the counter. "It's inappropriate."

"I thought I asked you to stop," he said. Plainly, as if he were used to getting exactly what he wanted.

He was.

"Interesting," Louise said. "I never said that I would do that."

He pursed his lips, displeased. "My patience is wearing thin, Miss Lloyd."

Louise pulled herself up as tall as she could. "You didn't hire me. Mrs. Wright did. I'm not doing this to annoy you. I'm trying to find the truth." She inhaled. She could do with a cigarette right now. "And I've been doing some research on you." She searched him for a reaction. To his credit, he didn't give her anything. "I had a nice long talk with Julie Cooper," Louise continued. She leaned forward on the counter. "And I learned the truth about what happened to her husband."

Under all of his bravado, Toussaint went pale. "You have no idea what happened."

"I do," Louise countered. "I read the reports. I read the interviews. And I talked to Julie." She paused for a moment, letting the weight of what she was saying sink in. "I know that you falsified evidence, that you sent an innocent man to jail."

"He wasn't innocent!" Toussaint snapped. The outburst of emotion made Louise jump. It was more emotion than she had ever seen from him. He caught himself, looking around. The three women were still in deep conversation and not paying attention to them. "He, too, was a terrible man. Julie was justified and I wanted to help her. Of course I falsified evidence. I wasn't about to send a battered woman to prison." He spoke so vehemently; Louise was almost surprised. It was obvious he cared deeply about Julie, that he wanted the best for her and did what he thought was right.

The most annoying part was that she couldn't blame him. If she were in his position, she would do the exact same thing. There was no denying it. He had done the right thing.

He stepped away from the counter, a little shocked. "How did you find out?" he asked.

"I told you, I read the reports and the interviews. And I spoke to Julie. It was easy to figure out. And if I could do that, think about what else I could do." She kept her voice even, neutral, as if she were advising him on the best hair product. She smiled thinly. "I think it's in your best interest to not threaten me anymore. I wonder what your boss would say." There was no way she could reveal what she knew, not without sending Julie to prison, and freeing the man who had gone in her place. It was a precarious position they were in. But Louise hoped he understood what she was saying. She hoped she wouldn't have to make it clearer. He watched her for a moment, weighing all of his options. He couldn't even be angry. She had just done the same thing he did to her.

Knowledge was power.

They were in a stalemate. She could see him trying to figure a way out of this, but in the end, he relented. "Fine." It was less of a word and more of an angry sigh. "You win, Miss Lloyd."

She eased into her real smile, not the sweet one she saved for customers. "I am so glad we're on the same page," she said. She straightened up again. The French women were approaching the counter. "Now," Louise continued, "if you don't mind, I have a job to do."

Toussaint had lost, and she had won. He left as the women stepped up to the counter, and she turned her attention back to her job. She replayed the victory in her head over and over, for the rest of the day. She had won.

But then why didn't it feel good?

◁◈▷

THE BEST PART about having her friends was that there were two more sets of eyes for Louise to use.

She, and Emme, of course, had met Rafael and Schoonmaker at their hotel suite. On the third floor of the hotel, it was just a little less opulent than the suite Mrs. Wright was in.

But it was still big and beautiful.

They spread out in the sitting room, accompanied by a huge fireplace and overstuffed velvet couches. Emme was on the couch, Louise stretched out on the floor. Rafael and Schoonmaker shared a large dining table just a couple of paces away. They had a record player, a Victrola from the last century, playing in the background. The music filled the space as everyone read.

It was comfortable. If Louise squinted, it was just like living at Schoonmaker's sprawling manse.

That was the only place she had felt at home, really at home. And it wasn't that there was a maid and more room or food than she knew what to do with.

It was the only place she really could just be herself.

Emme was still decoding Iris' journal entries. She had a patience for it that Louise did not. It wasn't that Louise really needed the information for the case. Changed from her workday, Emme wore a pair of wide-legged trousers and a blouse that buttoned up the back. Louise was half reading, half staring at her.

"Do you think this is an invasion of privacy?" Rafael asked. His shirtsleeves were rolled to his elbows, suspenders hanging free. He had his legs up on the chair next to him. He was sort of reading, but had gotten bored, and was mostly playing with a deck of cards.

Every so often, Schoonmaker looked up at him, a dizzying look in his eye.

"Do you think it matters if she's dead?" Emme asked. Emme and Rafael were getting along like a house on fire. She made him laugh with almost everything she said.

Rafael looked at her. "I guess you have a point."

Emme smiled.

Louise flipped through her letters. She was finally on early this year, when Iris' letters had slowed down. She knew, now, of course, that Iris always planned to keep writing her mother, that she planned to leave Paris and was finding a place to be before she died.

And it was something she would never have the chance to do now.

Iris' story would always be unfinished. Louise wondered, constantly, how Iris would be remembered. She hoped it would be as more than a society wife.

It seemed that Iris worried about that too. She wrote her mother in these last few letters about not being happy.

Not being happy enough.

Louise read through Iris' words, her private thoughts, with a pain of understanding. The letter she was reading was after the show debuted.

> It wasn't what I thought it would be . . . granted, I guess I don't know what I thought. But none of the pieces sold, and the papers were less than kind. I thought I was going to make waves. But no one sees me as a serious artist.

Reading her words sent a shiver through Louise's spine.

"Hey." Emme broke the pleasant silence around them. Her eyes were wide. She had pushed her glasses to the top of her head and was staring at Louise. "Iris was going to quit." Emme had her notebook next to her, a page she was using to decode the jumbled words in Iris' journals.

"She was?" Louise asked. She sat up, feeling a creak in her bones as she did so. She raised her arms above her head.

Emme wrinkled her nose. "She's talking about moving on."

"So, she doesn't say quit in so many words," Louise said. Her heart was thudding in her chest. "She could have meant anything."

She read the bit of the last letter out loud. Schoonmaker watched them, a frown on his face and his dark eyebrows knitted together. He was her favorite person to talk things over with; he always listened, taking all the information in before saying anything.

He lit a cigarette, chain-smoking copiously. He had been reading Iris' letters from the beginning. "Maybe she was thinking about leaving her husband," he said. "That could be moving on."

"She was." Louise closed her eyes. All she could see were the tangled knots in front of her. "She wanted Estelle Callaghan to go with her. She was in love with Estelle, not Philip."

"And we're sure Philip didn't kill her?" Rafael asked.

"Unfortunately."

Rafael laughed. Emme was still frowning at her pages. With all the effort in the world, Louise pulled herself up and went to sit next to Emme. Emme, holding her pen in her mouth, flipped frantically through her pages. The journal Emme was working on, much like the letters, ended abruptly and without notice. Louise took the sketchbook and flipped past.

Emme was indeed reading the last entry.

It was accompanied by a drawing of a sun over a horizon. Iris didn't work in landscapes. But her attention to detail was careful as always. The drawing was done in simple ink.

Louise stared at it. Even this drawing managed to capture something she didn't know she was feeling. Emme took the journal back before Louise was ready to relinquish it.

"That's a shame," Schoonmaker said.

"She was brilliant," Louise said. She read the last letter again. She had been piecing together Iris' life and feelings from her own words.

Emme put her pen down. She closed the sketchbook and turned to Louise. Every time they made eye contact, she thought about their kiss. It was still enough to raise the hairs on the back of her neck.

But then she thought about Clémence. And she was confused all over again.

Louise handed over the letters. "She wasn't happy. She wasn't in love with her husband. Maybe she thought she was doing the right thing." It was a decision Louise could never understand.

*Feb 5th, 1928*

*Louise,*

*It's a new year, and I am feeling better than ever. I know this is late, but Rafael wrote you earlier. I've been meaning to write more, but time has gotten away from me. It's that time of year where nothing happens. It's when you're going to sleep at three in the morning on January first, and you wake up and it's February.*

*I've never been a resolutions sort of man, but I wanted to build something real. I love the club and all of my other ventures, but Lou, let's face it, I'm an old man now, and I need something stable.*

*But things feel good. I've hired a new woman to help run my holdings. You'd like her. Her name is Sarah. She's smart and loves to keep me and Rafael in shape. I needed a you, and I think I found that in her.*

*Anna is engaged, and I didn't even know she was attached. I've just realized I never actually talk to Anna.*

*Rafael tells me I shouldn't worry, but truthfully, it feels futile writing to you if you never respond. And I'm worried. I think he is too.*

*I can't help but really wonder if this is what you wanted. Either way, I miss you.*

*I hate this time of year. All the festivities have passed, Christmas is over. I've never been a big fan of Christmas, but now I can give my siblings everything they want. That makes me feel good. This time, I was able to give your sisters everything they wanted.*

*That felt good too.*

*It sometimes feels like I have all this money, but nothing truly good to do with it. I'm thinking. I don't know about what yet, but I am thinking.*

*I hope you're well, that this new year is being good to you. I hope you've made one hundred new friends and you're the most glamorous of them all.*

*I love you.*

*I love you so much.*

*Forever yours,*
*F. Schoonmaker*

# 37

⊲⋈⊳

ESTELLE WAS MISSING from the meeting at the apartment before the debut of Margaux's show. Louise was dressed to impress, with a bottle of wine and a box of beignets that would be picked at and never finished.

With Iris gone—or maybe it was like this all the time; Louise didn't really know how to tell the difference—Margaux was the one in charge.

And with her show about to open, she was lapping up the attention.

The window had been fixed. She had to wonder who paid for that. But now, it was like Iris had never been there. No trace of her anywhere.

"Louise!" Jeanne had welcomed her in. There was no art happening today. Glasses of champagne were passed around. "It is so good to see you!" She was greeted like a sister in this pied-à-terre every time she walked in.

Jeanne hugged her tightly. Louise had no choice but to hug her back. Jeanne was the youngest of the group, barely twenty years old. She was still wide-eyed and almost innocent, and Louise felt the deep need to protect her like she wanted to protect her sisters.

"What are we celebrating?" Louise asked, as if she didn't already know. But the chances of these women drinking champagne in the afternoon for no reason was high.

"I have a show," Margaux trilled. "It debuts on the weekend. All my paintings will be seen by everyone. *I* will be seen by *everyone*."

Louise got the sense that Margaux didn't care much for the mechanics of the work, pouring herself into the canvas. She wanted the attention. Any way she could get it.

"In fact," Margaux said, moving to kiss Louise on both cheeks. She smelled like a bright and happy floral perfume that was slightly overwhelming. "You should come. Bring everyone you know. Tonight, we are celebrating."

She knew better than to mention Iris right now. Louise took her glass of champagne and hung back, watching the other women. But as one of seven women in the room, it was a little hard to hide.

The record was playing scratchy jazz, and it made Louise want to dance.

Many things made her want to dance.

"Another?" Sabine asked. She was the nicest, Louise thought, aside from Iris.

She was the nicest now.

Louise had been nursing the same glass of champagne, letting the other women get drunk. She preferred to keep her wits about her.

But she nodded, allowing Sabine to take her glass and fill it again. Margaux was still at the center of all things, the women cooing over her show. "What will you wear?" Jeanne asked.

"I don't know. Mother thinks I should get a new dress."

"This is the best excuse for a new dress," Sabine said as she handed Louise her glass back.

"I suppose." Margaux prevaricated, drawing it out. "I need you all to come too."

"Of course." The women all agreed. Louise took a sip from her glass, feeling the bubbles rise to her head. Margaux pushed a hair from her face, picking up a pastry to nibble at.

They were always careful to not get messy drunk, even here, even in private. Even now, with all the excitement. "My mother also says I should make sure the papers are there." Margaux exhaled through her nose.

"Where's Estelle?" Louise asked.

"I guess she's at home?" Marion said. She had been quiet up until now. She was sitting at the window seat, her head against the newly replaced pane of glass. "We haven't seen her around in a while."

"If she doesn't come back, we'll have to add a new member." Margaux was frowning at Louise, annoyed at having the attention taken away from her.

Sabine lit a cigarette. "Give her some time. She's still grieving. Aren't we all?"

Margaux was still frowning. "Of course we are. Iris was a marvel. But she wouldn't want us to sit around and be sad for her. Who has the time for that?"

It sounded glib, but the girls laughed. Louise did too, a couple of seconds too late. Margaux's decisive gaze slid back to Louise. "I think I'd like you to take photographs of the evening. Just for us."

It was a test, and Louise knew she had to tread carefully. Being there would be an asset, and if Margaux wanted this, then she would have it.

Louise swallowed hard. "I would love to," she said eventually.

Margaux squealed, akin to a little girl. She always got what she wanted. Louise didn't know if anyone had ever said no to her in her life.

The evening passed in a blur of champagne, dancing with the radio in the background. A rock weighed heavy in Louise's chest. She didn't know what it meant, but she was going to find out.

# 38

LOUISE DIDN'T VISIT Lucy as much as she should have. In fact, Louise did everything she could to avoid seeing the older woman. The truth was that even though she had made inroads, she still didn't know what to tell the lady. She knew Schoonmaker had checked in, but Louise had to do it too.

The Suite Imperial was just as big, just as empty, just as opulent as the first time Louise visited. She kicked her shoes off, letting her stockinged feet sink into the carpet. The silence seemed to ring around her, the loudest thing in the room.

The bedroom, too, was quiet. The cleaning crew had been coming in to provide fresh towels and clean tables and surfaces.

But Lucy Wright was still in bed.

The older woman was lying prone, under a thick layer of blankets. Louise almost didn't see her when she stepped in, nearly invisible.

Louise sat next to the bed. She didn't know what to say or how to say it. Iris' letter was the only thing on the bedside table that didn't belong to the hotel.

"Mrs. Wright," Louise said softly. She went to the kitchen, poured a glass of water—she would never be able to understand that this hotel room had a kitchen—and brought it back.

"It's Louise Lloyd." She kept her voice quiet. "I'm so sorry I haven't visited." The last thing Louise wanted, when Celia died, was someone around her, talking. But the women she had lived with then didn't care about that. They had come into her room, bringing food and water and telling her about their day. She had brought a couple of Iris' journal sketchbooks with her, intending to read them out loud. But now that she was here, she wasn't sure if that was the right thing to do. If someone had read Celia's journals to her, she would have just been in more pain. Louise didn't know how to judge how Mrs. Wright would react.

So instead, she kept talking. "I should come more, but . . . I don't know. I think I just want to have the most information when I tell you. But I will say that Iris' death was a murder, and I think the police are covering it up. I don't know *why* yet. Nor do I know who killed her. I have thoughts though." Louise stopped, trying to gauge a reaction from under the comforters. She wondered if Lucy was even awake. "I know Schoonmaker came to see you," Louise continued, feeling more awkward by the second. "He sends his love. Aggressively so. He told me that you're a friend of the family too. I didn't know that. He never tells me anything, and then gets surprised when I don't know anything about him. I guess he could say I'm the same way. But he's been looking out for my sister, and I don't even know if he has a sister. He must." Louise stopped talking again, realizing that she lost her train of thought. She leaned back in the leather chair, lighting a cigarette.

"I thought I'd read to you from Iris' journals, but I thought that would hurt more. I've been reading everything you gave to me too. She's funny and smart. And I think she loved you more than you knew. She writes about you a lot." She had put the two hardcover books on the floor next to her. She picked one up too. "Did she always draw? How did you know she was meant to be someone?" It was something Louise was desperate to know the answer to. When did Iris' brilliance make itself clear? How did she know that her daughter was someone special?

Would Janie have seen the same thing in Louise? How would Janie have nurtured her talents? Louise couldn't dwell on the past.

The blankets moved, and Lucy, skin raw and bleary-eyed, emerged.

"She was always amazing." Her voice was strained, quiet. Her gaze fell on Louise as if Lucy had no idea who she was. She reached for the glass of water, and Louise handed it to her.

"She was always a genius. I could never do anything to dissuade her from what she wanted to do." Lucy sat up. "Fox has two sisters. Elizabeth and Amelia. The rest are boys."

"Oh." Louise was unsure of what to do with that information. "Thank you."

Lucy nodded to her cigarette. Louise lit one for her.

"I am so sorry," Louise said again. "She was incredible."

"She was." Lucy's gaze, a little sharper now, fell toward the books Louise had brought with her. "May I?"

Louise nodded, handing them over. "She was always moving so fast. I could never keep up."

"Why did you want her to marry Philip?" Louise asked.

Lucy was quiet as she flicked through the pages, stopping at a line drawing that could only be a distant drawing of Lucy herself. Lucy traced over it with her fingertips. "I thought it would be good for our families. I would never make her do something . . . I thought they loved each other."

Louise leaned back, dropped her butt into the nearest ashtray. "What do you mean, the police are covering it up?"

Louise inhaled. She wanted to light another cigarette. "Inspector Toussaint has his own reasons for not investigating fully."

Lucy frowned. "Oh."

"I can't go into more detail. Did she ever mention *La Mort des Artistes* to you?"

"Not in any letters. Why?"

Louise explained everything she knew about the secret society. She did light herself another cigarette. Lucy didn't reveal her own thoughts.

"Thank you for doing all of this," Lucy said. "I know you didn't want to."

"Anything for a friend, or a friend of a friend," Louise said. "I don't mind it. I want justice for Iris as well." She sat for a while longer, watching as Lucy went back to sleep. Before she left, Louise refilled the water glass and replaced it on the nightstand. She took the journals back.

And she didn't know that that would be the last time she spoke to Lucy Wright.

⌁

LOUISE ONLY HAD one album of photographs developed.

But luckily they were her favorite ones.

Photos she had managed to take in her last few months of living in Harlem, amid all the wild things that those days had brought.

She pushed open the cover. She had taken the film in Harlem but hadn't developed it until she had lived in Paris for a month, when she was homesick and empty inside.

Even though they were all black and white, they glowed. She had caught Rosa Maria much like Margaux had caught Philip, in bed, no clothes, blankets at her waist, reading.

There were others, of Rosa Maria writing at her typewriter, pencil between her teeth. Rosa Maria in the bathroom of the little apartment they shared, grinning in the mirror.

Every photograph was like a stab in the heart.

Rosa Maria had hated it, but not really. Louise had done her best to catch her in candid moments. It was art, just like her writing.

And Louise wasn't the *best* at photography. She knew that. She wasn't about to have a whole gallery of her work. But this was enough.

Louise was sitting in the pied-à-terre, stretched out on the couch, on her back, with her album on her knees. There was to be an informal meeting, after the one at the Blanchets'. Louise had wanted the moments alone in the place, and even with the radio on, it seemed to echo around her. She flicked through the photographs.

The final one in the album was the first one she had taken with the camera, her birthday.

Her and Rosa Maria and Rafael and his then-boyfriend Eugene on the couch in the little apartment, laughing, smiling.

A world away now.

She closed the album. She had opened a bottle of wine—she would never get over how truly incredible alcohol was in France—and had poured herself a glass. She wanted these moments alone to prepare herself.

She just had to talk about her work without crying.

About thirty minutes later, Jeanne, Margaux, Sabine, Lili,

Estelle, and Marion traipsed through the door. They were varying levels of tipsy, Marion being the most, Margaux being the least.

"Louise!" Marion squealed, arms wide and open to pull her close. Marion even smelled like alcohol, overpowering the light perfume she wore. "We missed you!"

"You didn't," Louise said.

"We did!" This was Jeanne, also drunk. "We were crying out! Louise! We need you! And you're here!"

Louise drained her glass of wine and poured herself another. She needed to catch up.

"What is what?" Margaux asked. Louise had come to learn that these informal meetings were late and an excuse for the women to drink and talk. Margaux had spotted Louise's album, still alone on the couch. Without waiting for an answer, Margaux picked it up, flicking it open. "Who is this?" Margaux tilted her head, lips pursed, eyes taking in every bit of the photograph. She had an incredible eye for detail.

Margaux could just stand to be nicer about this. Margaux flipped the album out so everyone else could see. The photograph of Rosa Maria, reading in bed.

Louise blushed.

"This is nice. Intimate," Margaux said. She carried the same weight as her mother: an opinion everyone wanted to be favorable.

"It's my work," Louise said.

"Let me see!" The other women rushed forward; Sabine was the one who got it from Margaux's grasp. The women passed the book around, flicking through, making comments, laughing as they did.

It was the most naked Louise had been in this pied-à-terre, and she regularly had her breasts out.

"Who is this?" It was Estelle who asked this time, her voice soft.

"An old friend of mine," Louise said. She wasn't sure she had ever said the word out loud. That realization hit her like cold water to the face. "My girlfriend. My only girlfriend."

Estelle looked up at her, her eyes wide.

"We ended things when I moved; she ended things."

"Did you love her?"

"Madly."

They sat, pouring more wine. Margaux pored over the photos with the same eagle eye as her mother. They both had very decisive taste, something that was obviously inherited. "I think you have potential," Margaux said.

"That's a very nice compliment," Lili said, taking the album from Margaux. "She's very exacting."

"I'm still really just starting out," Louise said. She was four—almost five—glasses of wine in with very little dinner to speak of. And as every woman went through her photographs, she wanted to do nothing but run and hide and tell them it was a mistake. But they seemed pleased.

And to find Iris, she had to get closer to these women.

"You need a better camera," Lili said. "This is good, but I think you can get better."

"I can't afford anything better."

From across the circle, Margaux and Sabine shared a long look.

"We'll have to see to that, won't we?" Estelle added. It had been a long time since Estelle was at one of these meetings. She was still dressed in black, quiet and tired. She seemed to retreat into herself, just like Louise had done when Josie died.

But Estelle was making an effort. That alone was admirable.

"You've been holding out on us, Miss Lloyd," Marion said. She had the album now, and it was going slowly around the circle. "You've just been letting Lili paint you. You should be taking photographs of us."

"I'd like to," Louise said.

They all seemed to share the same look at the same time, something Louise was missing entirely.

She drained her glass, setting it on the table right next to her. This was the most at ease she had ever been in this pied-à-terre, and most of that was because of the alcohol. But these women, who were so kind and funny—one of them was a killer.

Louise would do well to remember that.

# 39

⌐◇⌐

THE LITTLE BOX was, like the first envelope, at the door when Louise got to work. It bore her name, was wrapped in nondescript brown paper. Allaire was the one who handed it to her. "What is it?" Louise asked. She had been, uncharacteristically, late that morning, and had had to skip seeing Clémence at the café. She took the box from her boss and allowed him to unlock the door.

"I think you'll have to open it," Allaire said. Behind her, Jessie yawned. Clara was smoking, her last before the day started. Allaire never let them smoke in the store. He barely allowed them to smoke in general. Allaire pushed the door open, and they entered the store. The stillness was always the best part of the day: right before opening and right after closing. With the drapes over the counters and the floor clean and gleaming, it was always a reminder that every day was a new day. Every evening, when the door was locked and the customers were gone, it was like an exhale. Coming in was like the inhale. The beginning of the dance, beginning of the day.

When they went in, Allaire went directly to his office, and Clara disappeared into the staff room. It was the same thing they did every morning. Louise began to remove the covers on the counters, folding them up and putting them behind the till. She wiped the counters down, making sure the glass was gleaming. All the while, the little box watched her from the till, where she had left it.

"Did Allaire ever get you anything?" Louise asked Jessie, who was the closest to her.

Jessie was removing her light coat and hat, leaning into the nearest mirror to check her lipstick. "I don't think that's from him." She turned toward Louise, happy with her appearance. Part of working here was making sure they were, as Allaire put it when Louise was hired, "putting their best face forward." That meant wearing every cosmetic available. Jessie was amazing at makeup. Louise was still stumbling over the technique of it, and Jessie made it look easy. "I think it was just here, wasn't it?"

"Huh."

Jessie turned back to the mirror, shoving Louise from her mind. "By the way, I think you should be in the back this morning. We still have orders from yesterday to wrap." That was something Louise didn't mind at all.

Louise made her way to the staff room and removed her own coat. She hung it up, and then sat at the table. She put the box on the table. She stared at it for a moment, unsure of what to do with it. She pulled the ribbon, black, and tied with the same amount of care she took when she did customer orders. Louise ripped through the plain wrapping and found a white box stamped with an infinity symbol.

Pausing at the box, Louise looked around. She was alone, but she couldn't be certain that Clara or Jessie wasn't watching. They loved to get into her business, but they weren't really friends. Just women who worked together. Outside of this store, she wasn't sure what they did or who they did it with.

Louise opened the box, holding her breath.

A bracelet was on top of a folded piece of paper. She picked the bracelet up, inspecting it. The delicate links, the emeralds inlaid with diamonds. She knew that bracelet. She had seen it on the wrist of every *La Mort des Artistes* member.

She flipped it over. It was cold and heavy in her hands. She still had the one she had found on the ground by the apartment building.

And now she had this one too.

The small engraving of the infinity symbol glinted under the light. Louise raised it, trying to take in every detail.

Louise picked up the note. She checked the time; the clock was hanging on the wall. She had fifteen minutes until opening, but she was going to be in the back anyway.

It was typed, nondescript. And it was a short missive.

*Mademoiselle Lloyd–*

*Welcome.*

Louise turned it over, looking for anything else on the card. But that, aside from the address to the jewelry store on the back, was it.

That was all.

It was obvious what this was, but it seemed to come out of no-where. Louise had barely shown the women her work, and she barely devoted any time to it.

And there was the other issue: she wasn't an artist. She was trying to solve a murder.

She put the bracelet on, feeling the cold, heavy weight. This was officially the most expensive thing she owned now, even though she couldn't keep it. She just wanted to feel it for a moment. She would keep it on for the morning and take it off at lunch. She shoved the box and note into the pocket of her jacket, furious at the people who decided her day dress shouldn't have pockets. Then she slid her white coat on and got ready to start the day.

Louise settled in the back room, a small list of orders on the table, ready to be packaged up. With every move she made, the bracelet slid up and down, hindering her work. It seemed to hold her back in a way. Maybe that was just the guilt she felt, seeping into the core of her being. She had to take it off, putting it in the pocket of her white coat. Louise had to roll the sleeves of that coat up, otherwise they were too long.

*Welcome.* The word followed her. What else? Was that it? Was she officially a member of the society now? She was grateful to be in the back. She had so many questions and no way to answer any of them.

# 40

THE OPENING OF Margaux's show was a star-spangled affair. Louise had made good on her promise and had dragged Rafael and Schoonmaker along.

In fact, many people Louise knew were there, including Tootsie, Queenie, Ditsie, Monty, Ciarán, and Emme, all in various degrees of formal dress.

And in the center of it all was Margaux. She wore a gauzy white dress with billowing sleeves. It shone under the lights, dancing and twinkling. In her hair was an ornate crown, made of gossamer-thin wires and made to look like the constellations in the night sky.

It was stunning.

The rest of the society women, Jeanne, Lili, Marion, and Sabine, were all wearing black. They were all crowded around her, ready to serve her every whim.

The first thing Rafael did was find glasses of wine. He passed them out; his bow tie was askew, but Louise didn't fix it. She had an inkling that he liked it like that. She gratefully took a glass. The idea of being social was making her skin itch. "Seems like a grand party," Rafael said. He lit a cigarette. Even now, Louise was noticing women's reactions to him. It was nice bringing him along; it meant she wouldn't be noticed.

"Sure." Louise was trying to spot Alphonse in the crowd. She knew he would be there, and she wanted to know how the show was going.

She had seen him earlier, as the night started, accompanied by his darling wife. Louise hadn't known he was married. She had never thought to ask, and that was on her.

"You're not loving it?" Rafael asked.

"It's not that," Louise said. She looked around, scanning the people and the art. She and the Moulin Rouge dancers had already gone through all of Margaux's pieces, critiquing them as if they knew anything about art. It had been fun, wandering about looking at the paintings. But that had taken thirty minutes, and she had a long stretch of the evening to go.

Margaux had painted a *Last Supper*–type painting, as Iris did, but with herself in the center. There was the one of Philip, reclining in bed with a cigarette. There were seascapes that she had painted at Île de la Grande Jatte.

Louise had gone through them quickly, finding that the majority of them were *fine.*

Louise had, at Margaux's request, brought her camera, but felt awkward taking pictures of people she didn't know. She took a few of Margaux, the society girls, and Rafael and Schoonmaker, and then held it tightly.

Louise sipped from her glass. Schoonmaker was in a deep discussion with Coralie, and even from her vantage point, Louise knew he was charming the hell out of her. Rafael was still next to her. She had trailed off and hadn't realized it. "I think I'm just tired." That was the truth. She had been spending long days at work, then long nights reading about Iris and trying to solve her murder. Those two things left very little time for her to do anything else.

Doris' band was playing, adding ambiance to the evening. Louise wondered how much an evening like this cost.

"One more hour, then we can go home," Rafael said.

"Did you ever think we'd be counting the minutes until we go home?"

Rafael wrapped an arm around her shoulders, pulling her close. He kissed her temple. "It's a sign we're getting old." Louise had to slap a hand over her mouth to keep from laughing.

"Lou!" This was Ditsie, a little tipsy and alone. "I lost Queenie and Tootsie!" She was clutching a glass of wine like it was her lifeline.

"Okay, let's go find them," Louise said. She reached out to take the other woman's hand and as she did, a chiming sound called the attention of everyone around.

Margaux was standing, tapping a butter knife against a wine glass. "Everyone, everyone!" Her voice filled the room as easy as air. Everyone turned to look at her. She was grinning, but not in a way that insinuated happiness. She was smiling in a way that insinuated that she had won. "I wanted to thank you all for coming. But first, I wanted to talk for a moment about Iris Wright. As you know, she . . . passed recently, and she was a very close friend. She was an artist in her own right, and I miss her . . . I like to think she's watching from wherever she is now. I would like to call a toast. To Iris."

"To Iris!" The room yelled back.

Louise looked around again. She spotted Toussaint watching

from the back of the crowd. He raised his glass toward her. Louise nodded in response.

"Who is that?" Ditsie asked in her ear.

"That is a man I know."

"Introduce me, please!" Ditsie looked up at Toussaint, and too bold by half, winked at him. Rafael hid a laugh behind his hands. Toussaint looked unnerved.

"After the speech," Louise said, although not many people were paying attention to Margaux anymore. Her tribute to Iris was enough.

Emme was jotting everything down. Louise knew it had to be in her strange shorthand, making sure she didn't miss a word.

"Do you have a crush?" Rafael asked, his lips near her ear.

"Thank you so much for coming," Margaux was saying. She was still trying to hold the room in a captivated silence, but she was failing. Somehow, Louise knew that Iris would have no trouble keeping their interest. "Enjoy!" The room seemed to relax. Louise drained her glass.

"Be quiet," Louise said to Rafael. She stepped away from him, taking Ditsie by the wrist.

"Inspector," Louise said kindly, catching his attention. "How nice to see you." She had to wonder what his motivation for being there was. She hadn't talked to him since she threatened him at her job.

"I hope you're well, Miss Lloyd."

"Have you met—" Louise began.

Ditsie cut her off. "Sarah Anne Baker."

Queenie, Ditsie, and Tootsie were all named Sarah, hence the nicknames. Two Sarah Annes and one Sarah Marie. This was Louise's first time hearing Ditsie's surname.

"Daniel Toussaint, this is Sarah Baker," Louise said. She knew that Toussaint wouldn't be able to handle Ditsie. She would eat him alive.

Louise wandered back to find Rafael. She lit a cigarette, exhaling smoke. Rafael was in deep discussion with Schoonmaker, their heads tilted together.

Louise left them alone to take another look at the art.

⊰⊹⊱

THE EVENING ITSELF dragged on, but there was one more notable appearance.

That of Philip Montgomery.

The hour for Louise and Rafael to leave had passed, and yet they remained, lingering as people left. Doris and her band played on.

And the last person to arrive, after most of the people had gone, was Philip. Louise didn't think she'd see him. But there he was, in a tux, looking cold and dashing. Louise watched as he made his way toward Margaux. Whereas the society girls were gone, Louise was sure Margaux hadn't moved at all.

Louise was yards away, and she couldn't hear them, but she watched. She was smoking a cigarette, on her third glass of champagne, and she was thinking about kicking off her heels and holding them for the rest of the evening. She wore those shoes dancing all the time, a sweet pair with T-bar straps, but apparently, standing still was worse than dancing. They were pinching her feet. She drained her glass and immediately took another one from the passing waiter. She wondered if Iris' opening was like this. Whether Iris had wanted to go all out as Margaux did.

Rafael and Schoonmaker were in deep discussion with Queenie and Tootsie. Louise could see them from the corner of her eye.

Ditsie and the inspector had left, and Louise didn't want to know what they were doing.

Even Emme was gone. She had left about thirty minutes before, probably to write her fluff piece about the opening for the paper.

She kept her gaze on Philip. He and Margaux were talking, hushed whispers, their faces close together. Louise stepped forward, holding her breath. She wanted to know what they were talking about, but that didn't matter. Philip reached over, lifting Margaux's chin with a delicate tenderness she had never seen from the man. Then Margaux rose and kissed him.

In front of everyone.

But no one was paying attention. The few people who were still there weren't even looking. It was just Louise. They kissed for so long that, eventually, she had to look away, a blush rising to her cheeks.

It was so public, and yet so private. Louise was the only witness.

Iris' body wasn't even cold yet. It had barely been a month since her death, and Philip was already, publicly, moving on. Louise turned back. They had fallen into a quick and quiet conversation. Louise wished she could do more than watch.

She lifted her camera, taking photograph after photograph of Philip and Margaux together. She had gone through two rolls of film, giving them to Schoonmaker to keep in his pocket for her. Louise lowered her camera. Philip and Margaux were in their own little world. She said something flirtatious, lowering her gaze as she did, and Philip laughed, the noise rising above the polite whispers of conversation around them. That got the attention of the crowd, and the murmurs began to change.

Louise could feel it, the tide shift. The conversation was now not about Margaux and her art, but about Margaux and who she was spending her time with. Philip cleared his throat, as if he was going to say something and then didn't.

He whispered something to Margaux and then he left.

Louise kept watching, her eyes trained on Margaux. She watched as Margaux drained her glass and then got up as well.

Before she knew what she was doing, Louise was following her. She kept her camera up, just in case. Margaux exited the showroom, out into the cold night air. The cool air kissed her skin, and Louise kept up with Margaux's quick pace. The cold didn't seem to bother her at all. She reached up, removing the crown from her hair. She shook her head, all while keeping the same pace. She turned the corner and stopped at a waiting car.

Philip was leaning against it, smoking. Louise took a chance on getting closer, her breath caught in her throat. Margaux stopped, facing Philip with crossed arms. He was focused wholly on her. Louise had to wonder what that was like, having someone's undivided attention. They didn't kiss again, and for that Louise was grateful. But he was telling her something, so soft and earnest. Louise couldn't believe it was the same man she knew. She could see their profiles. Margaux laughed softly, then reached up to wipe her eyes. Louise couldn't get closer, and, outside at night, the photographs she took wouldn't turn out. So, she watched and smoked. Philip and Margaux stayed on the street for ten minutes, and then slid into the car. He opened the door for her.

Louise wouldn't be able to keep up with a car. But she knew it had to be Philip's. She turned around, lighting a cigarette on her way back toward the gallery. The night was over; Margaux had left. Then they could go home and drink.

As she stepped back inside, Schoonmaker caught her attention. "Where did you go?" he asked, wrapping his arm over her shoulders.

"I think we should go," Louise said. "The night's over."

"Hey," Schoonmaker said. He was addressing Queenie and Tootsie. "Do you all want to come back to our hotel for a nightcap?"

Queenie and Tootsie nodded in unison.

"Come on, then," Schoonmaker said. "Get everyone you know. We'll drink until the sun comes up."

# 41

THE ONLY WAY to finish a night was to settle into the Ritz suite with her friends. Louise made drinks, starting with a round of French 75s, and passed them out. Queenie and Tootsie, along with Doris' band, Ciarán, Monty, Lili, Jeanne, Sabine, and Marion, whom they had found outside of the gallery, were scattered around the suite, kicking off shoes and stockings and hats and outerwear.

Someone turned the record player on, filling the room with music.

Rafael was at the heart of the conversation, always at ease when surrounded by a bunch of beautiful women. He said something, and they all laughed. Schoonmaker took a drink from her. "He lights up a room."

"Yeah," Louise said. "He really does."

"I could watch him forever," Schoonmaker said.

Louise looked over her shoulder at him. He was staring at Rafael, hopelessly lost. Rafael looked up, meeting Schoonmaker's eyes. Louise had never seen Rafael smile like that, one that was utterly unselfconscious, that lit up his whole face. She had never seen him like that in her decade of knowing him.

She sipped from her own glass, watching for a moment. She was so grateful to be on the outside. She had kicked her heels off and now was allowing her feet to sink into the carpet. She wanted to be rooted to that spot forever. Louise clutched her camera, then raised it, not wanting to forget a moment of this.

"What do you think? Honestly?" Lili asked. She, Marion, Sabine, Monty, and Ciarán were in another small group, discussing the show.

"Gauche." Sabine was smoking. "Everything she paints is . . ." She exhaled a large plume of smoke, tilting her head back toward the ceiling. She closed her eyes while she did.

"Boring," Marion finished. "No heart. No life. Nothing she does is interesting. She just got this show because her mother paid the gallery." Louise stepped over to the group.

"Is that true?" she asked, unable to resist good gossip.

Sabine looked over at her. Louise didn't know if Sabine liked her, even now. She was a woman who was hard to read. Her body language, her face never gave anything away. Louise had never seen the woman smile. Sabine largely avoided the pied-à-terre. Louise had only seen her a few times, and then, she never really said much. It wasn't that Louise *needed* Sabine to like her. She just wished she had an inkling either way.

It was Lili who took over. "That's what we heard," Lili said. "Coralie was talking to the gallery man—"

"Alphonse," Louise supplied.

"How do you know his name?" Marion asked.

"I'm nice to people."

"Alphonse," Lili continued, bringing the attention back to her. "She was saying she would come in tomorrow and pay him the balance."

"And Margaux thinks she got it on what? Merit?" Sabine asked with a scoff. "Embarrassing."

"Her mother would do anything for her," Jeanne added. She had been in deep discussion with Rafael, but now wandered over, clutching an empty glass. "I wonder if that's healthy."

"I wouldn't know," Louise said. This was the most candid she had ever heard the other women be about art and a woman in their ranks. She had spent a *lot* of time around women. She knew that they could be vicious.

She just hoped they hadn't talked about her work like that when she left the room.

Louise had to guess that it was also part jealousy. After hours of watching Margaux lap attention up, she was a little annoyed too.

Lili looked around. She drained her glass. "Anyway, she's not as good as Iris. Come on, Jeanne. Even you have to agree. Iris had that *it* factor. Margaux is a pale imitation."

"Her toast was so . . . cloying." Jeanne groaned.

"And did you see the painting of Philip?" Marion added. "Her dead best friend's husband? How . . ."

"Gauche," Sabine repeated.

"They're having an affair," Louise said. "Isn't that obvious?"

Every woman looked at her, dumbfounded.

"No," Lili said.

"How do you know?" Sabine asked. Now, a catlike smile was growing on her lips.

"I've seen them," Louise said. "Together, at a party." The mental image of Margaux on her knees was one that would never leave her. "He's also given her a ring. He *kissed* her tonight."

Lili and Marion shared a look. Sabine lit a new cigarette. "How long has it been happening?" she asked with a plume of smoke.

Louise swallowed. "That I don't know," she said. "But I think they're really in love."

"Margaux has never really been in love. With anyone. She just wants to see and be seen." This was Marion.

Sabine looked back at Louise. "How did you know about the ring?"

Louise swallowed hard. "I had a meeting with Coralie, and when I was looking for the bathroom, I found Margaux's home studio. It was right there." It was mostly the truth.

They seemed to take this as fact.

"How much do you think Coralie paid for this show?" Lili asked.

Louise turned away from the group then. She wandered over to sit next to Ciarán on the couch. They needed another round of drinks, and it was Rafael in the kitchen making them this time.

"What are you writing?" Doris asked.

Louise rolled her eyes. "Don't bother. He's not told anyone. But I hear him typing away all night at *something*."

Ciarán took a sip of his drink, the last dregs. "My big brother owns a pub. You know that?" he asked. "Back home in Cobh. I didn't want to do that for the rest of my life."

Louise didn't know that. He was the one person who talked about his past less than Louise.

"So, you're writing a play about the pub?" Doris asked.

"No." Ciarán scoffed.

Louise looked back at the group of society women. They were still talking, quietly, heads bowed together. She wondered what they were talking about. There had to be more gossip about Margaux.

She knew that Margaux couldn't have gotten that show on her own, but finding out her mother paid for it made sense. She didn't know why Alphonse didn't tell her so.

Maybe Coralie paid for discretion. Louise would, if she were in the same position. She took another drink from Rafael and took a sip. She felt herself settle, trying to forget about Margaux and Iris and everything for a moment.

Tomorrow she could get back to it.

⌖

WHEN LOUISE GOT home in the early hours of the morning, the cab dropping her off with a squeal of brakes, Clémence was waiting on her balcony. The few flights of stairs were a Herculean effort, Louise lifting her body weight with every step. It took longer than usual for her to get up to her apartment, and when she saw Clémence, she collapsed onto the stairs below her.

"I've missed you," Clémence said.

"It's been a while." Days. It had been days. With Iris, and work, and the appearance of her friends, she had been visiting the café less and less.

Clémence sat down beside her. The closeness made Louise's nerves stand on end.

"I've missed you too." Louise nudged Clémence gently.

Clémence pulled out two cigarettes and lit one for Louise. "Where were you?"

Louise exhaled smoke. "The opening of an art show, and then Schoonmaker's suite."

Clémence nodded, taking this in. They didn't talk for a moment. It was so late, the sky was that inky black that happened before the sunrise. Louise had seen this time of day a lot, but it was best with this vantage point. There was something so breathtaking about the view from her apartment building. "Do you wanna go inside?" Louise asked. She began to rise, and her whole body yelled in displeasure. She was tired. She was drunk. And she wanted to spend time with Clémence.

"Not yet." Clémence exhaled.

Louise agreed. There they sat, side by side, waiting for something—or nothing—to happen.

"Oh, I decided to not audition for that play." Clémence continued. "You were right. I don't want to have to pretend to be a chicken. I'll find something else."

"Good," Louise said. "You deserve better."

Silence again. Louise smoked. "Do you want something to drink?"

"Just stay here for a moment. Sit with me. You're not good at staying still, are you?" Clémence asked.

"No." Louise tilted her head back, closing her eyes. "When I was young, I was in charge of my three siblings. My sisters. There was always something to do. And if I slow down, then . . ." Louise trailed off. She didn't want to complete that sentence.

Clémence wrapped an arm around her shoulders, an effort to keep Louise in one spot for at least a minute longer. Louise relaxed into Clémence's grip.

"You don't have to explain. I wish I wasn't an only child. I wanted to have at least five children."

"You wanted to be a mother?"

"That's how it would happen," Clémence said. "But I was a kid, and there are so many other things I want before that." She leaned her head on Louise's shoulder.

There, in the night air, she felt closer to Clémence than anyone else in her life. Clémence understood. She hadn't felt that since Rosa Maria.

And that was the last person Louise wanted to think about at that moment.

She stubbed her cigarette out, exhaling the rest of the smoke. She didn't know what to say, but that didn't matter. It was hard to get herself to stop, even just for a moment. The world they were living in meant that she could be anyone, do anything, and there never seemed to be a chance for her just to relax. For her to be *herself*, with no eyes or judgments on her.

Being herself felt more and more like a performance. Everyone wanted her to do something, be something. It was worse in Harlem, when she was Harlem's Hero. Her father wanted her to be a mother; strangers had wanted her to be more like that fearless young girl.

Coming to Paris was supposed to be a fresh start. She would never admit it, but she resented Schoonmaker, just a little, for bringing Iris and Lucy into her life.

They had work in mere hours. "Penny for your thoughts?" Clémence asked. The two women moved so they were facing each other; Louise against the wall and Clémence against the railing. The moonlight glowed, making Clémence look ethereal. Every time Louise looked at her, something deep in her stomach sparked.

"You'd be a wonderful mother," Louise said. She meant it too. Clémence's smile was sort of sad. "I hope so."

Her dark eyes locked onto Louise, and Louise found that she couldn't—or didn't want to—look away.

In the next millisecond, Clémence leaned over and pressed her lips to Louise's. There was a part of her that wasn't expecting it. She froze before leaning into the kiss, letting herself dissolve into the other woman.

They were out in the open.

They were two women.

They were kissing.

It took a moment for that to connect, and when it did, Louise pulled away. She looked around, as if anyone was awake and watching them. She had seen other men and women be with each other, fearlessly and openly.

And she forgot that it was different here.

"What?" Clémence asked.

Louise leaned in for another kiss. She supposed she had thought about this moment since she stepped into Dauphine's Café. Clémence moved so she was practically on top of her, her body weight warm and welcome. She settled her hands at the small of Clémence's waist, almost impossible to find in her drop-waisted dress.

And eventually, they had to part. "It's late." Louise couldn't bring herself to speak above a whisper.

"I need to get back home." Clémence slowly pulled herself away. "Come back to the café."

"I will." Louise watched as Clémence turned and fled down the stairs, her own private Cinderella. She pressed a hand to her lips, still burning. Louise took her time getting back into her own apartment. She wanted to treasure that moment for the rest of her life.

She thought she would never be able to move on; her first few months in Paris had been akin to a monk's existence.

But now she could see that there were possibilities everywhere. And that was exactly why she had come here.

*Feb 14th, 1928*

*Happy Valentine's Day, sister!*

*I've been well. This year is shaping to be the best yet. I still don't love my elocution lessons, but I do love everything else. It's hard, but it's so fun. I'm content to be in the background, and I take formal dance classes five days a week.*

*I'm sure, if you read any of our letters, you'd know that Michael moved away. Or I guess I moved away. He still has the house. I moved in with some women from the studio.*

*We're all contract players, and it's funny to think about.*

*I haven't written in a while, and I have to admit that life has just gotten busy. I've decided to stop hounding you about writing me back, and just hope that you're at least reading these. My roommate is a woman named Veronica, and we get along all right. I hardly see her, she isn't on screen, she works in the cutting room. Our hours are all crazy.*

*But she's kind and funny. You'd love her. She's so smart. She reads all these books; I think she's read more books in the few months we've roomed together than I've ever read. She's intuitive, too. I like to talk to her a lot.*

*AND I make my own paycheck.*

*(Well, I get paid in cash, but it's all the same, isn't it?)*

*I think about what Daddy wanted for me, and us, and I think about all the possibilities. I think about what Michael wanted. And he was fine with it not being what I wanted. I just let it go on much too long.*

*I'm sending some photos along. I had photographs taken, and I don't recognize the girl in them.*

*I have a big and exciting life. Now that I think about it, and I do a lot, it's all I've ever wanted. I want to climb mountains and jump and fly. I want to make mistakes and fight and win.*

*I want a world that will allow me to do all of that.*

*It's a good start, though.*

*Veronica says that we have to go to dinner tonight. It's Valentine's Day, and we can't spend it alone.*

*But I thought I would write you first.*

*You're never far from my heart.*

*With my love,*
*Josie*

# 42

⟐

WHEN LOUISE ARRIVED at the hotel, it was full of police and reporters. She could tell the difference, but they were all men, milling about.

Louise looked around for Emme, hoping that she would be there and that she could explain. But the only reporter she recognized was Christopher Braithwaite, Emme's story stealer. No doubt Emme was in the office, typing up his work.

The men didn't see her, didn't notice her. The Suite Imperial was on the first floor, and she could tell that that was where the chaos was coming from.

She tried to get closer, moving slowly. Her heart was stuck; she wasn't sure it was even beating. All she could do was fear the worst. Louise searched the faces again, looking for someone she knew.

Toussaint was there, but she hadn't talked to him alone since she had threatened him. He was in a deep discussion, a frown on his lips. She wished she could get closer. Toussaint looked up; Louise froze, as if not moving would make her invisible. But of course, he saw her. He motioned for her to cross over to him. She narrowed her eyes and shook her head. His frown deepened. Louise raised an eyebrow, crossing her arms over her chest. She could do this all day. She was pushing her luck, but he knew where she stood. All she had to do was lean over to the nearest officer and pretend to tell him what she knew.

But she couldn't do that.

Louise won. Toussaint crossed over to her, blocking the crowd with his body. He tilted his head down and looked her in the eye. "What are you doing here?" he asked.

"My friends are staying here," Louise said. He glared at her, as if he was trying to decide if she was lying to him. His eyes scanned her face. "And Mrs. Wright. I was going to see her. What's going on?"

"She died late last night."

The words hit her like an anvil. The realization shuddered through her.

"What happened?" Louise asked.

"When was the last time you saw her?" Toussaint asked.

"I didn't do this."

"Answer the question."

Louise swallowed hard. His gaze had turned hard, steely. "A couple of days ago. I haven't been checking in with her as much as I should have been."

"What was she like when you saw her?" he asked patiently.

"Almost catatonic. I made sure she drank some water. I . . ." Louise omitted the fact that she had Iris' journals. She didn't want to give that away. "I asked about Iris, and I'm not sure I helped that much. When I left, she was awake."

"And you didn't talk to her at all after that?" His questions were persistent. His eyes didn't leave hers. There was something about his gaze that made her blood run cold.

Louise shook her head. "I was about to go talk to her. I wanted to make sure she was okay. What happened?" She asked again. He had not answered her question.

He inhaled. In that moment, he looked exhausted, ages older than he really was. "We don't know yet. There was no foul play involved."

"How do you know?"

"She was alone in her room all night."

"How can I trust you?"

His eyebrows knit together, and he lowered his voice. "You're playing with fire, Miss Lloyd. You can trust me because I said so."

Louise tried not to react. She bit her tongue, biting back her responses. The fact that he was wrong about Iris, had manipulated an investigation to set a woman free. A noble reason, but still, she didn't know if she could or should trust him. So, instead, she looked around. The crowd was starting to disperse.

An officer, a young redhead, approached. He spoke quickly and in French. "Inspector, the examiner is moving the body now."

"Give me one more moment to deal with Miss Lloyd," Toussaint replied. The officer nodded, and Toussaint looked back at her. "You can trust me." His voice was quieter now. He leaned forward to speak directly into her ear. "You know everything about me. I don't have anything else to hide."

"Why didn't you speak out about Iris' death?" Louise asked.

"You know I can't." She didn't know that. But she saw genuine fear in his eyes. "If I did that, it would mean the end of my career." He spat the words out. Literally, a drop of spit landed on her cheek.

She wiped it away.

"Think, Miss Lloyd. Coralie Blanchet could ruin me. She's one of the most influential Parisian women. And I'm just an inspector with the police." His eyes were hard.

She didn't know how she didn't realize that. Coralie Blanchet could ruin him, if she wanted. It wasn't just the salon. The Blanchet family poured money into donations and fundraisers in Paris. Whatever Coralie wanted, she got. Louise didn't know if the older Blanchet was that vindictive.

But the younger one might be.

Louise couldn't trust him. She knew that now. But she wasn't going to say it. Louise took another deep breath. It was a lot to take in that morning, and the day had barely started.

"Okay. I won't say anything," she said. Her heart was pounding. She never meant to be a keeper of this secret. She didn't want it, and it put her in more danger. But the way he was looking at her, he was pleading.

"I promise. You can trust my word."

He wrinkled his nose at the dig. "I need to go."

"Okay." Louise stepped back, adjusting her hat. She watched as he swept away, hands in his pockets. He moved fast, as if the world had to bend to his will. Louise stayed there for a moment longer, watching Braithwaite run toward the phone. She wanted to linger, in case he was calling Emme.

She turned to the elevator, taking it up to the floor Rafael and Schoonmaker were on. When Schoonmaker opened the door, Louise breezed past and sat down at the phone. She picked up the receiver. Sitting on the couch, she could finally process what had just happened.

"Lucy Wright died last night," she said.

"What?" Schoonmaker asked. He moved toward her. "What do you mean?"

"Exactly that. She died last night. I don't know why. But . . ." Louise trailed off. She couldn't sort her thoughts out. "I need to call Emme."

EMME WAS . . . QUIET. But this was different from her normal quiet.

She was speechless.

They sat around the table. Schoonmaker had decided that they needed something to do; they were playing cards.

"That's terrible," Emme said eventually.

Louise had told the story, broken up by a large amount of alcohol. Now, she was staring at her hand, which was not great, and trying to figure out if she should bluff.

The last twenty-four hours were hitting her hard.

The show, kissing Clémence . . . *kissing* Clémence. Now Lucy was dead.

It was a lot for one day. And somehow, she had to go to work tomorrow.

Rafael was watching her, his dark eyes narrowed. "How are you feeling, Lovie?"

She opened her mouth to respond, but what came out was a small scream.

Schoonmaker raised an eyebrow. "You need to sleep. Did you get any sleep last night?"

"No." She put her cards down.

All she could think about was Lucy. Lucy, dying alone in an opulent hotel room, a world away from her family.

Lucy, who just wanted to know what happened to her daughter.

She took a deep breath, closing her eyes. Every so often, she felt a panic rising up in her, a wave of *something* she couldn't control, couldn't even name. The emotion rolled through her like a hurricane, and she didn't know how to deal with it. It took everything in her to pull it back to a place where she could concentrate.

How was she supposed to do anything if she couldn't deal with her own emotions?

"Lovie." Rafael's voice was soft, bringing her back to the present. "Are you okay?"

She exhaled through her mouth, and looked around at the three pairs of eyes, all staring at her with varying levels of concern.

It hit her immediately: she didn't want to die alone. She didn't want to be alone.

She pushed her hair from her eyes. "I'm fine."

"Once more, with feeling," Rafael said. She looked up at her oldest friend. His eyes were digging into her, willing her to tell him the truth. She gnawed at a fingernail, feeling it fold between her teeth. "I'm fine."

"I know you don't want to hear this, but what are you going to do?" Emme asked.

Louise considered the fact that she could just quit. She could stop. She could let Iris' killer get away, let Iris become a footnote.

But she wasn't a quitter.

Lloyd girls weren't raised that way.

Louise lit a cigarette. "I wish Lucy could have stayed around a little bit longer." She was scared that Lucy's ghost would follow her, joining Gilbert in haunting her.

*March 5th, 1928*

*Lou,*

*Happy birthday, sweetheart. It's hard to believe that you're twenty-eight now. This year has passed so fast.*

*Is it strange that I think we're closer now? In letters, I can tell you anything. Even if you don't write back. So, I'm going to take the chance to tell you some things I would never tell you in person.*

*The first is that I think you're so brave. I don't know many women who could do what you do. You've been challenged so many times, and you've only ever come out stronger.*

*The second is that you're so giving. I know you had to raise the twins while I was allowed to be a child. You had to grow up way faster than you deserved. And you never let that stop you.*

*The third is that you're brilliant. You use your mind in ways I could never imagine. You're constantly thinking up things, and I'm always in awe.*

*Happy birthday, and I'm so grateful I had a sister like you to show me the way. I know we haven't ever been close, but that doesn't mean you don't inspire me.*

*Now. I'm including monthly photos of your niece. Celia Jane is going to be a year old soon, and there's a photograph for every month so far. She looks like you, which means she looks like Mom. She's so clever, too. Just a brilliant little girl. I tell her stories about her auntie all the time, but I don't think she believes me.*

*I'm writing to say happy birthday. And I love you.*

*Your sister,*
*Minna*

# 43

◅▽▻

LOUISE HAD GONE over this story three times, and Emme still needed details. Emme's eyes were narrow, a telltale sign that she was still processing information.

"And Toussaint?"

"Hates me," Louise said. Emme wrinkled her nose; Louise's joke was not appreciated.

"What does this mean?" Emme asked. She held her hand out, Schoonmaker gave her back her notebook.

"You write a lot," Schoonmaker said. "And I can't read any of it."

"That is on purpose." Emme was busy flipping through pages. She found a blank page and wrote something down.

"Braithwaite already knows," Louise said.

Emme glowered, staring at her page. "He's probably writing the story as we speak. Then he'll want me to type it up."

"He was there when I was," Louise said. She paused, lighting a cigarette.

She had thought that Emme would help her organize her thoughts, but she seemed as lost as Louise was.

"Are we sure that whoever killed Iris didn't come here and kill Lucy too?"

Louise had considered that. "I don't know if anyone but me and Iris and Estelle knew Lucy was here. I think it's just an unfortunate coincidence."

Schoonmaker had spent two hours on the phone, contacting his family overseas, trying to tell them that Lucy was dead. She didn't know if he had succeeded; she and Rafael had given him time and space.

And now they were sitting around this table with more questions than answers.

"I don't know if Toussaint will tell me. He already hates me," Louise said. "But he seemed confident that there was no foul play . . ."

"That's what he said about Iris," Emme said.

Louise nodded. He had been wrong, but she would wait, see what happened.

She wished she could have solved Iris' murder before this happened.

"Should we go over the suspects again?" Emme asked.

"I don't think we're needed for this," Rafael said. They were finishing dinner, sitting over mostly untouched plates and empty glasses of wine.

"No," Louise sighed. She felt herself wanting to just lie down and sleep. She picked up her water glass, taking a long sip.

Things had changed so much, and she still wanted to talk to Clémence.

⊲◊⊳

THE INVITATION SAID to wear black. Louise did just that, a slinky number that she hadn't had the chance to wear yet.

When she got up to the apartment, it was dark. Candles were lit everywhere, on every available surface.

And Margaux, Sabine, Lili, Estelle, Marion, and Jeanne were all standing, waiting for her. They, too, were all wearing black. They were all grinning at her. Louise closed the door behind her. The hair on her arms stood up, and her body hummed with nerves. She hadn't known what to expect from the invitation, but it wasn't this.

Lili handed her a candle, and Estelle lit it.

"Welcome," Lili said. Above the orange glow of her candle, her eyes were wide and excited.

"Sister," Estelle said, her voice low and steady. "*La Mort des Artistes* was begun to help generations of women become the artists they were meant to be. And now you, Louise Lloyd, will join the sisterhood. Do you accept?"

Her mouth was dry. Candle wax was melting and dripping onto her fingers, burning for a moment before cooling down.

"Sister, do you accept?" Margaux asked. Above her candle, her eyes were narrowed, as if she were waiting for Louise to say the wrong thing.

"I accept." What else could she do? She hadn't meant for this to go this far. Louise cleared her throat.

"Repeat after me," Marion said. Louise had to wonder if they had practiced this. "I, Sister Lloyd, promise to uphold the standards of *La Mort des Artistes*. I promise to support my sisters in times of strength and in strife. My sisters come first."

Louise repeated the words, her voice shaking as she did. Every woman was staring at her, boring through her until she thought she was doing all of the wrong things.

"Now the blood pact," Margaux said. "Give me your hand."

"What?"

"She's joking," Lili said softly. "We wouldn't do that."

Louise took a deep breath, letting her heartbeat settle back down to normal. Margaux's eyes were still narrowed, glaring at Louise.

"Good," Jeanne said. They were all standing in a semicircle in front of her. "The glass?"

Marion put down her candle and handed Margaux a shiny silver goblet. "We all drink from this glass to bond." She took a sip and handed it to Lili, on her left. Louise was last. She held her breath and took a sip. It was red wine.

"You're one of us forever now," Estelle said with a wink.

"That's all?" Louise asked. She had been humming with nerves since she had received the invitation the day before. She had been imagining all sorts of worst-case scenarios, the last of which ended with her falling through a window like Iris had.

But that was it.

"There's just a lot of pomp and circumstance," Estelle said. Lili turned on the lights, Marion blew the candles out. "The founding mothers had it written that we welcome all new members like this," Margaux said. "I don't know why."

"What do we do now?" Louise asked. She blew out her candle and placed it on the table.

"We drink," Estelle said. Jeanne was already pouring glasses of wine, handing them out.

"Welcome," Lili said. "It'll be nice to have another forward-thinking artist."

"Thank you," Louise said. She sipped from her wineglass.

"The last person we initiated was Iris," Lili said with a sigh.

Sabine rolled her eyes. "It's always about Iris, huh?"

"No . . . I've just been thinking about her," Lili said. "She would have loved you, Louise."

Beside Lili, Estelle was quiet. Louise was never sure how much the other women knew about Iris and Estelle's relationship. Every time Iris was mentioned, Estelle seemed to go pale.

Sabine looked at her. "Maybe we should focus on Louise tonight."

"Right," Lili said. "You're right. Sorry." The mood changed in an instant. And the night would never recover. Sabine was still glowering.

"One more thing!" Jeanne was drunk. She was rarely not drunk. She was handling a box, neatly wrapped, like Louise would at her job. She took the box and pulled the wrapping away.

A new camera. Without a matching lipstick, which Louise thought made it *that* much more professional.

It was serious and black and heavy.

"Thank you." Louise felt tears prick her eyes. The smallest gesture of kindness and she was on the verge of tears. It was really nice. But it was more than that.

"Welcome, kid," Sabine said.

"You're one of us now," Estelle added.

Louise took her time, opening the box and checking out her new camera. The group had broken into factions now, with Marion and Sabine disappearing, and Margaux and Jeanne in a quiet conversation.

Apparently, the celebration was over. Louise was fine with that. All she wanted to do was go home and go to sleep for hours.

"Wait," Lili said. She took Louise's hand and pulled her over to where the easels were. "I'm not really done with it yet, but I wanted you to see it." She pulled out the canvas and set it in front of Louise.

Louise was staring at herself. But a more beautiful version of herself, one where her hazel eyes gleamed, and she looked slightly surprised at the viewer. Around her neck was a gleaming necklace.

"It's amazing," Louise said.

"Better than photography, right?" Lili asked.

Louise nodded.

"You look incredible," Estelle said. She had wandered over.

Louise took another sip of her wine. "It is beautiful." It was all she could think to say, but it was true.

"I think it's my best work so far," Lili said proudly.

"I love the way you captured her smile," Estelle said.

"Well, my model has such an enchanting smile," Lili said. "Louise, how do you feel?"

"Good," she said. And it almost wasn't a lie. "I'm glad you had me."

"Me too," Lili said.

"Louise!" This was Margaux, crossing over to her with another glass of wine. "Now that you're one of us, I have a favor to ask. That rich guy you're friends with?"

"Schoonmaker?"

"Yeah, him. I want him to invest in me," Margaux said.

"Margaux, are you sure?" Lili asked.

Margaux glared at her. "Of course I'm sure. And Louise doesn't mind, does she?" She turned back to Louise.

Louise cleared her throat. "Of course I don't mind. I can talk to him."

"Great," Margaux said. "Let me know when you do." She flounced away, leaving Louise a little bewildered.

"I guess we're already showing our true colors," Lili said quietly. "Let's get you another drink."

And she needed it.

# 44

WHEN LOUISE ANSWERED the door, the last person she thought she would see was Estelle Callaghan.

It was after work, after her welcome celebration. Louise had just narrowly avoided a hangover, but she was still a little annoyed at everything.

Ciarán was hovering behind Estelle, smoking a cigarette, trying to look casual.

Louise stepped out onto the landing, closing her door behind her.

Louise looked around. "Do you want to come in?"

Estelle nodded. She opened her door, inviting Estelle in.

She left Ciarán out.

They sat at the table, close proximity. Louise kicked her shoes off and lit a cigarette. "Did you hear about Lucy?" Louise asked. "She passed away."

Lucy's death had been marked as natural. Just like her daughter's, there had been *no foul play involved*. That somehow made it worse.

Lucy would never know what happened to her daughter.

Louise wished she had more time. She wished she had gotten to know Iris. Reading her thoughts simply could not compare.

And the one thing Louise came back to was that, with her death, the world would be deprived of an amazing artist.

Her works that were shown were just the beginning.

And now she was unfinished.

"When Iris died," Louise said, "she asked me to find out what happened to her."

Estelle's eyes narrowed. This close, Louise could see she wasn't wearing any cosmetics. She looked young, lost.

"Did you?" Estelle asked.

Louise omitted the fact that Estelle was a suspect. "I think so. I didn't mean to deceive you, but you six women were the closest people in Iris' life."

"What have you found out?" Estelle asked. She leaned forward.

There was something about human nature. People were interested in the most horrible things. Louise could describe the fall, how Iris' body had hit the pavement, but she didn't.

The most gruesome details of Iris' life, her end, was what people would remember about her.

Instead, Louise changed direction. "She loved you. She adored you." That much was true: Estelle, in writing and in drawing form, covered Iris' journals. "She thought you were incendiary."

Estelle's smile was slow. "I like that."

"Me too. Can I show you?" Louise got up, pulling out a couple of the large sketchbooks, placing them on the table. "You said she was wearing a red dress when you met. Do you remember what you were wearing?"

Estelle closed her eyes. "Champagne dress with long sleeves, I think."

Louise flipped the book open, pointing to a sketch.

Of Estelle, with longer hair, in a champagne dress.

Estelle took the book, turning it toward her, utterly speechless.

She stared at the sketch, which took up a whole page. Louise had seen it before, and it had brought her to a full stop.

She knew it was Estelle the minute she saw it, and, while Iris had still been playing with style, she could *feel* the way Iris felt, even after that first meeting.

"That night, we left Duke's to go to the apartment. And then I left to go pack. I went home, and by the time I got back . . ." Estelle trailed off. "She was gone. I kissed her good-bye, I said 'See you soon,' and then . . ." She stared at the drawing. A tear dropped onto it, and she wiped it away.

Louise got up, handing her a glass of water.

"Something stronger?"

Louise obliged, pouring a glass of gin, adding a little club soda to it. "Who did you leave with?" Louise asked.

Estelle sighed. "Sabine. We left together. And Margaux and Jeanne were left."

Louise put the glass in front of Estelle. She drained it in one sip, and then stared at the glass in her hand.

Without thinking, Estelle threw it on the floor as hard as she could.

The glass shattered, seeming to rock the entire building. Louise had no doubt that it could be heard right down to the ground floor.

"I am so sorry," Estelle said. "I don't know what came over me."

Louise paused. "It's okay," she said. Then she took another glass and smashed it on the floor too.

The act of it, the sheer ludicrousness of breaking something, was amazing. Then she picked up a plate. Louise didn't have much in the way of dishware, but what she did have was rarely used. She threw the plate on the floor as well. Estelle was grinning now.

"Feels good."

The knock on the door brought them to a stop. "I'll clean it up," Estelle said.

"I don't have a broom. It's fine," Louise said. She opened the door to see Ciarán, concerned.

"What are you doing up here?" he asked. "Is everyone okay?"

"We're fine," Louise said. "Do you want to come break a plate?"

Ciarán considered her, his eyebrows knit together. "Have you been drinking?"

"No," Louise said. He didn't believe her, and she could see it on his face.

"Leave us alone, Ciarán." Estelle joined Louise at the door. "We're fine."

He looked between both of them. "Estelle, how are you really?" Louise thought that maybe Ciarán was Estelle's Rafael, in the way that she could never lie to him.

"I'm okay, or I will be."

Louise didn't even believe that.

⧖

THE LAST THING Louise wanted to do was visit the Blanchet salon. She felt more like an outsider than ever after telling Estelle everything.

But Ciarán had begged her.

She had asked Estelle, between girls, between *sisters*, to not blow her cover. Estelle had promised.

Louise was surprised to find that Schoonmaker was there, too, sitting right next to Coralie, looking right at home. And then she understood why Margaux had wanted an introduction. Dinner went smoothly. She was happy to see Estelle there, wearing a day dress and flat shoes.

After dinner, as always, they went upstairs for dessert and readings. Margaux, fresh off of her show, was still basking in praise. "Louise!" Margaux had greeted her with a wide smile, two kisses on the cheek. "How have your photographs turned out?"

"I still have to develop them."

"Hm, we should use the darkroom. Make it into a party," Margaux said. She was always looking for a reason to have a party.

That was how Louise knew they were of different worlds. New York flapper girls just partied.

"Of course." Louise could smell the alcohol on Margaux's breath. She was too close and drinking too much. "Whenever you want." Margaux's eyes narrowed, trying to figure out what Louise meant by that. Then she eased into a smile, bright and brilliant, one Louise knew she had captured at the party. Margaux took both of her hands in hers. "You're not wearing the bracelet."

"It's too expensive for me to wear every day. I'm not used to it."

Margaux smiled, an almost sinister turn of her lips. "You must have been really poor."

Louise didn't know how to take that, but she didn't have to. Coralie called them all into the solarium, and the meeting continued.

Margaux sat next to her mother. Louise sat next to Schoonmaker. He had been busy throughout dinner, charming anyone who looked at him. Even now, there was a handful of people vying for his attention.

"First," Coralie said, "I have to say that the impressive and generous Fox Schoonmaker has offered to support two lucky artists here. He's here tonight to . . . see what we're offering." A smattering of applause. Margaux sat straight up, eyeing Schoonmaker with more interest.

"It'll be something casual," Schoonmaker said. "I'm still in the process of working everything out, but I'll be happy to reveal more details as they come."

"Moving on," Coralie said. "We're beginning with a reading from Ciarán Dunne."

This is why Ciarán had begged Louise to come; he wanted her to help read his new play. It was a little exciting. It had been so long since *Darling Girl* that people were beginning to think he would never write anything again.

Ciarán stood, Margaux moved so that he could command the room. Everyone applauded.

"Thank you," Ciarán said. He took a moment, looking around the room. "After the success of *Darling Girl*, I didn't know if I would be writing anything again. But . . . I think I've done it. It's about an actress torn between her love and her marriage."

"How dare you." Estelle rose to her feet. She had been quiet all night, but now, her voice shattered the silence around them. She was glaring at Ciarán. If looks could kill, he would have been dead on the spot. "You're writing about Iris? How dare you? Who gave you the right?" She moved closer to Ciarán, the rage of one thousand suns behind her. Ciarán actually stepped back.

Every person in the room was holding their breath.

Instead of saying anything, and Louise didn't know what he *could* say that would temper her, Ciarán stepped forward and wrapped her in a hug. He murmured something in her ear, and Estelle broke down into sobs.

It was a moment before Estelle could control herself. The room watched, waiting with bated breath for another outburst. But Ciarán kept talking to Estelle, quietly, and the sound didn't travel around the room.

Louise looked away, uncomfortable with the display of emotion in front of her. When Estelle sat back down, it seemed as if the matter was over. They had put it to rest. She looked over at Schoonmaker, who was staring at her. He smiled. She smiled back.

"Tiny, can you help me with this?" Ciarán asked. That was why she was there. He refused to read the pages himself.

Louise was no actress, but she could see that this play would be another hit. Ciarán wrote in such a clear, confident way. It was the same way Iris painted, a way that showed he totally loved it.

And the months of stress, the months of agony—it had all paid off. Applause. In the years since *Darling Girl,* his writing technique and skill had grown by leaps and bounds. And he was writing about Iris.

He'd be the talk of the town.

Louise dipped a small curtsey when she had finished reading. Then she turned to Ciarán. "I think I have the perfect actress to star in this."

Ciarán looked her over. "I'd like to meet her, then. Have her prepare something dramatic. Nothing Shakespearean."

Louise nodded.

It was the least she could do. She promised Clémence an introduction long ago.

And Louise knew that Clémence was perfect for this. It could be her big break.

She pulled away. Coralie had already moved on, critiquing a woman's still life painting. She watched as Ciarán sat down next to Estelle, falling back into a quiet discussion.

"You're supporting artists now?" Louise asked Schoonmaker.

"Just two. And I want that play."

Louise bit back her response, knowing Rafael wouldn't like that. But it wasn't her place to get in between.

She resumed watching Margaux, leaning in to give her advice to another artist. She had changed since Iris' death.

And not for the better.

Margaux looked up, smiled, and laughed as someone said something. Louise needed another drink. She couldn't wait until she never had to come back here again.

She lit a cigarette. Margaux tossed her head back in a laugh.

Louise hated her.

# 45

LUCY'S DEATH DIDN'T make the papers. She didn't know why she was expecting it to, but that made it all so much worse.

Louise arrived at Dauphine's Café thirty minutes early, like usual. She hadn't slept, so she was subsisting on coffee and cigarettes.

Clémence was behind the counter, looking equally ragged. She was normally perfectly put together.

"Hi," Clémence said.

"Hi." Louise sat at the counter. Clémence already had coffee waiting for her. She poured two cups and pushed one toward her.

"We should talk," Louise said.

Clémence frowned, wiping an invisible spot on the counter between them. "I don't think we need to discuss anything." Clémence didn't look at her. She reminded Louise of Celia in a way. Whenever she was nervous, or avoiding something, Clémence would start babbling. "It's gonna be busy today; I think it might rain. I have to make sure everything is clean."

Louise let her rattle off the list of things she had to do, patiently sipping at her coffee.

"Are you done?" Louise asked, five minutes later. Clémence stopped, leaning on the counter. She took a deep breath. Louise needed another cup of coffee.

"I think we should talk," Louise said again. Clémence exhaled, refusing to meet Louise's eyes. She wanted to talk about the kiss, but she got the sense that that was what Clémence was avoiding. "Ciarán Dunne wants to meet you. I told him all about you, and I think you'd be perfect for his new play. He said to prepare something dramatic. No Shakespeare."

"Huh."

She watched Clémence's reaction, trying to gauge if it was a good or bad one. "I can help you pick something, if you want?" It came out as a question, but she wasn't sure what else to say.

Clémence nodded, a smile. "Of course. I thought you wanted to talk about . . ."

"I do . . ."

"We can't do it here," Clémence said. "My parents." She looked around, and Louise understood her panic.

She lived in fear of her own father, and she could only imagine what he would do had Joseph found her kissing a girl.

"Come to my apartment after work," Louise said. She thought she was begging, but she didn't care.

Clémence's eyes met hers, and for one frozen moment, she was breathless.

"Okay," Clémence said. "Aren't you going to be late?"

Since she had begun at Allaire's, Louise had never been late once. It was a record she wanted to keep, but she didn't want to leave the café.

—◁▽▷—

AND, AT SEVEN o'clock on the dot, Clémence was at Louise's door.

It had been a long day. There was a détente between Clara and Jessie, but there had been more customers than there had been in Louise's entire time at Allaire's.

Her feet hurt. She was hungry. She had a headache.

And all of it went away when she saw Clémence. Ciarán had come outside, and they were talking. Actually, Clémence was reciting, and Ciarán looked enamored. She had pages in her hand and was reading the same pages Louise had a few nights ago at the Blanchet salon.

"Lovie, my word," Ciarán said. She preferred him calling her Tiny to using her middle name. "Where have you been hiding this one?"

"I told you," Louise said.

Ciarán nodded. He looked very serious, his eyes still on Clémence. "Well, Tiny, you are always right."

"We're going now," Louise said, unlocking her door. Clémence handed back the pages and followed her inside. Louise closed the door behind her and dropped her bag where she stood.

"You look exhausted," Clémence said.

"You're so kind."

She had wanted to talk. There were so many things she wanted to say, but the first and only thing she wanted to do was kiss her.

So Louise did.

There were a lot of things she couldn't be sure of. But she was certain about this.

"You wanted to talk." Clémence's voice was soft against her lips.

"And I can't remember about what."

Clémence stepped away, and Louise fell forward, catching herself before she hit the ground. "We should talk." Clémence sat at the table.

Although she was still in her work clothes, Louise opted to sit on her bed.

Her headache was returning.

"I can't do anything too . . ." Clémence trailed off, sorting through the words she wanted to use. "Intense. I don't know what is going to happen, but I can't settle down."

"I know," Louise said. "It's not what I want either. I want to have fun."

That was, after all, why she moved. She wanted to find herself. She wanted something different.

"I don't want anything permanent." Louise said it, and she didn't know if she believed it. But she felt it and that had to be good enough.

"You know I have a husband."

"I kissed Emme!"

"The reporter?"

Louise nodded. "We're even. I just like spending time with you a lot." She got up, crossing to her tiny kitchen table. She sat on it, hoping it could support her weight. "For the record, I am so much better than your husband."

"Really?" Clémence's eyebrows raised. They had been dancing around this for months, since the first time she walked into Dauphine's Café. There had been that instant moment of attraction, and she was never able to fight it.

But then she met Emme.

How was it possible she was torn between two different women?

This had never happened to her.

"Yes," Louise said.

"You're confident."

"Confidence is my middle name."

Clémence laughed. "Okay, Lovie."

Then Louise leaned down and kissed her, and everything else fell away.

Clémence's lips were soft and sweet, and kissing her now felt just as good as it did a couple of nights ago, on the landing of the stairs.

"We should do something," Clémence said softly. "I can't believe you live above Ciarán Dunne."

"I know, he's very irritating," Louise said. "Do you really want to talk about him right now?"

"I do not," Clémence said. "Merde," she added softly.

This was the first time she had had a woman's hands on her body since Rosa Maria.

And when that hit her, when she really realized it, Louise pulled away. Her heart was racing.

Merde, indeed.

*April 15th, 1928*

*Lou,*

*This is late. I know this is late. I just wanted to write to tell you happy birthday, and I got all anxious about it. I don't know* why *exactly. We can do this, even though you didn't write me for mine.*

*It's okay.*

*I hope it was nice. I'm over a month late. And last year for your birthday, we were at the Dove, right before everything went to shit. That is still, weirdly, one of the best nights of my life.*

*Or, at least, right up to the murder.*

*I hope you haven't encountered any murders in France.*

*Also, I've met someone. A man. Named James. I really like him. And I wrote a book. And that may amount to nothing, but I keep thinking of all those nights in our boardinghouse with you watching me write. You believed in me, and I am always grateful for that. I regret how things ended between us.*

*I'm so sorry.*

*James is a banker. He is the oldest of four siblings, all boys. He is intelligent, loves to read, but is a terrible dancer. He makes me miss you, in a strange way. I'm not sure you two would get along. You would question everything he says. You'd get used to each other, I think.*

*That is why I haven't written in a while. (Rafael tells me you never respond, anyway. I take it he guilts you about it, but it doesn't work if you don't read the letters.)*

*I am happy for you, and I hope you can be happy for me too. And James. James and me. I think it really could be my future. I wasn't sure if I wanted to be a wife or not, but I think I could be for James.*

*You and I just wanted different things. That's not a bad thing.*

*Happy birthday.*

*I hope twenty-eight is the best year for you yet.*

*With love,*
*Rosa Maria*

# 46

〜〄〜

THEY MET AT Estelle's house. Instead of the pool, the place Louise had first met her, they were on a patio in the late-afternoon sun. Estelle was sitting at a lovely wicker table, along with Lili. Louise was last to arrive. For this occasion, she had put the bracelet on. She wasn't used to the weight. She thought that someone would try to snatch it while she was wearing it.

She sat down at the table. There was a modest tea spread. Estelle had a sketchbook open, and Lili was sitting in a chair, her small face tilted toward the sun.

Louise had been the last to arrive because she had to convince herself to go. She couldn't pull this off by herself; she needed the help.

Lili and Estelle were the only two women in this group she trusted. "Estelle," Louise said.

"You're here."

Louise leaned forward, pouring herself some lemonade. "Mary will do that for you," Estelle said, without looking at her.

"I can pour my own lemonade," Louise said. "And I need to ask both of you a favor."

She had their attention now. Louise picked up her glass, feeling the bracelet slide down her wrist as she did. "I need you to host a dinner party. Members only."

"Why?" Lili asked. Her eyes were on Louise.

Estelle looked at Lili. Louise thought that Estelle would have told her everything.

"I waited for you," Estelle said.

Louise exhaled. She would have to start at the beginning. And she did, while Estelle and Lili listened. She had to go through the story, from Lucy arriving in Paris, to Lucy's death.

"So, this whole time you were . . ." Lili asked, an eyebrow raised.

"I didn't mean to get so involved," Louise said. "But yes, I was investigating."

"Huh," Lili said. She tipped her face toward the afternoon sun, again. "So, what do you need from us?"

"I need you to hold a dinner party and invite every current member of the society," Louise said.

"Why can't you?" Estelle lit a cigarette.

"I'm pretty sure all of you don't like me that much."

Lili laughed, loud and clear, then smacked a hand over her mouth. "That's not true. You're one of us."

"You're laughing," Louise said. "And I don't think anyone would come if it was from me."

Estelle and Lili shared a look. "Are you sure about this?" Estelle asked. "I mean, what makes you so sure it wasn't one of us?"

Louise looked right at her. "I'm supposed to believe you pushed the love of your life out of a window?" She stopped when she realized how that sounded. "No, I mean, I just need all of you together in the same room at the same time."

"I can have the invitations written out," Lili said. "What time would you like?"

"Whatever is convenient for you?" Louise never knew what time would work for everyone.

"Should we cater it?" Lili asked.

"What sort of party is this?" Estelle asked.

Louise didn't know if she should try to temper their expectations.

But then again, it would be a party.

"I've got it all handled," Louise said. "Your only job is to send out invitations."

"And collect responses," Estelle added.

"Exactly."

Estelle picked up a tiny sandwich, biting into it. For a moment, everyone was quiet. Louise leaned back into her seat, picking up her glass of lemonade.

"Why did you agree to find Iris?" Lili asked. She was in the process of lighting a cigarette.

"It was a favor," Louise said.

"I would have politely said no," Estelle said.

"I considered it."

"Do you even like photography?" Lili asked.

Louise nodded. "I'm not great at it, but it's fun."

Lili considered this. She didn't say anything for a moment.

"For what it's worth," Estelle said, waving Mary over, "I do think the other girls like you. We're just all . . ."

"Ambitious, but that's not a bad thing. It's hard to be friends with the people you're competing with."

"Iris understood that. She never sabotaged any of us. Even

when she had the chance to." Lili closed her eyes. "I think she really would have liked you."

"I don't know about that," Louise said. "I wish I could have gotten to know her better."

She knew the ins and outs of Iris' thoughts and life, but she still didn't know the woman.

But she could solve her murder, and that had to count for something.

# 47

⌖

MARGAUX WAS THE last to arrive.

She did it sweeping in, wearing a powder-blue evening gown, outdressing everyone else's cocktail wear.

Margaux was so late that Louise was beginning to think she wouldn't show up.

But the invitation was worded in a way that made it seem Margaux was going to be lauded for her artistic expression.

It was easier to get Jeanne to show up. Louise eyed the woman now, sitting at the table, drinking from a flute of champagne. She looked bored.

Louise had been at the apartment all afternoon. Lili had proved instrumental in getting everyone there. The invitations had been sent anonymously. Louise hoped that would draw all of them to her. And this was important.

The rest was up to her.

Margaux looked around. "What is going on?" She sat down at the table, at her place.

Sabine leaned forward, picking up her champagne. "We were all called here."

"Was it my mother? No one else knows we keep this place," Margaux asked. Under her frothy gown, there was steel.

Louise took a sip of her own champagne. She had wanted to keep a clear head, but she was on her fourth glass and feeling the stars rise to her head.

She leaned forward, commanding the attention of the table. Estelle was to her right, looking scared and plain. Lili to her left, cool and controlled.

Beyond this table, Emme was in an adjacent sitting room, close enough to hear and write down everything that was said.

"I called this meeting," Louise said. She wasn't used to being in this room without the record player or the radio on. The silence seemed to hum around them, loud and oppressive.

And now five pairs of eyes were watching her. "I want to talk to you all about Iris." She rose with a champagne glass. Lili and Estelle were the only two people who knew the whole truth. "I was hired to find Iris Wright." She tried to control her voice, although it was shaking. "And after she died, her mother asked me to find out what happened to her."

"It was a suicide," Jeanne said slowly. She was looking around the table.

"That's what was reported," Louise said. "But Lucy thought differently, and I did too."

"What are you saying?" Sabine asked. She wasn't drinking, a glass of water was set in front of her.

"I called you all here because one of you killed Iris Wright." Appropriate gasps, except from Estelle. Louise took a deep breath. She needed a cigarette. Her hands were shaking now too. Her mouth had gone dry. What was she doing? Why was she doing it?

She wanted Iris and Lucy to rest easy.

That was why she was doing it.

She picked up her champagne glass and drained it.

"You think one of us killed Iris?" Sabine asked slowly. "We all loved her."

"That's not true." Louise began to walk around the table. "One of you was having an affair with her husband. One of you hated her so much because she was achieving what you couldn't. One of you loved her with everything you had, but not all of you *liked* her."

Now she had their attention. Every woman watched her, all mirrors of blank expression. "You all keep your secrets, and I was hired to oust them." She was well acquainted with women and their secrets; she couldn't be a chorus girl without learning who drank too much or who didn't like who.

But this group was more intimate. It was harder to delve into their secrets, their inner lives.

And they were so close.

"Margaux is with Philip, you told us," Lili said. Margaux blanched, the first real emotion from her since she sat down at the table.

"Iris didn't love him," Margaux said. Her voice shook.

"And that makes it okay?" Lili asked. "She was your sister."

"All of this is bullshit," Margaux snapped. "Are we letting this woman tell us this obvious story? She is trying to tear us down after we let her in." The other women shared a look, drawing out the moment.

"So, Philip didn't write you, telling you he loved you, and give you a ring?" Louise asked. She pulled out a photograph she had taken at Margaux's show. One of Margaux and Philip in a close embrace. Margaux's face turned red.

"But this isn't about Philip," Louise said. "This is about you women. *La Mort des Artistes*. Sworn to support and help each other." She stopped beside Lili. From where she was standing, she could see the canvas Lili was working on, her own portrait.

"And Iris was about to quit. She was about to leave altogether," Louise said. "She didn't want this life. She didn't want to be part of this society anymore. She was going to move on."

She had to respect Iris for that decision, knowing that she could do something else, be anything else.

And the world would never know now.

"That night she died," Louise said, "she told one of you, and that woman pushed Iris out of the window." She placed the bracelet she had found on the tabletop. "Iris took this bracelet with her."

"We all have ours . . ." Jeanne said, her eyes rolling around the table.

"Because this woman bought a replacement to cover it up." Louise pulled the bracelet she had found out of her purse and placed it on the table. "I thought it was Iris'. Hers had some missing stones. But the coroner said she was found with hers." Louise looked at her wrist. Her bracelet was still safely on. She thought about selling it when all of this was over. "I love what these represent. I love that this means something. The sisterhood. The women who want to be incredible at what they do. Iris told one of you." Louise looked around the room. "After the rest of you left that night. And it was just Iris and Marion." Everyone's gaze slid toward Marion, whose mouth dropped open.

"I . . ." she stammered out.

"I know it wasn't you." Louise's heart was racing. Every woman was looking at her. "One of you came back. The woman who never actually liked Iris. Never wanted her in your special little club."

"Margaux!" Lili was staring at the other woman, her eyes wide and scared.

"How can you believe this? Iris killed herself." Margaux was lighting a cigarette. She shook the match, looking at Louise with icy eyes.

Was she wrong? She squeezed her hand into a fist. She tried to steady herself. She wasn't wrong. The bracelet. Her jealousy. The affair.

"And then you blackmailed Toussaint into writing this off as a suicide. 'No foul play involved.'"

"She was going to quit. And that would have been such a waste of talent. She had it all, and she didn't even want it," Margaux said. She couldn't have been drunk, but her voice shook. She backed away from the table.

Louise's heart pounded.

"She was going to give it all away. She was incredible and I just . . ." Margaux trailed off. She was pacing back and forth, spit flying from her mouth. She was looking around, breathing fast and hard. "How could she not see that she had everything. Effortless talent. And I have to get my mother to pay for me to have a show." She looked toward Louise. "I'm a Blanchet. That means something. You wouldn't know, but my mother? Me? I'm someone. And this *American* just comes in and takes everything and then she wants to quit."

"Did you fight that night?" Louise asked.

Margaux looked around the room, a caged animal, wild and unpredictable. "She told me she was leaving. For good. And I thought I should be happy for her. But . . . I just got so angry. I tried to get her to reconsider. She just laughed at me and said I could have Philip. Like he's a thing. A prize. She never cared for him. She was Mrs. Montgomery for convenience. I want to be Mrs. Montgomery because I love him.

"So I pushed her. We fought and I pushed her. I watched as she fell, hit the ground. I didn't know she had taken my bracelet with her until later." Margaux looked around. Her eyes were wide. She was fiddling with her bracelet, easily opening the clasp. The bracelet fell to the floor, forgotten.

"Did Toussaint know?" Louise asked. It felt wrong to talk. If she said anything, it would stop Margaux and the spell would be broken.

Margaux exhaled cigarette smoke. "Of course he didn't. But he asked, and I needed his help." She dropped her cigarette butt into an ashtray. "And I am not going to let you . . ."

Louise would never hear the end of that sentence. When it was clear what Margaux was going to do, Louise tried to stop her.

But she was a moment too late.

Margaux ran at full speed to the newly replaced window, and Louise nearly followed.

She would never get the sound of her body hitting the ground out of her head.

*May 10th, 1928*

*Louise,*

*I don't know how to begin this letter. You haven't responded to many, or any, of my other letters. I'm sending this with Rafael, so at least I can hope you'll read it.*

*I thought about having Josie send this letter to you, but I can't do that to her. I have to send a letter to her too.*

*I need you to read this and then react. Please, Louise.*

*Father is sick. I don't know how sick, but I have seen changes. He keeps denying it, but it seems as if he's aged a lifetime in months.*

*I thought you would want to know. I need you to know. I don't know what to do. He won't listen to Aunt Louise or me, and I need help. I just need you to tell me what to do. I don't know. I'm scared.*

*He's slower, older, more tired. But he refuses all help.*

*I've just thought that maybe you don't want to hear this, maybe you don't care. But I'm not asking for him, Lou. I'm asking for me.*

*We've always had our differences, I understand that. I hope you would help me because we are sisters. We are family. We are bonded together, for better or for worse.*

*I don't know what to do or when to do it. He won't listen to me. And I just want to warn you, I guess. I suppose he could die before this reaches you. And I guess if that happens, I'll have to call Rafael.*

*A lot of things can happen. But I need you to write me back.*

*I don't think I've ever been this scared in my life. I know whatever happens, I'm going to need you.*

*Your sister,*
*Minna Scott*

# 48

TWO MORNINGS LATER, Emme's story was front-page news. Louise stayed over at the hotel with Rafael and Schoonmaker. They had been waiting to help Emme with the story, while Louise talked to the police, clearing everything up.

The papers for the day after Margaux had died had already been sent to press, and they couldn't change it, but Emme was promised a front-page story. And she got it.

Louise had slept on the couch of the hotel room. She didn't want to be away from her friends. The big hotel room felt more like home than her apartment. And when the paper was delivered, Schoonmaker held it aloft, reading every word they had written.

"You are famous, Lovie," Rafael said. He had called up for breakfast, pastries that were warm and flaky, and mimosas, a new invention of champagne and orange juice, something that had become Louise and Rafael's favorite drink to have in the morning.

Who needed coffee when you could have champagne?

She could not believe that there was a point in time when she couldn't stand drinking champagne. Parisians seemed to drink it morning, noon, and night, finding inventive ways to have it.

She had to respect that.

Louise sat on the couch, her legs crossed under her, wearing a very expensive pale-pink shirt that she had slept in.

She had begged Emme to leave her name out of it, but without Louise Lloyd, it was only half the story. So, she was staring at her name, in print, again. The story would spread. From the English papers to the French ones, and all Louise could hope was that it wouldn't affect her. She wouldn't be anonymous for much longer.

"I have to go to work," Louise said. She didn't want to talk about it.

"Play hooky," Rafael said. "I could use you." The idea was tempting. She wanted to stay in the hotel all day, do nothing and talk with her friends. What she really wanted to do was hide. She could spend the day in this luxurious hotel room, and no one would find her.

Louise sighed. Room service was delivered, and Schoonmaker handed her a mimosa. She took a sip, needing a cigarette. "I need clothes," Louise said.

Schoonmaker and Rafael shared a look, a quick smile between them. "We got you some things," Rafael said.

Schoonmaker disappeared into the bedroom and returned with a small collection of day dresses.

"Are you serious?" Louise asked.

"You are our Lovie," Schoonmaker said. "And you won't let me spoil you in any other way."

"Because I don't need it," Louise said. She took another sip from her glass. She was thrilled.

"And you've been staying here more and more," Rafael said. "Now you won't have to go back to your horrible little apartment."

Louise selected a dark-purple drop-waisted dress with a necktie. She had enough time to bathe, dress, and go to work. But she needed another mimosa first. Schoonmaker read the story, out loud, again.

They were proud of her. It was nice to have the support when all she felt was exhaustion. Nothing. She should be so pleased. But all she could think of were the lives that had been lost.

Three of them, and for what?

She had no cosmetics with her, but she worked at a place that was considered the holy grail of cosmetics. Once she was dressed, she strapped on her shoes and pulled herself together.

"Lovie," Rafael said. "Are you okay?" He was watching her. He hadn't stopped watching her, as if she would collapse if he took his eyes away from her. He was hovering, which she didn't know if he realized.

"I just want to go to work, then go home."

Rafael frowned, lighting a cigarette. "Call me when you get home." He moved to pull her into a tight hug. "I love you." His voice was soft.

It was the same sentiment twice. Louise was grateful for it.

⌄▲⌄

THE DAY LOUISE was hired at Allaire's was the only time she had been in the office above the sales floor. That morning, after the rush that came with opening, Jessie came to her. Louise was behind the counter, staring at a fixed point in the distance, trying to figure out what she wanted to do next. Getting through the day seemed like a good start.

"Allaire wants to see you," Jessie whispered. It took a moment for Louise to even register the other woman was talking. "I'll cover the till."

They didn't really need it. There was no one in the store, but Allaire hated the till to be vacant.

"Upstairs?" Louise asked.

Jessie nodded.

Louise exhaled and climbed the golden stairs to the office door. She knocked twice, and entered after she was bidden to do so.

Allaire was behind his wide oak desk, framed photos decorating the walls. He had shelves with every product he had ever sold, and his windows looked onto the rolling Paris avenues. The walls were painted a soft pink, and two chairs faced the desk. Allaire wore glasses low on his nose, which he now removed. "Miss Lloyd. Please sit."

Louise did as she was told, feeling anxiety grow in the pit of her stomach. She liked Allaire. He had always been kind to her, and she had sort of thought of him as a father figure.

But the small frown marring his face told her that this wasn't going to be good.

"I read about you in the paper this morning," he began.

Louise froze.

"It's nothing," she began to say. "It's just a little . . ."

Allaire raised a hand, halting her speech. She didn't like the way he was looking at her. "Louise, I think you have been an exemplary salesgirl. But I have to let you go. You will be given a month's severance, and you are dismissed immediately."

"Wait," Louise said. "I need this job. If I don't work here, I'll lose my apartment."

"Louise . . ." He trailed off for a moment, composing what he was going to say. "I see a lot of myself in you. But when I hired you, I told you that the best salesgirl was one who didn't draw attention to herself."

He had said that. Louise had disregarded it. The whole reason she had moved to Paris was for anonymity. She thought she would be the ideal Allaire's girl.

But that had changed. She couldn't even blame him. She sat for a second, still shocked. She wanted to plead her case, but a month's severance would help a lot, and if she argued, he may change his mind. She looked back up at him, unsure of what to do.

Moments ago, her next hours were so clear.

"I'll escort you down to collect your things," Allaire said, rising from his chair.

"Please, don't," Louise said.

He regarded her as if she was a bomb that was about to go off. And maybe she was. Maybe, given a chance, she would destroy the store. "Miss Lloyd," Allaire said, but he didn't finish his sentence.

She took a deep breath, deciding to take the next ten seconds one at a time. She thought about going back to the hotel, but she wanted her bed. At least she knew that Ciarán would be home, and that she could spend time with him.

"I think I'll take over the floor," Allaire said, mostly to himself. Louise couldn't even look at him. She pressed both hands flat on the cushion of the chair, using every ounce of her energy to pull herself up. The world revolved around her, and she was seeing in triple vision.

He followed her down the stairs and stopped at the till to inform Jessie what was going on.

Numbly, Louise entered the break room, taking up her coat and hat. She stopped for a moment, taking it all in for the last time. "Louise!" Jessie was behind her, eyes wide, her hair falling into her face. Without saying anything else, Jessie crossed the space between them and wrapped Louise in a hug.

The move was so unexpected that Louise didn't know what to think of it. But she hugged Jessie back. She didn't think that Jessie liked her that much. "I'll miss you. Who else will want to take the stockroom?"

Louise laughed, despite herself.

"I'm so sorry," Jessie said. "I'll talk to him!"

"It's okay," Louise said, although it wasn't. She was constantly making herself smaller for the comfort of everyone else. "I'll see you later; I should leave."

"Wait, Clara will want to say good-bye."

"Tell her for me." Louise didn't want to linger. The longer she stayed, the more it felt as if her heart was being tugged from her body.

"Okay," Jessie said.

It wasn't lunchtime yet. Louise put on her hat and coat, sliding her gloves on last.

She didn't say another word as she left the store, hearing the distinct chimes announce her exit.

# 49

C IARÁN ANSWERED HIS door. She knew he'd be home. He was half dressed, no shirt, and looked exhausted when he opened the door.

"Detective Tiny! Shouldn't you be at work?"

Louise pushed past him, looking for the cat. "I got fired." Saying it out loud was like putting the final nail in the coffin. Her entire journey home, she had been avoiding telling herself the truth. It stung. It would sting for a while.

He didn't say anything to that. She wondered if he had ever been fired from a job. This was her first time, and it didn't feel great. She sat down, allowing Irving to jump up on her lap.

"I've been working since I was sixteen. What am I going to do?" Louise asked. He watched her, lighting a cigarette.

"What do you want to do?"

"Today?"

"No, I mean, if you could do anything, what would it be?" Ciarán asked.

"Do I have to answer that now?"

He shook his head. He was quiet, thoughtful. "No. Just think about it." He set a glass of water down in front of her, and she picked it up, draining it.

On her lap, his cat was purring. And for a moment, she let herself try to relax.

Ciarán leaned on the counter, his arms crossed over his chest. "I read the story. I think Emme's a talented writer. And I think what you managed to do was admirable. Not many people would change everything about their lives as a favor to a friend of a friend."

"Everyone would."

"I wouldn't."

"You're selfish!"

Ciarán laughed. "Maybe so, but know that you're formidable, Detective Tiny. You do things people can only dream of."

She was grateful he didn't ask her if she was okay again. The question was asked of her far too often, and she never knew how to answer. This was the first time he had spoken so highly of her, at least to her face. He crossed over, wrapping his arms around her. She hadn't realized she was panicking until that moment.

"Can I take a nap?" Louise asked. "I don't want to go upstairs yet."

He nodded toward the bed. Unselfconsciously, Louise removed her shoes and dress, stripped down to her slip. Her clothes were left in a pile on the floor behind her. Ciarán undressed as well, crawling into bed with her. He began to stroke her hair, the way she had stroked his when Iris had died. For a moment, she resisted his touch, so used to caring for other people. He was murmuring something in her ear, melodic and lyrical, allowing her to relax just a little.

"Breathe, Tiny," Ciarán said. His arm around her was a

comforting weight. She closed her eyes, trying to imagine herself falling asleep. She rolled over so she was lying on her back, Ciarán's arm now over her stomach. From her peripheral vision, she could see him watching her, intent with concern.

"Please stop staring." Louise moved again so she was sitting up. She reached for his gold cigarette case, never more than five inches away from him, and lit one. For a minute, that's all she did. Now that she was lying in a bed, with nothing to do but sleep, she was filled with a nervous energy that rattled around in her like a beast in a cage.

"I can't. I'm worried about you. I've never seen you like this," Ciarán said. But, to pacify her, he did close his eyes.

"I'm just . . ." She trailed off.

Louise recognized this feeling. She got caught up in something, solving a murder, and then it was over, and it felt as if she had nothing to do. The world had come crashing to a halt. Last time this happened to her, she moved to Paris.

She couldn't just pick up and leave again.

She exhaled, sending smoke toward the ceiling, before lying back down.

"You're just what?" Ciarán opened one eye, falling on her.

"I don't know."

"Yes, you do."

She wrinkled her nose. She didn't know, and she didn't want to say. "Can we talk about anything else? Anything?"

Ciarán took a moment to ponder it. "I think your friend is going to invest in my play."

"Schoonmaker? Really?"

"Do you know anyone else as rich as he is?"

Louise shook her head. "That's amazing. He's wonderful. He's just so caring. And the pages you had me read at Blanchet's? They were transcendent."

"I know Iris wanted to quit. Sometimes I . . ." he trailed off, carefully putting one word in front of the other before he spoke again. "Sometimes I think about moving back home. Working at the pub. But if I wanted that, I would have stayed. I would have been happy."

"How often do you talk to your brother?" Louise asked.

"How often do you talk to your sisters?" Ciarán asked. "That's not my point. My point is I *understood*. But this new play. I think it could be really, really great."

Louise sat up, crossing her legs. She pulled a pillow into her lap. She lit another cigarette.

"Do you love what you do that much?"

"No." The only time Louise had loved what she did that much was when she was running a nightclub. That was what came easily to her. She loved working with her best friend every night.

And although she loved the predictability of Allaire's, it didn't give her the spark.

"Then you need to find something that does. This was a blessing in disguise."

She opened her mouth to say something, but she didn't know what. She lay back down. "I'll let you sleep on that," Ciarán said.

⋖╫⋗

IT WAS DITSIE who would deliver the last bit of news in the Iris Wright saga. She came to their Le Chat Noir table, looking wholly undone. She had mascara streaks down her eyes. Queenie and Tootsie shared a look; it was often as if those three shared a brain.

Ditsie sat down at the table with a sob.

It was the most emotion Louise had ever seen from any of these girls. Ditsie wasn't wearing her glasses.

"What's wrong?" Doris asked. Louise caught Doris' eye across the table. It was all women that night, and it was a relief.

"Daniel gave up his job," Ditsie said. "Or he's going to. He told me before the show, and I cried all the way through it! I can't stop crying."

"Oh," Doris said. She clearly had no way to follow that up. She lit a cigarette, then picked up her glass of wine.

Women-only evenings weren't rare, but they did have a certain tradition. None of them ate. They all smoked and split bottles of wine.

And the most important part was that every topic was on the table.

With no men around, they were free to talk about anything and everything.

Unfortunately, that topic was usually men.

Presently, Louise gripped her wineglass, staying silent.

Louise hadn't even known that Ditsie and the inspector were slightly serious. In the time Louise had known her, Ditsie had never had a man. But this was different, and she knew it. Louise took a sip from her glass. Ditsie had stopped crying. Tootsie pushed a glass of wine toward her.

"Why is this upsetting you?" With Ditsie out, it was up to Queenie to be the rational one.

"I love him," Ditsie sighed.

It wasn't the first time Louise had seen a woman on her knees for a man. Louise lit a cigarette.

Toussaint resigning. That was news.

"Did he say why?" Louise asked.

"He said he had to make something right."

Louise exhaled cigarette smoke. "You need to talk to him." She could see why Ditsie, the most romantic woman she knew, had fallen for the inspector.

Ditsie frowned. "Can't you just tell me?"

Louise shook her head.

"Dits, I've seen how he looks at you. He thinks you've hung the moon," Tootsie said.

It was nice to be around women, and simple problems. There was no murder to solve here.

"I have to go see him now," Ditsie said. She rose from the table, brushing off her dress skirt. "I have to go talk to him."

"We should go with you," Tootsie said.

Ditsie looked at them both, considering it. "Fine, but you can't come in."

Doris looked around as they left. "I should go too. Work tonight and tomorrow."

"Me too," Louise said, before she remembered she got fired. She had nothing to do tomorrow. An endless stretch of tomorrow and tomorrow and tomorrows were in front of her. She'd find something.

"Are you okay?" Doris asked. She and Louise weren't close, but Doris was perceptive. "I read that stuff in the paper."

"It's nothing," Louise said. "I'm just glad that everything has been put to rest."

Doris nodded, taking a last swig from her glass. "Do you want to come to the club tonight?" Louise wasn't dressed, but that didn't matter.

"Of course. Let me call Rafael and Schoonmaker." Dancing would help, spending time outside of her claustrophobic apartment would help too. She hadn't even been unemployed for a day, and she was already bored, skittish like a caged animal. She needed something to do.

Dancing would fix that, and everything would look better in the morning.

If she said it again and again, that would make it true.

She hoped.

Louise drained her glass, wanting to make that phone call. "Let's go," Louise said. There was nothing else she could—or wanted—to do.

# 50

LOUISE SAT AT the counter, watching Clémence clean the café. Louise had spent the day alternately relaxing and whipping herself into an anxious spiral.

She had been without a job for twenty-four hours, and so far, things had been fine.

Louise had spent all afternoon at the café, reading and smoking and drinking coffee.

"You could help," Clémence said.

"I could," Louise said seriously. "What do you want to drink?"

"My parents found the alcohol," Clémence said.

"Damn."

"I'm moving out, but what I meant was you could help me by putting chairs on tables."

Louise sighed and pulled herself off of the counter, doing as she was told.

"How are you feeling?" Clémence asked.

When Louise arrived, nearly six hours ago, she had made Clémence promise not to ask. But now, as Clémence swept the floor, she was going back on her word. Louise watched as she swept, her head down, lips pursed. Clémence had taken her apron off, revealing her button-up shirt and soft pair of trousers. There was a ruby clip in her hair, keeping it from her face. Clémence stopped, looking up at Louise. Her eyes, brown and bright and brilliant, locked onto Louise's.

Louise had succeeded in putting one chair on one table, but she stopped now, crossing the space between them and pressing her lips to Clémence's.

Clémence kissed back immediately, their bodies meeting and melding together. Their connection was fire, it was alive, she knew it was.

It was all she could think about, now that they were alone. Clémence's parents had left an hour ago, leaving their daughter to close and clean the café. Clémence was all she could think about a lot of the time.

Now that she was unemployed, maybe she would devote her time to studying Clémence. How she wrinkled her nose when she thought, how she bit her lip while studying lines. How she laughed when she was caught off guard.

Louise wanted to know everything about her.

She didn't want anything serious, but that didn't mean she couldn't have fun.

"We do need to talk," Clémence's voice was soft. Heat was radiating around them.

"We've done enough talking." Everything between them had to be named, had to be figured out. "Where are you moving to?"

"I don't know yet, but it won't be here. Ciarán says I can stay with him," Clémence said.

"And your parents are okay with that?"

"I didn't mention the Irish writer who drinks a lot."

Louise laughed. "Makes sense." Clémence raised an eyebrow, her full lips turning up at the corners.

They were the same height, making it easy for Louise to press her forehead to Clémence's. She didn't have to move to do it. "We should go to my apartment," Louise said.

Despite everything, she felt good. She felt ready for whatever life gave her next.

# A
# LETHAL
# LADY

NEKESA AFIA

READERS GUIDE

# QUESTIONS FOR DISCUSSION

1. Louise Lloyd has left everything she's known in Harlem behind to start a new life in Paris. Have you ever started over in a new location? What were your biggest challenges? What did you enjoy the most about the experience?

2. Louise's neighbor Ciarán is an important part of her new life. What do you think of their friendship? How does it evolve throughout the book?

3. Louise's friends from Harlem use letter writing to stay in touch throughout her time in Paris. Why do you think it is hard for her to write back? Is there anyone you would want to write a letter to? Why?

4. Lou receives letters from her sisters Minna and Josie. How would you describe Louise's relationship with her sisters? What do you think about the new developments in their lives and how they might affect Louise?

5. To help find Iris and learn more about what has happened to her, Louise joins an elite group of women artists. What do you think of her decision to join their ranks? Have you ever taken a class or joined a group to explore your passion?

6. Iris' work awakens a newfound love of art in Louise. Have you read a poem or book or viewed a painting that captivated you in a similar way? Who was the artist? How did you feel?

7. Schoonmaker and Rafael make a surprise visit to Paris. How does this visit affect Louise? How do her friendships with them compare to the new friends she's made in Paris?

8. Despite being from very different backgrounds, Iris, Emme, and Louise all struggle in different ways to live the lives they want to live as women in 1928 Paris. Discuss the obstacles they face to live their truth. How do they work to overcome those obstacles?

9. Detective Toussaint makes choices that greatly affect the outcome of the initial investigation into Iris' death. Do you understand why he made those choices? Do you think he did the right thing?

10. Louise's life in Paris at the start of *A Lethal Lady* is very different from how we see her as the book ends. Discuss her evolution throughout. In what ways do things get harder for Louise? In what ways does her life change for the better?

# ACKNOWLEDGMENTS

First, as always, thank you to me. Writing this book was hard and I persevered.

This book would never have thrived without the absolute patience of my editor, Michelle Vega. Thanks also to my Berkley team, including marketing, publicity, copyediting, and production. Thank you as well to my agent, Travis Pennington.

My family has always been my number one support team, and I could not do this without them. I am so grateful to have a strong foundation below me.

The best friends a girl could ever have: Sarah Strange (Who's like us? Damn few), my sweet knife wife Molly Clark, Allan Perkins, Lauren Park, Comet Girlie Vika Hendersen, pterrible dinosaur connoisseur Vincent Briggs, Cristina DaPonte, Lor Maroney (sorry I never eat), Rachel Kellis, Jay Jeanes, and Lou Villarruz.

I am so lucky to be in the middle of a community that is so inspiring, even when I'm lost. Thank you to Lev Rosen, Emily J. Edwards, Allison Epstein, Megan Collins, and Amy Suiter Clarke.

Big huge thank-you combined with sorry to the friends, spouses of friends, and friends' pets whose names I stole for this book.

Without the Berkletes' support, I would have given up so long ago. I love you guys, and I am so grateful to be your collective child. Can I stay up late tonight?

My fellow Charm School students: thank you for providing years of laughs and discussion. I am so sorry all I do is talk about my books.

Special thanks to Cat's Eye Café and the Bathurst/College Starbucks. This book would not be done without me having a place to go.

And finally, thank you to you. Your messages, your emails, your posts may have gone unanswered, and I am so sorry, but know that your support is everything to me. I literally could not do this without you. You make it possible to live my dream and I am so thankful.

NEKESA (Nuh-kes-ah) AFIA (Ah-fee-ah) is a Canadian millennial who is doing her best. When she isn't writing, she is either sewing, swing dancing, or actively trying to pet every dog she sees. The Harlem Renaissance Mysteries is her debut series.

## VISIT NEKESA AFIA ONLINE

NekesaAfia.com

⌾ NekesaWritesBooks